Ripping across the U.S., the U.K., Russia, Iraq, Dubai and finally to a dramatic ending in a remote part of Uzbekistan. This story defines the phrase quote "Revenge is a dish best served cold!"

A realistic thriller tracing the journey of two parents and their determination to balance the books after suffering a devastating blow handed to them from a truly evil family.

Recruiting the help of loyal comrades and friends who each provide their own key skills and expertise for this quest. They achieve not only a righteous pay back for the perpetrators but deal an incredible blow to the forces of evil flooding our World.

Based on some real characters each with their own unique niche to fill the group become inextricable linked together, culminating in a crescendo that will leave you wondering. – "Just how much of this *really* happened?"

A unique blend of fact and fiction awaits in …

THE SHAMAL

Dedicated to Natallia Vinahradskaya for giving me the encouragement to write this book.

With grateful thanks for their invaluable input to:

    Captain Brad Johns RAAF

    Staff Sargent Collin Wanley

    Flight Engineer Alexi Molchenka

In fond memory of David Allport from us all …… "Cheers Mate."

Arthur Tyler – Author

Donald Dirnberger - Editor

TABLE OF CONTENTS:
FORWARD: 2
CAST OF CHARACTERS: 5
BACKGROUND:
PLANE: A90 EKRANOPLAN 7,8
    MAPS: MIDDLE EAST ROUTE 9
        TITAN AND VENUS 10
        KASHMAR 11
PROLOGUE: THE EMAIL 12
CHAPTERS:
1 RING STINGERS OR ALI'S STORY 16
2 THE WADI 28
3 ESCAPE 43
4 INSIDE THE AGENCY 48
5 THE ARRIVAL 63
6 THE PLAN 80
7 ALL ABOARD 94
8 THE OFFER 110
9 BACK IN THE USSR 120
10 TIMELINE 129
11 THE REUNION 139
12 THE BRIEFINGS 148
13 "ROMEO THIRTEEN" LIVES 164
14 COME TOGETHER 171
15 THE EVE 188
16 TAKE THE MONEY AND RUN 195
17 NIGHT FLIGHT 233
18 THE DELIVERY 275
19 THE AMBASSADOR 302
20 BALANCING THE BOOKS 311
21 IMAGINE 329

Cast of Characters

- *Mathew Donnelley* –US Special Forces, US Marine Corps. (USMC) – Retired. Father of Thomas Donnelly USMC.
- *Maria Donnelley* – Matt Donnelley's wife. CIA analyst head of financial section Gulf States and Mother of Thomas Donnelly USMC.
- *Major Lord Stuart Henry Bonham* – Former SAS Major who had served with Matt previously in Central America. Retired: living in Dubai.
- *Tommy "Tit" Jones and his colleague "Sarge"*– Tommy "the tit" is borderline mad, he knows it and enjoys it. He is a character, charismatic, always a joker, loyal and dedicated professional at the flick of a VERY instant switch. Tommy is part of Stuarts SAS team with the long-suffering Sergeant of the team who is the opposite to Tommy and had his sense of humor removed at birth.
- *Natasha* — Qualified in Engineering with a "red diploma", Natasha fled the Ukraine after the collapse of the Soviet Union and got a job "working" for Lecho at the Kremlin nightclub. She is also in love with Stuart.
- *Lenna* – A Ukrainian blonde bombshell, Lenna is in Dubai to earn enough money to return to the Ukraine and live comfortably. - doing ANYTHING she can to make money and also working at the Kremlin.
- *Usman Al Ghazzal* – A Dubai "local", extremely wealthy but not well liked by the Royal Family who are suspicious about his ethics. Owns many jewelry shops in the Gold Souk and dealt heavily in the property boom.
- *Khalid Al Ghazzal* – Usman Ghazzal's son - as distasteful as his father and a fanatic to boot.

- ***Lecho Dudayev*** – Runs the Chechenia Mafia from Dubai – but at the same time he keeps his nose clean in the United Arab Emirates. Dudayev is rich, dangerous, and well connected with underworld elements throughout East Europe and the ex-CIS states. Most of all he is greedy.
- ***Bradley Johnstone*** – Ex-military pilot, entrepreneur on the side, a drinker and fighter for fun. A former RAAF and Special Services pilot, he now runs his own air freight company in Dubai — OZZAIR.

A90 Ekranoplan Onlyonok

Flight Map: The Full Route. A map used in planning the project.

Map Titan and Venus: A map used in planning the project.

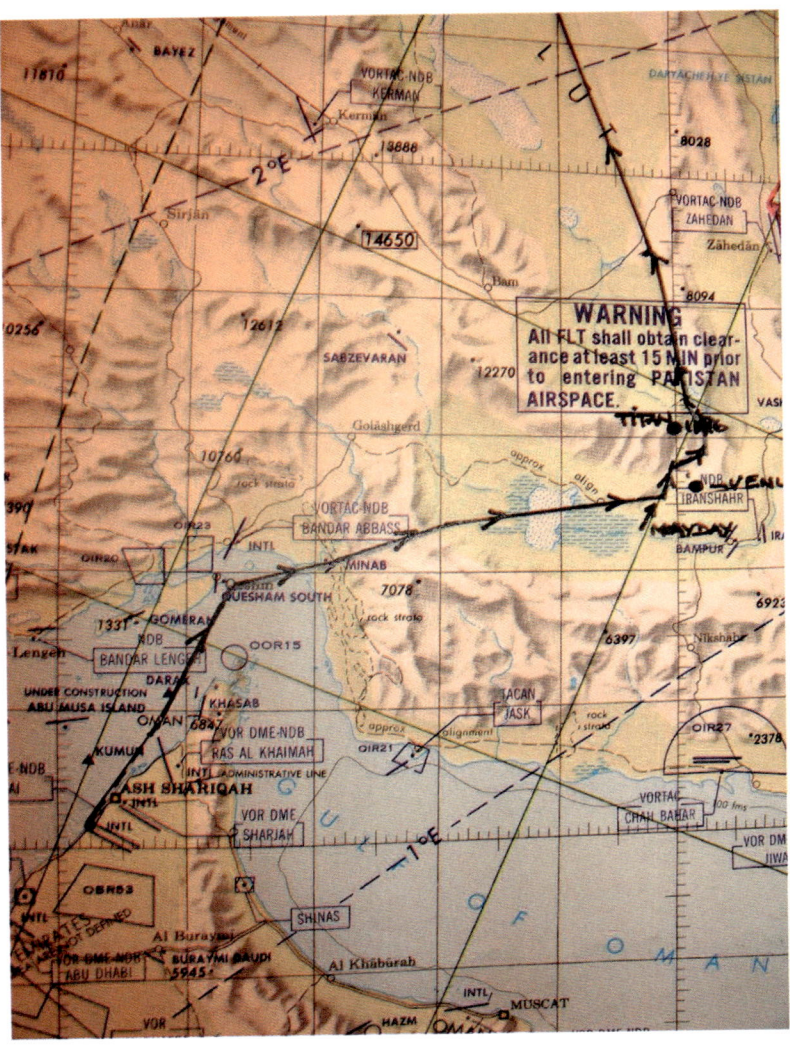

Kashmar Cable Marshed Map: A map used in planning the project.

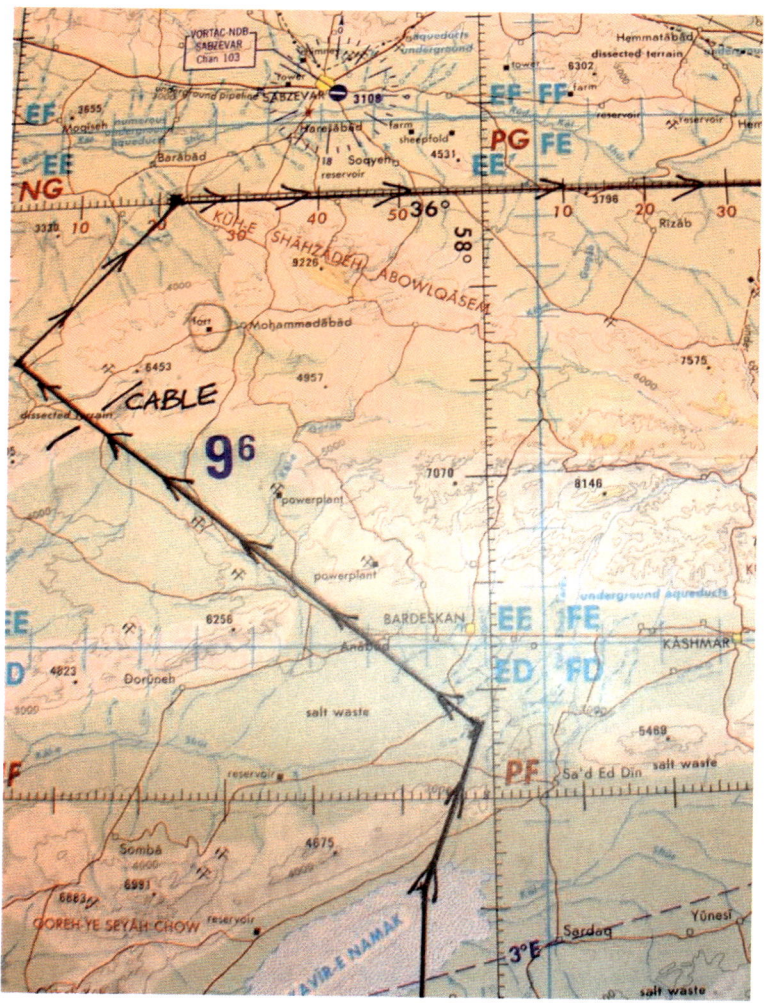

PROLOGUE: THE EMAIL

Three days before Christmas.

Matthew Donnelly flicked the computer on and went into the kitchen of the family holiday cottage on the green and damp Virginian coast to get his wake-up coffee. Looking out of his window over the quiet grey harbor wrapped in its wet early morning mist, he yawned at the start of another flat boring day, just three more of these grey days to run before returning home to Washington for a traditional white Christmas.

Stirring the coffee, he glanced at the framed picture of his only son, Thomas, as it hung on the drab wall as his portable computer wound itself up and eventually rang out its tone, "You have mail."

Sitting at his desk he took another sip of coffee he flicked and yawned his way through the usual junk mail and then came to "*Hi Dad*" an email from Thomas

Matt talked to himself; he did that a lot lately "And about time too Son. Where the hell have you been?" having not heard from his son for almost three weeks now, Matt had started to get worried. Thomas had been in Iraq for almost two months with his unit and had only contacted his father twice to let him know he was OK.

The page opened and Matt read

Hi Dad,

Things are fine here in Iraq, just the way they <u>should</u> be.

I thought you would like to know how I am doing. The attached pics will show you what I mean.

Your ex son

Tomas hahhahaha

Matt was confused "What the hell does he mean "*ex*" the crazy little……" but what he saw next changed his life forever.

Instantly and automatically the "attached Picture" opened itself. In perfect high-quality resolution Matt looked into the green eyes of his only son, Thomas staring back at him from the picture. The difference was that now they eyes were dulled; they were the eyes of his dead Son. The picture showed Thomas's head being clutched by a gloved hand as it was hung to pose for the perfect picture. It had been severed from its body.

"no……..no…no,no,no,no,no…."
Matt was frozen; he was locked to his son's dead gaze, the lifeless eyes of his Boy, his best friend, his life. What seemed like a minute happened in a second and a minute became an hour. He couldn't breathe, he was numb, and he didn't feel the coffee fall and burn his leg. He vomited without warning or control.

Almost falling Matt spun back from the computer, stumbling across the room knocking over a side table as he ran into the kitchen and vomited again in the sink full of used plates. For the first time in his life panic had taken him over. The horrible and helpless feeling that wells up and takes over all control grabbed his very being.

Thoughts flashed through his mind like flashes from a camera. Thomas at 3 years old, graduation, his first rangers' uniform, conversations, echoes from his sons' life, his mom…

"Oh my God" the realization started to dawn, if Matt had received this then had Maria? "Oh my god, she's at work."

Frantically he tried to dial Marias number; he couldn't remember it even though he knew it by heart. Then he couldn't find the book with it in even though his hand passed over it twice before he saw it.

"*Get control*" thought flashed through Matts mind; he knew he had to.

Eventually the switchboard number was answered. "Langley Centre"

"Maria Donnelley, quick, it's an emergency, I'm her husband quick!"

"Yes sir, please hold while I put you through" the voice was unperturbed, it seemed like forever to connect and when it did, it just rang and rang for what seemed like another lifetime.

"Hello" eventually and very quietly came back, it wasn't Maria, it sounded *wrong,* but Matt didn't realize.

"Maria, I need Maria, is she there? This is Matt" The nervousness was ringing out in Matts voice, he knew it and didn't care, he needed to warn his wife

"Matt…..Oh Matt…. this is Katie" there was a pause

"Katie I need……" he was interrupted

"Matt, something terrible has happened, Matt?…" another pause

The realization kicked in as Matt sank his head "Oh my God No" Maria had just opened her email too.

CHAPTER 1: RING STINGERS or ALI'S STORY

England February

At 5.30 p.m. in a dark cold February night. Ice cold drizzle made the Northern English roads neither properly wet nor properly dry. Constantly Ali needed to use the screen washers of his old Mazda to see where he was going in the already dark winter's night. He hated February; it never ever seemed to get light. Working in his Uncles popular restaurant seven nights a week, Ali seemed to pass through the whole month of February without seeing daylight. It was a normal English February, cold, dank and depressing.

And so, he made his way to his Uncles restaurant, the *Dil Shad Tandoori Indian Restaurant and Take Away*, High Street, Bradford, Leeds

Ali Ramadan needed some time alone to tell his uncle, who was his guardian, that he had made an important decision. He knew his uncle would be pleased. But he planned to wait until his shift as a waiter at his uncle's restaurant had ended.

At 11.00 pm as usual, the Friday night Lager louts started to pour themselves into Asian restaurants all over the UK and the Dil Shad was not immune to its share of the ritual onslaught which would see bad behavior ranging from ordinarily bad-mannered drunkenness through to the most blatant racisms and brutal violence. Ali, as with every other employee just worked in the hope that all they would need to manage on this night would be the usual and predictable insults and bad behavior, rather than out and out violence.

Ali was ready when a band of six swaggered in; its leader who mistook his hanging beer belly for muscles was more than happy to reply to Ali's offer of showing him to a table for six persons.

"Fuckin spot on Gunga Din" he answered, and the overweight slob patted the top of Ali's head "Learned how to count with coconuts did yer Sambo?"

The band loved their leader, but not as much as he loved himself, and followed him to the table.

They were there to spend a week's hard-earned cash. Having collected their hand outs of dole money, or state benefits payment, they had managed to top up this free gift from the British Taxpayer, by stealing two car radios from a local multi story car park.

The electricity bill money that a seventy-five-year-old pensioner had safely hidden beneath the clock in her living room was predictably easy for them to find, as they burgled her house in a neighboring suburb of the cold wet City of Bradford. The old ladies four hard saved ten-pound notes had topped up their weekly earnings nicely.

"Hey, fuckin Osama, fetch us six buckets of Heineken and a dozen poppadum's'"

Ali smiled, hated them, and returned five minutes later with the drinks. Then again with the small mountains of the light wafer thin crispy popadums. Making room on the table between the various chutneys and Yogurt dip Ali leant forwards to remove the single red rose in the vase which formed the central decoration of the table. As he reached for it, the yob opposite beat him to it and pulled it away from Ali`s grasp, towards his own equally bulging belly. Ali smiled, reached further and then felt a handful of popadums slap downwards onto the top of his head. Exploding in a shower of tiny pieces, even covering the leader and his fellow slobs too. The couple sitting at the next table wasn't excluded from the small explosion of crispy wafers but knew better than to complain. A wiser decision was for them to see the funny side and laugh at the joke too.

The beer belly was amused at his joke as always "Fuckin Ell, you *dirty* bastard. Yer fuckin dandruff's everywhere"

Oh, how witty and funny the joke was to the band of six. As Ali turned, still trying to contain the situation, trying to hold the acceptance of a joke he heard

"This'll fix it, good for dandruff" and Yob one up ended the yogurt dip onto Ali's "popadommed" head.

Escaping to the kitchen Ali's Uncle passed him as he headed for the table. An old hand with almost thirty years of humiliations under his belt, he knew how to cool things down and having a broad Yorkshire accent himself, somehow made him more acceptable to the Neanderthals.

"Whooo..Steady on lads, I'll need a new fuckin vacuum at this rate"

The yobs were satisfied, their joke had been funny, and the Owner had more sense than to make an issue out of it. Their natural superiority had been asserted.

"Some more popadums lads? And six *ringstingers* (*1) with onion bhajees correct?" Uncle predicted.

"An` six fuckin pints as well pal" came back another beer lout's addition to the order.

"No problem lads" and Ali's Uncle returned to the kitchen.

Seeing Ali at the sink in the corner, he was in a mess. A fellow waiter trying to mop the Yogurt from the back of his shirt and shoulders. Trying to minimize the damage to Ali's crisp uniform of white shirt and black waistcoat that his mother had just got dry cleaned for him that very same day. Ali's hair was wet having just been rinsed under the tap. He turned to face his Uncle who, from his own years of experience, asked him with a genuine feeling of sympathy.

"You alright Son?" the Uncle asked, knowing the feeling of humiliation far too well.

His eyes filled with tears of embarrassment, hate and anger Ali had to tell his secret to the Uncle he loved and trusted.

"Unc, - I am going…"

Misinterpreting what Ali was about to say his Uncle held Ali's shoulders

His gaze fixed into Ali`s eyes as if to reassure him. "Calm down son, just calm down…you know its normal for these shitheads, don't you? Just leave them to me I'll handle them, just keep away from them and it`ll be OK…Alright

"No Uncle, you don't know what I mean…I mean I am going" glancing at the others in the kitchen Ali leaned forward and whispered in his Uncles ear "I am going for Allah, for His Jihad Uncle"

Looking at his nephew eye to eye. The face of the Uncle just said it all. He was *Proud*. And now with tears of emotion in his eyes too he nodded firmly. There was no need for him to comment.

Smiling, actually beaming, he turned and asked the cook "Which is their ring stinger?" The cook pointed at the large pot on the cooking range as he spit into it.

The Uncle walked towards the cook "Put it down here" pointing at the floor.

The cook smiled and they all laughed, including Ali thorough his tears, as the Uncle urinated in the large commercial sized cooking pot.

When the "preparation" was finished and lovingly placed in the imitation silver serving dishes Uncle was more than pleased to serve it to his Clientele with a genuine smile.

Two were heard to say that these Pakis aren't good for much but good cooking…And days later, with his uncles blessing and the crisp bundle of 2,000 Pounds Ali was in London

1 A Phal Curry, or Ring Stinger, an invention by Bangladeshi restaurants to be the hottest possible curry available to the standard English drunk.

London
Finsbury Park Community Centre

On a speaking tour of mosques spread all over England, Oxford-educated Mullah Ibrahim opened his speech to a throng of Islamic studies students attending his lecture series in a London mosque. He has given this speech before; he knows that all he has to do is convince about five percent of the audience to take action, and he will have more than succeeded. His purpose: to find new recruits for the battle for Iraq, and for the war on the west.

"Do not ever be afraid of what you are facing. Always remember; never ever forget the one plain and simple truth…Allah Akbar! God IS Great – and that simple and pure fact is exactly what your enemies, my enemies and the enemies of the whole world and the *real* enemies of God do not understand."

The Mullah paused and looked around the class of young men as if measuring them for commitment and belief "Here, in my classes and readings, you will start to learn of the lies, the brain washing, and the deception that the west had laid forth on its own people, and on the world. You will hear about the tools used by the enemies of God even against their own children. You will be taught just how evil these people are, and you will be shown how they use one set of rules for themselves and another for anyone that opposes them.

Allah Akbar! (God is great)!

The Americans tell us that we should live in democratic states, that terrorism should be attacked wherever it rises, and that Jews should live in peace without any threat.

But these same Americans do not educate their people, they lie to them and they control them with constant deceit, they manipulate and brainwash their children by deliberately keeping them uneducated. For example, history is a subject that starts in 1920 with most Americans, and their knowledge of geography is equivalent to believing that the world is flat!

First, I will tell you of history. The real fact in history is that there was never a country called Israel, that is, until it was claimed to exist by Jews. In 1951, when they stole land from our Palestinian brothers and the United States recognized Israel as a sovereign state.

Who are terrorists? Israel. It was the Israelis who started the idea of terrorist bombings. It was they who attacked and killed hundreds of innocent Muslims as they stole Palestinian land. Israel is a state formed on terrorist acts, with terrorist guns, and terrorist bombs with all of the murders committed financed by American Jews. And yet, Mr. President and his people are firmly and absolutely dedicated against terrorist states. If this is the truth, why don't they bomb Israel?

They proudly claim that they have the right to bomb any terrorist no matter where they are on the planet, so why didn't they bomb the Irish community in Boston that was financing a hundred years of terrorism in England, or perhaps drop a bomb on southern Ireland where the IRA terrorists ran there to hide from the British Troops?

And yet they bomb Beirut – just like they have bombed Bekha, Baghdad, and Tripoli without even thinking.

The American people believe that Arabs persecute Jews because that is what they are told. Yet what really happened? What is the real history? Throughout 2,000 years it is the Europeans who have persecuted the Jews, not the Arabs. When Spain was under Arabic rule, Jews lived there, coexisted for hundreds of years even with their right to worship, and then when Spain turned away from Allah and Arabic rule ended, what happened? The Jews were persecuted and had to flee for their lives to the protection of the Muslim Arabic countries in North Africa.

In Britain, whole communities of Jews were exterminated by the English, hundreds at a time were slaughtered by the English and then.... well then came Hitler and the holocaust was the zenith of Jewish persecution in Europe, killing so many millions of them.

But where did Arabs ever persecute Jews? Can the American President answer that? Can he tell the truth that Arabs and Jews have lived side by side for thousands of years? Can he tell his people that?

The British Prime Minister or the American Poodle stands up so bravely and says that we, our people, should demand and embrace democracy. Did the British ask the Palestinian people to vote on the decision to invent a country called Israel and set it in the middle of the land which has been Palestine since the time of Moses?

His American owner tells us that he is also against any none democratic state. Then why don't they attack Bahrain, Saudi and Kuwait? Yet they can attack a democracy such as Iraq. *Why do they want to interfere with our culture, our way of life?* Why do they want to turn people against their royal families after they have cared and looked after their people with such compassion and kindness for a thousand years? Do they think that our princes, kings and sheikhs put themselves there as dictators when their countries were so poor? Don't they realize that the rulers were chosen because of the peoples' respect for them and the peoples' *wish* that they should be ruled by them?

What right do they have to even say these things to us about our history, our culture and our choices? To tell us these things is to be arrogant and bad mannered, to interfere in other nations sovereign rights is a sin and an insult. But then, after the arrogance is shown, after the insults are made, what comes next? A push, a harder push, then a blow, then a kick, then a shot? Where do they stop? Do they then go on to bomb your homes, your villages, your families? Ask the people of Iraq, Afghanistan, Libya, and Palestine to tell you. The answer is simple, it won't stop. Someone has to stop it!"

Ibrahim Al Mubi paused, catching his breath while letting the audience dwell on the messages he had just delivered. He then picked-up the "discussion" exactly where he had left it.

"All these questions you need to have answered. Here, it is my work to teach you, enlighten you, explain to you the real reasons why the infidels are acting this way against us, why they want this turmoil and killing, and you will be shown why they want total global control."

The mullah paused and again noticed Ali's face, the enthusiasm, the look of a true fanatic caught his eye. His speech had done the job, now time to lighten up and send the message home in a different way.

"Firstly, I will show you a video. I show it because it is widely believed amongst educated mullahs that there is a systematic "dumbing down" of the children in America. Of course, their President denies this, so let us see just how much his normal, free voting people understand about the World".

Mullah Ibrahim then stepped down from his podium, started a projector, and played a video made by an Australian TV crew in which Americans on the street were asked simple questions about the geography of the Middle East, the reasons for the war in Iraq, even questions about their own country that any citizen should have known. The blind sample of Americans interviewed demonstrated a numbing, self-centered, isolationist view of the world — they cared nothing about world politics or geography. All they cared about were themselves. One didn't even know which state KFC came from!

As the class rolled in the isles laughing at these ignorant and stupid Americans, the Mullah restarted his lecture.

"Yes, it is funny isn't it? But now understand why this is so evil.' He paused and then explained.

"If you take one generation, lower its level of education, then they will become parents who in turn will believe that their children are being well educated even at a low level. You do this to three generations, until anyone with a good education has long since passed away and what have you got? An uneducated people who will believe anything they are told simply because they don't know anything better. It is a brainwashing of entire generations of children and" Again with a well-timed theatrical he paused before adding an emphatic…."….and THAT is evil."

Quickly he moved on "Also, what a strange coincidence that Britain has slowly lowered its levels of education over the past twenty years. Their own Government admits that 25% of English children leave school and are illiterate or close to it. Examination papers have been made easier; standards have been lowered slowly but very surely over that same period. So, you have British children leaving school at 18 years old having sat examinations that a 12-year-old would have passed in the previous generation. Because standards have been lowered the pass rate has increased, therefore it shows what an excellent job the Prime Minister is doing with his nation's education!" At this, the Mullah allowed himself another chuckle.

Then, turning to the class "But are we Muslims illiterate? Are we uneducated animals as they show us on their TV?" Turning he asked the newest student, pointed at him and snapped his fingers "Ali, how many languages do you speak?"

"English, Hindi and Urdu master — oh, and some Arabic too, Sir" said Ali.

"And did you learn that in your English school, Ali?

Ali blushed, thinking how right his master is, and responded confidently "No sir!"

Then from where did you learn these languages Ali?

"From my parents; and I learned the Arabic from my religious teacher in Leeds, Sir. His name is Mullah Omar, sir."

"Thank you Ali. My point here, young men, is that they are the liars, they change their vile version of history, they keep their people uneducated and theirs is the evil empire; the axis of evil … ours is the Kingdom of God and in the whole history of the world, the universe, the heavens……ONLY God is right!

Allah Akbar!

By his third class with the Mullah, Ali had become a true believer in the need for a Jihad against a Godless west. And Mullah Ibrahim, as he had done for so many other Ali's in England, encouraged him to follow his conscience and to take strong action against the western liars and oppressors.

Ali was hooked and Ali Ramadan left England a week later, bound for Pakistan.

CHAPTER 2: THE WADI

One Month later, North West Pakistan

Ali, even more so than his new peers, loved the Camp. It was no more than a tented city huddling around a scattered collection of dhobi huts in a windswept oven called Mukhrar in North West Pakistan, but Ali loved everything about it from the weather to the food and the prayers. Most of all he loved the chance for once to be treated as an equal by everyone around him. He was at last with his real brothers. The Jihadists.

And here there were leanings too, teachers to educate them in the history of the West's constant plethora of lies, deceit and extortion of the Muslim peoples over many Centuries past. How to dismantle and assemble a Kalashnikov, how to shoot, how to play with explosives without fear, how to look for the best places to conceal bombs…the whole of the terrorist basic education.

Here Ali could drink from the cup of true education and his thirst seemed unquenchable. When not training he was sitting in classes, listening to older wiser men speak, when alone he would read his books. For Ali, the camp was paradise. How he wished he could write and tell his Uncle of his perfect world and how happy he was to be in it.

At last he was equal, a Jihadist, just as all his comrades were too, irrespective of race, background, upbringing or whatever kind of passport they held. They truly were brothers in the eyes of God and the love that Ali had for this new acceptance in life filled him with pride for himself and his newfound friends.

They shared everything, food, feelings, thoughts and secrets too, especially with Samer and Khalid, his new friends from Dubai who were his team members and it was in one of these secret moments, when Ali and Samer were together alone one sweltering hot humid night that Samer confided.

Samer sipped his Chai "Don't worry my friend, whatever happens I will bring you to my home safely…… Look." Feeling underneath the collar of his green combat shirt Samer carefully extracted something from a double sealed pouch secreted there.

"See?" Asked Samer "This will buy us out of anything"

Ali gazed upon the single most expensive thing he had ever set his eyes upon. Samer's insurance policy. A single diamond as big as a thumb nail - His Mothers Diamond. Perfect clarity and cut, a fully paid up 50 carat insurance policy.
Ali was amazed and Samer went on to explain about his Fathers involvement with the string of jeweler's shops in Dubai Gold Souk and how the Father of their friend, Khalid was the real money behind the incredible wealth of both families. About how it was God's gift and why the families now had to be good and to do their duty for God, to fight the Jihad.

Samer explained proudly how all Muslims were brothers, how he and Khalid's families helped with the Jihad and shared their wealth by providing arms from Eastern Europe.

Now it all made sense to Ali, how devout and committed not only his comrades but the whole of their families were too. He felt a comfort and wellbeing, knowing he was part of it all, part of them and not an outcast to ridicule anymore. Soon they were to leave for Syria and then at last they could cross into the land of war, Iraq.

Ali couldn't wait and slept that night dreaming of the heroic days ahead.

Syrian Border with Western Iraq.

Three months later the professionals, the British Special Air Service (SAS) were watching. As they had been for the last four days since they took over from the previous team who had lain in wait for the insurgents. Times were difficult for the SAS as well as every other hard-pressed regiment in the British Army which was now not hesitating to bring back ex-soldiers who had either finished their term of service after leaving the Forces upon signing a document agreeing to be brought back at any time the British Government so wished.

At forty-six years old Sir Stuart Henry Bonham, former career soldier and now a Major had been called upon yet again to do his part. He was only one of over two thousand ex-Army personnel that had received the same call back to service throughout the British Isles over the past three years. He didn't mind one bit, this is what he was good at, what he was born for, like many others from the Bonham family before him.

He'd had a good tour and now, as he squatted down against a rock wall with an almost perfect view over the Wadi a little short of twenty feet lower down, he considered what was earmarked as his last "escapade". They had ambushed the previous groups thanks to good intelligence sources and now they expected another, this was nothing new to the elite cadre.

Lying in wait and split between both sides of the cold, barren wadi were four SAS professionals. Further along towards the south were four more of their comrades, again split onto both shoulders of the wadi on slightly higher ground. It was a nice, sensible trap.

Just past midnight the first information came through on Major Stuart Bonham's earpiece from the Boeing 707 AWACS (Advanced Warning and Control System) thirty thousand feet above cruising to and fro, unseen in the black moonless night informing Stuart of the group of fourteen who had entered Iraq following the long wadi that carves its way into the heartland twenty miles south of Mosul deep into the remote, lifeless, stone dessert plain. Once the information started it kept coming. Updating itself every minute or so, including a heat sensitive picture taken from the aircraft showing the progress of the group and fresh news that now revised the number of them to twelve in all.

Stuart looked at a picture that had been sent down to his hand-held screen, made a mental note of how the group was positioned together as they followed each other along "his" Wadi and thought "Good, amateurs… too close together." He also noted that two were together at the front of the line, then a group of six followed by four more who seemed to separate themselves slightly but not enough.

Oblivious of what was ahead, slowly, cautiously the group moved along his chosen route led along the route by their local Iraqi scout Hammed with Khalid at his right and slightly behind him. Unknown to them they would soon be quietly walking straight past Stuart and his team.

At 0300 hrs., silent and invisible Stuart and his men looked down as the group passed by and it was at that same time that Hammed felt it – that special feeling and the shiver ran down his spine like iced water. Was it fear or premonition? He didn't know but non the less, the feeling, the sixth sense that he felt so strong meant he didn't hesitate. Without any warning he broke into a sprint, leaving all the new recruits behind except one, Khalid. Hammed knew where every gully and every ditch there was to be found and he intended to use them.

As soon as Hammed abandoned his charges, he was spotted and allowed to run. The group froze. Not knowing whether to follow Hammed, to go back or if it was a trap by Hammed. They broke the rules and shouted out to each other and without half a second passing brought down a murderous hail of fire on themselves from Stuart and his men.

A succession of six well placed grenades and a hail of bullets from the other three members in the team completed the slaughter in less than twenty seconds. As Stuarts group ceased firing, almost exactly on que, shooting began further along the Wadi.

Hammed running at full speed, having thrown his weapon away and backpack too ran into the cross hairs of the Scottish Sergeants infra-red sights. Khalid saw it all as he was running ten meters behind Hammed. For a split second it was like a dream so fast and also in slow motion. Khalid saw it happen saw Hammed stop dead in his tracks and then move backwards slightly. A surreal sight to Khaled as the bullet tore through Hammed's chest and blew a hole out of his back.

Six running strides more, when he was almost on top of Hammed is when he saw his head explode and felt the warm red shower that used to be his leader's life blood hit him in the face. He heard the noise and felt the blow in his groin. As if hit by a massive hammer he stumbled, but still he ran hardly missing a beat.

The whole event took less than a minute. As the smoke lay deep in the wadi, all that could be heard now was the sound of moans and prayers.

The Major heard the call on his earpiece.

"Sitrep boss" (*situation report*) Came through on Stuart's earpiece from the group leader 200 meters down the wadi.

"Go-head" was the snap reply from him

"One slotted *(shot dead)* and one runner (*escapee*) wounded, following his track now" Came the Scottish whisper.

In the mêlée one had escaped despite the efforts of a stocky Scottish sergeant who managed to let one instant glancing shot go towards the shadow sprinting behind the rocks and into the cover of the natural gulleys. Two SAS were dispatched to follow the trail of the one who had escaped. Looking for any signs to follow and finding precious little after three kilometers it was pointless. The SAS professionals determined that the risk was not worth the reward and returned to report to their commander but luckily, only after some blood was found at the early part of the trail and the Sergeant had carefully taken drops of it and delicately smeared it onto the glass plate before placing it into a sealed plastic container, no bigger than a book of matches.

Back in the Wadi long minutes passed…the moans from the two injured — and the sounds of their prayers being said. One prayer, ironically, was in English. As two of God's Soldiers lay on the ground, the only living survivors of the hell that had rained down upon them only minutes earlier, they did not see the team of SAS troopers' approach. The first thing they felt was a blow to the head and then they were rolled onto their stomachs as their hands were tied fiercely with plastic ties behind their backs. As the first was trussed into place, his pain and wounds completely being ignored he shouted out in a broad Northern English "English, English — I am English! Don't shoot me, don't shoot!"

From behind his head he heard a hard-cockney voice "English are yer son?" and then a whisper closer to his ear "Well…. that means you're a fucking traitor then doesn't it you cunt"

Within minutes, specially converted Land Rovers arrived at the ditch where the first team of SAS were evacuated, taking the two wounded Jihadists with them. A separate Jeep was loaded with the nine corpses, which were thrown on after being thoroughly searched. In the just ten minutes they would reach the SAS base camp, a makeshift huddle of six large tents.

Even during the bumpy ride, the two wounded had been given emergency treatment, not especially out of mercy, more so out of the necessity to keep them alive for questioning. Ones bowels had been pushed back into his lower stomach cavity and with the other survivor emergency swabs had been pushed hard down into the wounds that had ripped his lower backbone into a hundred splinters, plugging the fist sized hole where he no longer had any feeling.

Soon, Ali Ramadan lay, praying in English, flat on his back in a tent and looked up into the eyes of an SAS sergeant who half smiled at him as he "Well, well, well, lad you're a long way from home ant ya now? A very long way indeed eh?"

The Morphine and Amphetamines were doing their job. Ignoring him Ali pleaded "For fuck sake man, I'm fuckin' bleedin' …do something will you? I can't feel me legs, I think me back is broke man. Help me for fucks sake!"

His words were met with total coldness, no sign of compassion registered on the Sergeant's face. He's seen all of this before and he didn't give a shit about Ali who, in his eyes, was nothing more than a turncoat to the country he had been borne in.

"What's your name boy? Where you from in the North, …..Leeds is it?"

Tears start flowing down Ali's cheek. "Ali…Ali Ramadan……Yeh… Leeds. Look, I am fuckin hurtin man — God its hurtin! Please do something, for fuck's sake man, do something, come on".

The Sergeant's coldness didn't flicker. "Leeds is big, Ali boy — whereabouts in Leeds?"

"Scarborough Road — fff ffiteen Scarborough Road. It's in Bradford, between Bradford and Leeds. Please now, please!"

Another trooper arrived and knelt beside Ali-the-unfortunate. Wiping the fingers of Ali's undamaged left hand, he started taking fingerprints. That done, he took a swab from a plastic sterile phial in his medical kit and opened Ali's mouth. As the swab was jabbed deep down Ali's throat, probably a bit further than it needed to be and Ali wretched as the DNA swipe was taken.

The Sergeant's questioning of Ali continued fast, furious, and without any pauses. The inquisitor knew Ali's lack of blood would soon override his adrenalin, possibly sending Ali into shock. And that would not do, the Major would still want information.

"Which school did you go to, Ali? Got a car? What's the registration number? What kind is it? Ever been caught by the police? Where? What for? Where did you work? Who for? What mosque did you use? Who's your teacher there? Who recruited you? Where?"

Ali was answered all and every question, but he was also on the brink of passing out when another soldier entered the room, this time to take Ali's photo. Ali's photo was then instantaneously broadcast using the Internet to the Pontrailas Barracks in Herefordshire, England — the headquarters of the SAS. And GCHQ General Command Headquarters in Cheltenham, in ninety seconds, flashed a message back to the SAS soldier in the inquisition room:

Ali Ramadan date of birth 17.1.84 Social Security number PA02771414S Unemployed since school, left on date ….. Known student of Mullah Ibrahim Al Mudi, possible inspiration for the London tube terrorists. And so, on and so on…

Ali woke up quickly, the last amphetamine jab having kicked in. The Sergeant now had him riding high on speed.

"Answer me! You came to Syria via Pakistan last week. Where did you stay; who with; and how many others were there?

"Lots….. lots of us there…" and then as if to drop the question he started to quietly beg "Please…..please help me…We can pay you."
"Who sent you; when are they sending the next lot?" The Sergeants questions went on without pause.

"Where did you stay in Syria? How far across the border was it?"

Ali ignored the question "We can pay, honest we can…..please……..help…Samer will pay you, he's got a diamond

..From his moms' shop, his dads' shop… He owns a big shop in the souk in Dubai. …."

Ali was losing it, heading for confusion, his voice getting weaker and weaker he was sliding towards his own dreamland.

"Who ran away, who was wounded and ran away" the Sergeant hammered the questions in again and again

Ali was whispering now as his life was slowly bleeding from his body "The guide, Hamed …..ran off…… left us…. Khalid went as well….. fuckin bastards ..bastards ……please……….I……………."

"Khaled who? What's his full name?" The sergeant was hurrying now; he knew time was slipping away along with Ali.

"Khalid, his names Khalid…from Dubai…. Khalid al…" and then it was too late, Ali had answered everything he was asked but now after three minutes at high speed, Ali gently died as the Sergeant wrote down the name *"Khalid al (?)"*

The Sergeant hissed through his teeth "Fucking wanker…...Khalid al fucking who!" and got up leaving Ali's corpse sprawled on the floor lying in its own blood and excrement.

In the next tent, Trooper Tommy "the Tit" Jones was kneeling beside another boy, twenty-one-year-old Samer al Shataff. Try as he may, Tommy could not get much information from young Samer except his name which he gave immediately for some strange reason. Samer lost a lot of blood in the earlier exchange with the SAS and all the drugs, poking and prodding was yielding less and less results.

Over and over, like his dead revolutionary brother in the next tent, Samer begged for help. And as he felt his life slipping away, his hand shaking still in their plastic wire ties Ali nodded slightly towards his left side, down towards his collar, he was going for his trump card, his diamond ace in the hole.

"Please…in my shirt…the…. the collar…. it's something for you. Take it.." Ali's eyes seemed suddenly bright…" It's for you…to help me…take it.."

Tommy used his knife to prod under Samer's collar. As he turned the collar upwards the found a secret pocket stitched into the collar. Very carefully cutting away the fabric of the secret pouch he quickly found what was hidden inside and very quietly exclaimed to himself "fuuuuuck me!" In his grasp he was now holding a blood stained clear white diamond, close to an inch round.

" My ..my mother... give you this… it's for you to help me. Take it….. Take it…. Help me…".

Tommy looked at the boy. "Your mother gave you this to join Al Qaeda? Yes??"

The Sarge entered the tent and knelt beside Tommy, as Samer nodded — and mouthed the words…." Take. Take it…for me… for help, ok?...OK??"

Sarge spoke loudly, he knew the boy was drifting away, hearing his name called Samer eyes opened wide before they slowly and gently started to close for the last time "Samer! Samer!...what is your friends name, the one from Dubai, he ran away, what's his name? Khaled al what???"

Quietly Samer said the name "Khalid"

"From Dubai? Khaled who? What's his name? Full name"

"Ghazzal" the dying boy whispered "Al Ghazzal…now help me please help………………."

And Samer's eyes gently half rolled back and the lids half closed. At that moment, Samer Al Shataff was whisked off on his personal magical flying carpet to visit the land of virgins in the sky.

Unseen to the Sarge. Tommy took one quick look at the diamond and smiled before dropping it into his pocket and writing down every detail he had just heard in a tiny notebook kept lovingly just for this kind of job.

Turning to Tommy the Sarge asked "The one I questioned said this one had a diamond on him, did you find anything?"

Straight away Tommy jumped in with his reply "Not a sausage Sarge, fuck all, zero, sweet fanny Adams…I searched him properly, all except his arse hole, but that's mainly because he left that back in the Wadi"

The two had been teamed together for the last six years and it was no surprise when the Sarge stooped to lower and move his face towards inches of Tommy's face, looked him in the yes and whispered "You fucking liar Tit"

For once Tommy, caught "pants down" was serious and looked straight back at the Sergeant "Later. OK?" eying towards the other SAS troopers entering the large tent.

The sergeant nodded then snapped "OK lads, bag the fuckers and let's get back to base…..I'm starving!"

Two hours later at the Mosul camp, looking across the table in the canteen the three were almost alone. The chiseled face of Stuart was now washed and shaved for the first time in eight days. Still a little too hyper to sleep they had met for a hearty meal before turning in and sleeping through the next day.

"So, lads, that's it then, the shows over for us now. Back to civy street, Job done and dusted. Well done." Stuart said, "we'll get some kip and meet up tonight at 1800 with our reports, once they're in - we're off, OK?"

"On the lash (*drinking*) in Dubai Boss?" asked Tommy.

"Yeh why not Tommy, we deserve it I reckon, see ya later lads" and Stuart turned and left for his well-earned bed.

Waiting for their Major to leave the room Sarge looked at Tommy "Well Tommy?"

Inside his clenched fist Tommy retrieved the diamond from his trouser pocket, as if in school searching for his favorite marble he then passed the same clenched fist over the Sergeants open hand. The hand over would have been unseen even in a crowded room but at 0500 the canteen was empty.

The Sarge looked down into his hand which was halfway under the table. Tommy watched the Sergeants and mimed the Sergeants words "Faaaarrrrrkk in hell"

A minute later the Sergeant passed the stone back to Tommy.

"I don't like it Tommy, we should tell him" the Sarge was definitely uncomfortable with hiding anything from his Commanding Officer.

"We *will* Sarge, but not *yet* OK? Let's get to Dubai and officially de-mobbed first OK?" Tommy paused as the Sarge hesitated………" Tommy pushed a little harder "Sarge..OK??" Tommy was no fool, he had come up from the back streets, never had a penny as a kid until he joined the army at sixteen straight from school and what he had in his pocket wasn't going to be handed in for free so easily.

Tommy whispered urgently to the Sarge "Look Sarge, Look……., I aint givin this in. I aint handing it over to bleedin Her Majesty - no fuckin way. She's got enough sparklers in her hat already! This one's for us - not her. We've done our bit; we deserve it and well you know it"

The Sarge argued back "It doesn't go to the fucking Queen and *well you* know it Tit, it goes to the Crown, the Government"

Looking a mocked stunned look "Well in *that* case it's even *more* fuckin reason to keep it *innit*!!??"

Sarge was silent; his face was straight "Get your report done by 1700 meet me in my room. We'll work through them both. Don't make any mention of the jewelers in Dubai for now, just who the kid was and where he was from OK? It will float through easy. It never happened - BUT Tommy - As soon as we are out of the Army you, *will* level with the Boss. Understood OK?

"OK Deal" said Tommy " Besides, look on the bright side, we slotted eleven of them, only one did a runner and we've even got his name and blood sample so it's only a question of time before he`s slotted as well, so all in all, it aint really a bad score is it Sarge?'

The Sarge had to agree "Yep, fuckin good night all in all"

Tommy was relieved, he had got his reprise and it was time to get back into his "normal" role "Now is it time for beddy byes eh Daddy? Cause were allllllll going to Dubai tomorrow yeahhhhhhhh!!! Will you make sandcastles with me??? Please Daddy will ya???"

Sarge walked away leaving a happy Tommy Tit to sip his tea, shaking his head as he walked, he had to smile. Muttering to himself "I swear to Christ he's the biggest fucking nutcase I've ever met,,,crazy..stark raving.. Just doesn't give a flying fuck"

CHAPTER 3: THE ESCAPE

Baghdad

It wasn't really a cave, more like a hole in the wall behind a boulder that had taken a thousand years to move down the wadi to this exact, lucky place. How Khalid found the hole God alone knows, but he did, it just seemed to be there for him to bounce and fall into. He had found the river and doubled back almost running into the two SAS troopers than were stalking him. Just why he doubled back and how he miraculously stumbled into the cave was unquestionably a twist of fate that was, in Khaled's eyes, no less than the hand of God protecting him.

He wanted to cry, to scream but he knew that would be the end. He knew he was hurt, the pain in his groin shooting down his leg. And the pain came stronger now than before.

As Khalid looked outside the cave, he saw a silent shadow pass by. His heart jumped, the pain went, and fear took over and a burning tear ran down his cheek as he started to tremble uncontrollably. Alone, in silence he sobbed as he passed through the most painful night of his life, praying that the shadows would not return.

The next day he waited, he prayed, and he suffered and then at dusk finally took the risk to make his way out of the Wadi. He never remembered the farmer who found him and delivered him to the local midwife whose basic skills saved his life long enough for him to be smuggled into Baghdad and medical help arranged and financed by his Father in Dubai once he had received the news of his Sons plight.

Luckily for Khalid the bullet that had hit Khalid was a ricochet, slowing its speed but rotating the bullet itself like a tiny propeller that had ripped into his groin and glanced his left hip before finally exiting his right buttock. The pain was immense and the bleeding severe, but no deep surgery was required. He had been very lucky indeed and during his recovery it was easy to convince himself that the only reason for his survival was because he was chosen as something special and with a path of righteous glory ahead of him.

His colleagues and comrades, the Jihadists of Al Qaida, were quick to embrace him as their newfound hero. After all, he had survived a lethal attack purely by his own bravery and cunning and by the time he was on his feet it was a well-known fact according to his version that he had personally slain six of the attackers in the heroic battle too. Khalid the Warrior was on his way to stardom in the ranks of the terrorism, it was what he wanted more than anything else – fame and glory as a warrior of God instead of a spoilt little Dubai boy.

It was also what his Father and the Iraqi Liberation Front wanted too, but for quite different reasons. For Usman there would eventually be a massive payback from the new leaders once the Americans lost the heart for battle. He reasoned that sooner or later, the American people would turn against the idea of losing son after son in a futile war on the other side of the world. Sooner or later for sure they would decide exactly the same as they did in Vietnam and the Russians did in Afghanistan and they would pull out, leaving the country of Iraq open for someone else to financially rape. With the right investment now, in the form of a hero son, who could be in a better position for the gang-bang of Madame Iraq once the infidels had gone?

The chance for Khalid to join the hall of fame soon arrived and he was taken to the farmhouse forty miles North of Baghdad where three American soldiers captured a week earlier when their Humvee had been the target of a bomb buried in the road leading to Tuqqumdiem from Baghdad. Four had survived the initial blast but now only three were left and they were destined for a more useful purpose for the Iraqi Liberation Front now.

In the dim yellow lights in the living area his colleagues had gathered round a table and the general confusion of everyone talking at the same time went on as normal. Looking down onto the table Khalid views the personal possessions of each of the captives, wallets, watches, a crucifix, a wedding ring, a nude photograph of Mary Beth Adams a girlfriend of one of the hostages.

Leafing through the wallet of Thomas Donnelly and scrutinizing every tiny scrap of paper Khalid saw a note. *Dads new email mattthedon555@zorillion.com*

A flash of light in Khalid's brain and immediately he turned to the head jailer "Get their emails and passwords – ALL of them – Get everything, even this fucking *sharmutahs*
(Whores) too!" as he skimmed Mary Beth's picture across the table.

His ranting started "I want all of these pigs' families to know what happens when they send their sons against a Jihad"

Twenty minutes later Khalid was checking into the email accounts of all three prisoners, just to make sure the passwords and accounts were real before he murdered them.

In the large storeroom the hostages, all three men were trussed, blindfold, kneeling and bleeding. All had been beaten repeatedly for the past week and Thomas had endured eight broken fingers before he had given out his email and password details; his head was reeling, floating between pain and consciousness at times when the waves of pain passed through his broken body. He knew it was a question of time; perhaps giving out a password might buy enough time to be rescued, perhaps if the beatings continued the mandatory death sentence would be delayed giving just enough time for the Army he loved so dearly to find him alive.

The noise of people busy around him was unusual. Why weren't they screaming at him or beating him again. This time something was wrong, something was different.

A shout in Arabic, a different voice and suddenly the blindfold was yanked from Thomas's head. Peering into the light Thomas could see a man holding a professional TV video camera, lights were being set up, so was a vice technician complete with headphones and boom. And standing in front of him, Khalid al Ghazzal in his impressive black kabala and Thomas knew that now, the time had run out, he had seen the videos of others that had gone before him.

Another shout in Arabic from Khalid and Thomas was dragged, still trussed in a kneeling position, to the centre of the room. Cameras and lighting were all being checked. They were ready to roll, and Khalid pulled down the black balaclava to hide his face.

Lights, action and the list of crimes against Iraq, Allah and the Muslim world started to be read out in Arabic by the hero Khalid over the kneeling Thomas Donnelly. Pulled to his feet, the movement sending a shock wave of pain through his body of broken bones as Khalid ranted.

"You piece of American shit" as the first blow landed on Thomas's already fractured cheek bone and as Khalid arched himself backwards and grabbed the soldier's lapels to deliver more pain into the boys already broken face.

Screams rang out, especially but this time not from Thomas but from Khalid and then the beating began again. Reeling into unconsciousness from the hammer blow on his temple that caused the fatal aneurism was a blessing for Thomas. He was dead before they sawed the head from his body.

CHAPTER 4: INSIDE THE AGENCY

CIA Northern Virginia

Following Maria Donnelly's nervous breakdown, the usual military screw ups in bureaucracy and the necessity for extensive postmortem procedures the funeral of Thomas Donnelly was finally concluded. The whole process had taken four months as Thomas's killers had dumped his body and head in a hidden shallow grave which wasn't discovered for weeks.

Three days after the funeral Matt and Maria sat together, it was time to reply to the many letters of condolence they had received from so many of their mutual friends, colleagues and acquaintances from all over the world.

They leafed through the letters, choosing who should answer which, Maria came to one, it was a personalized letterhead and in the centre at the top was a small embossed English coat of arms, the shield with a red dragon to the left facing a white lion on the right with the family motto in a scroll written in Latin beneath it. Maria quietly passed it to Matt.

"It's from Stuart; you better answer this one OK?"

Matt took it and looked at the Coat of Arms, Lord Stuart Henry Bonham of Martley, Worcestershire better known to Matt as Major Stuart Bonham, SAS. Who he had served with in Central America twelve years earlier, then again in the first Gulf War after some marvelous string pulling had been achieved by his old friend and comrade. He read Stuarts letter.

Dear Matt,

It was with great sadness that we heard the news about Thomas; our hearts go out to you and your Wife at such a sad time.

From the three of us here, Tommy, Sarge and Myself we want you to know that our sympathies are with you.

Of course, we can only try to imagine what you're both going through, but also know that you will be strong.

Always remember, we are here, we are with you.

Our deepest sympathies,

Stuart, Tommy and Sarge

As Matt started his reply letter, he thought of the three comrades who had left the British Army recently and were now living in Dubai. He knew of Stuarts business attachments operating "private security" in Afghanistan and Iraq, protecting mainly civilian specialist contractors and construction workers, but also clearing some of the old soviet mines from farms and rural areas too. He made a brief reply to Stuart thanking him for the note and said he might want some help soon before turning his attentions again to Maria.

Like many other nights, Matt held her in his arms, neither had slept well, both cried in their sleep, their regular nightly torture when the vision of Thomas's face came back over and over again. Every time she looked at Matt she saw Thomas, to her their eyes were identical, green, lovely - Unique.

But after the funeral, the look in Marias eyes had also changed. It was not the gleam it had been in her previous life. It was different changed forever. Matt knew only too well that she would never be, could never be, the same again but this look now had turned from shock, to mental trauma, to grieving and was now piercing. It was a look of a single pure, cold emotion. - Revenge.

A week later Marie had returned to work, at least by now she could contain her grief enough to resume some sort of normal life. Inside she knew, it was a fact, deep inside she would mourn forever. Hatred helped, and the hatred she had for the killers, the vengeance she wanted for her only son couldn't be described. It was the very fuel of her entire existence now.

Initially her Bosses helped, she was given a fairly wide berth by everyone. No one really knew what to say or do to help her, just act as normal as possible was the general consensus. And on her part she tried to do the same, to be normal.

She knew the video of her dear Thomas existed, knew that it was "in the system" and knew it had been analyzed for clues, leads, anything that could help. She hadn't seen it and never would. The image of the email that had opened on her computer three months earlier had not only thrown her without mercy into her terrible complete nervous breakdown but had also been burnt and branded deep into her mind; she saw it every day it would never and could never, go away.

Unknown to her husband Maria met her friends Julia and Nadia every day. They were all determined to find out who had killed Thomas and one day bring him to his just end. News was constantly flowing in from Iraq and information centers throughout the Middle East. The general consensus was that the group that had executed Thomas and his comrades were led by a newcomer to Iraq. Voice recordings of the video, the killer's stature and every snippet of information leant towards this probably being true.

For a week they analyzed every known insurgency and speculated on other possible entry of potential Jihadists. Julia had been active and eventually looked at Border interceptions and then one caught her eye. Soon she had narrowed the search down to the three link names submitted into British Intelligence by the SAS team reports. Ali Ramadan was quickly verified as real, his British passport secreted in his left shoe sole had helped that move along easily. The names Samer al Shataff and Khalid al Ghazall had proved a God send revealing long suspected links with a man who had been monitored by the British MI5 four years earlier, a certain Mr. Usman al Ghazall – Father of one Khalid al Ghazzal.

And real proof had surfaced too; the blood collected on the plastic slide in the Wadi confirmed a match to the Ghazall family. Not that proof was exactly what the CIA needed, they were not a Court of Law, and they were the CIA. Trying to dig up more about Usman lead Julia to circulate a many different requests for information to their various colleagues in different countries. Anything on Al Ghazall of Dubai? Was the basic question.

Following the exchange of a few messages, MI6 and MI5 in London both came back with information for Julia. Photographs, know associates, favorite restaurants, Hotel bills, shop receipts and copies of his phone bills and Credit Card statements all came back from London. So did Usman al Ghazall's DNA profile, easily collected from a hotel room in London four years earlier by British Intelligence.

Julia's dossier on Usman was growing by the day now.

Nadia Khoury a Lebanese born Christian should have been a model instead of an interpreter. She was the archetypal eastern beauty. Fluent in Arabic she worked closely with her pier, John Macintosh a dedicated film buff and photography expert. Anything, absolutely anything to do with the oldest celluloid through to the most advanced and ultra-modern in photography world was Johns passion.

At lunch a week or so later Maria explained "I know, I know. It's been analyzed and there's nothing coming up. But please Nadia, you know Johns the best at this, please can you get him to run through it again? This time you've got more information. You know his probably background, listen for his accent, any word that may give any indicator at all…absolutely anything Nadia…. Please?" Nadia couldn't say no.

That same afternoon Nadia and John went to work. They were professionals and knew that the shock and disgust of the horror on the screen would divert and numb their technical scrutiny; they knew that they could only work at 100% when the shock factors had been removed. And it was Nadia and John who sat and watched through the execution of Tomas Donnelly so many times, over and over again until it was almost a *normal* thing to view.

"It's been reworked, in a few places, but this is the main one, look….." John moved frame by frame at the portion of the video which showed the eventual executioner at one point after pulling the wounded soldier to his feet, bracing himself as if to do something, then the video was cut.

He mumbled "Why the cut?...Why?"

Nadia mind flashed back almost immediately to her University days and The Square in Glasgow, Scotland

"Oh, I know what he's going to do …. look…. he's going to head-butt him! Watch!"

"What the fuck? …Why?" John stared at the screen trying to work out what was going through his mind "What sick fuck would want to head butt the guy?"

Nadia sneered "Easy, …it's to show how brave he is"

"Brave? Head-butting a guy that's trussed up like a Thanksgiving turkey?" What do you mean?" John was puzzled at Nadia's comment.

They sat and sipped coffee and Nadia explained "When I graduated in Beirut, my dad sent me to Glasgow University, its Scotland, not England, big difference you know"

John was uninterested, still looking over and over at that section of the video sort of subconsciously listening without even knowing.

"Anyway" Nadia continued "It's a great place, Glasgow, I loved the people there, it was voted the Cultural City of Europe too did you know that?"

John didn't answer but still Nadia continued "Some gorgeous hunks there too, mmmm well, the one guy I used to date, proper Scot, gorgeous, natural body know what I mean?"

"Yeh, whatever. What's this to do with it Nad? You're putting me off" John was getting aggravated with her story as he continued his frame by frame search.

"Well, I'm telling you. See, the Scots don't like the English, you know for Brave heart, William Wallace…errr OK Mel Gibson and all that stuff? And my boyfriend explained it to me. About a Glasgow Kiss"

John leaned back from the screen "Nad, no offence but ..your pissing me off now who gives a fuck about Scotsmen kissing English guys, Jeeeez"

"No John, listen, the Scots would start fights in the bars in Glasgow, usually they would fight each other, God they were wild guys but, if they could find anyone English they would always choose to fight with them first. And if they could they would always try to use the same sort of trademark, it was called a Glasgow kiss, a head-butt"

"Great" now John was really pissed off "So after all that I now know that the Scotts are racist bastards who enjoy sado games with British tourists..wow..great"

"English tourists, the Scotts are British too. Oh, forget it ..what I mean is that the head-butt is a way of showing that they're not afraid to hurt themselves as long as they hurt their enemy more. See what I mean? The guy here" pointing at the screen to the hooded figure " He's the one making all the condemning speech in the first part, reading out Thomas's crimes as an American, then he's the one who wants to show everyone how brave he is..*but*..after – I mean if he did the head-butt - then he's a lot quieter and doesn't say so much. See? It hurt him, he hurt himself when he tried to head-butt Thomas - he isn't that brave. Now understand?"

John stopped, turned and looked at the screen, Nadia's story was sinking in, she had spotted something - a male ego. John had missed it and missed the fact that the executioner had been quieter after the point where the video had been cut and pasted. *"Quieter after? Quieter after?"* went through Johns mind *"Why quieter after?"*

Nadia left to get more coffee from down the hallway. John was a film buff, a technician but definitely not a bar brawl expert. He needed advice. Picking up the phone he dialed an extension number.

"Hey Godzilla"

Marine Major Pete Erikson answered, "Hey fuck you too John, how you doing?"

John got straight to the point… "Pete, head butting? I want to know about it….."

Pete laughed "Anytime John, come right on down and I can show you. What kind of nose would you like?" Pete had a Marine's sense of humor "Wide, very wide or ear to ear?"

John exaggerated the Bronx accent on purpose "Fuck you Rambo, I am serious, help me out here will ya or no more homo porn for *yooz* anymore, kapish?"

Pete just loved his friend *subtle* wit "OK go ahead, what do you need John?"

"Head butting, is that what you go for, the nose?" John was squinting at the screen, phone in one hand as he craned his head looking at the executioner's delivery of the movement.

Duly Pete answered what he thought was a stupid question "Of course! *Your* brow needs to connect with *his* face, not his head; otherwise you can both get hurt. Idea is to hurt the other guy a lot more than you hurt yourself John, didn't they teach you anything at school?"

Still staring at the screen Pete was drifting trying to hold two trains of thought "No. I mean yes, but..fuck..listen. What happens if you do it wrong? I mean how can it go wrong? Is there any sort of special training that you meat heads get taught or what?"

It's a good job they were friends, Pete had knocked teeth out for much less comments against the Corp and he also understood that John was probably involved with something less than tasteful.

John still flicking through the video as he spoke updated Pete.

"We've picked up on something…he Thomas Donnelly thing…we think his executioner head butted Thomas before killing him. I need to know what the score is, the A to Z on head butting"

"Ah. That one" Pete replied in a serious tone now he knew where this was leading, he had seen the video too

"Yeh, that's the one. What do you think?"

Pete switched on now he knew what John was picking up on. "Well I saw it and the kid did great. He knew his time was up and he didn't crap himself. He showed true balls if you ask me. As for that fucking asshole who head-butted him, he's a goddamn coward and a fucking amateur. Even with the kid trussed up he must have missed the face almost totally because Thomas`s face didn't show any damage to his nose. That must mean that the guy missed. You look at it and you will see. Understand, if the guy doing the headbutt isn't used to doing it, or is afraid, then the first thing he will do is to close his eyes, a sort of natural reaction, knowing that some pain will be his too…know what I mean?"

Johns fingers were already working on the mouse under the screen, zooming in, X100 into the eyes of the black ski mask.

Down the phone to Pete immediately and in the very last frame before the cut he saw it "Yes! He closed his eyes. Definitely they closed"

"Yep, that's what I said. A coward and an amateur" Pete was pleased to confirm.

"Gimme more Pete, what could have happened if this guy screwed it up? I need to know, just run stuff past me" John could smell it; something was here, at this point in the video, something they had to cut and edit.

"Well….first, check out Thomas`s face, I know you can do it with all your gadgets, I just saw the vid once, but look at Thomas, first determine did he see the headbutt coming, even a quarter of a second is enough to react. He was a young fit kid in the Rangers." First check that out. If he had any warning he could have flinched, tried to duck or turn his head sideways and down a little. Can you see?"

John was already there as Pete had been speaking John was zooming, forwards and back to the right frames.

"No I can't see anything Pete, the bastards have cut it" Johns mind was racing trying to imagine the "cut" part of the video as Nadia placed a fresh coffee on Johns desk, sat and listened to the conversation on the speaker as she cupped her mug in both hands and sipped.

John needed to know "Pete, what options would the kid have? He was trussed up".

"Not too many John, in fact, only one I can think of but even that wouldn't have gotten him out of that kind of corner"

John paused, one option, of course it was all the poor kid had left and as he thought it, Pete said it……..

"Bit the motherfucker"

John was working, his head swimming in realization and he put the phone down as he was thanking Pete "Call ya back……Thanks" turned to Nadia "Quieter after, I know why he was quieter after"

"He hurt himself?" Nadia asked.

"No. Thomas hurt him. Thomas bit him, Look"

Quickly he flicked through the key frames and explained what Pete had passed over to him and how it was fitting together. Zooming in and using computer graphics to analyze close ups of Thomas's lips he could see it. Even though Thomas had obviously been wiped with a rag or a cloth John could now see blood in the fine lines of Thomas's dry lips.

"Play his speech after the killing, just want the sound OK, clear as you can in the headset, just let me listen" Nadia directed then started to listen, her eyes closed, she wasn't translating, that was easy, she was in pure Arabic mode, listening to the spoken Arabic for the tiniest inflections. She would direct John, he would rewind, pause, press play and then stop. Over and over again. After fifteen minutes and having marked key positions in the soundtrack, they went back to the beginning Nadia telling John,

"The list, when he was reading out the list of Thomas's crimes, number one this, number two that.."

"It's in Arabic" John complained, thinking to himself *"how the fuck do I know when he says this or that?"*

"Doesn't matter, go back till I say stop, then go forwards"

Almost immediately Nadia's eyes still closed listening intently in the headset "That's it, mark that, back, no back, no.. OK stop, play, That! Mark it"

She took off the headset "Telatha… he said *the-latha* instead of telatha"

"What's telatha?" John asked.

"It's a number, or rather it's the Arabic word for the number three and she counted and showed on her fingers Wahid, Etneen, Telatha – One Two Three, he said telatha before he killed Tomas and afterwards too, but he said it differently afterwards, sort of, how can I say it with a, you know when people can't pronounce the words clearly, what's it called"

John stared at her, "A lisp, …he's lisping in Arabic?.. You can tell?"

"Yes" Nadia clicked her fingers and scolded herself for forgetting the word "Yes that's it, a lisp, he's got a lisp after he killed Thomas, I can hear it"

Nadia confirmed it "I've heard it before, in Majayoune, my village in South Lebanon. When my Brother Imad was climbing a pine tree he banged his head on his knees as he tried to sort of jump out of the tree and his teeth went through his top lip. He sounded like that for ages after, with a *yeldug,* that's our word for it…a lisp"

They looked exhausted, tired out but very, very pleased. At last they had something. Tomas had bitten his killer and had bitten him on the mouth.

They sat there and must have looked stupid, they didn't care, and they repeated the word telatha over and over again. To lisp as the word was pronounced only happened when the top lip was pinched. Thomas had bitten the top lip.

Even though it was midnight all departments were open and running at full strength. The CIA doesn't close, ever.

John spoke into the telephone after flicking through the Internal Directory to find the extension of someone in the medical department; basically, he had gone to the CIA Orthodontic specialist.

After explaining who they were and what advice was needed the doctor on the other end was pleased to help with a simplified layman's version about scar damage to the mouth and lips. In a nutshell, he explained that the bottom lip could sustain more damage than the top one due to the mass and elasticity of the flesh. The bottom line meant that any scar would be far more evident on the top lip than the bottom one. Also, it could be reasonable to expect that the scar would be more disfiguring and permanent. And if the scar was severe enough then most definitely it would lead to the person having a lisp.

" Great many thanks Doc, say; can you put me through to somebody helpful in the Autopsy department? I need a big special favor" John was moving fast and thirty seconds later the doctor in Autopsy Records section was flicking through Donnelly – Thomas – Mathew - beheading files on his computer.

"Were swabs taken? From the body or head?" John asked

"Yes, from both, sixteen from the head including inner ear, nasal passages, throat, what was left of it, gums basically covered the lot. From the body…"

"No. - no need The head swabs are the important ones. We need them analyzed, its urgent. Can it be done?"

"Well, yes I guess so, but we will need the right paperwork. We're pretty thorough you know" The Doctor said proudly.

John lied through his teeth "You'll have it by noon tomorrow, but can you please start on it now? I need to know is there any trace whatsoever, any, of anyone else's blood in there"

"Sorry, I need the paperwork, have to have it"

The New Yorker could think on his feet "Doc, if there's someone else's bloods in there it's from Thomas Donnelley's killer. I need it and I need it to nail the asshole now within hours or we might miss him"

The Doctor paused. "Gimme your direct email, you'll have it by morning that's the best I can do OK?"

There was no time to waste but now John just had to wait as he leaned back in his chair hands behind his head he looked at Nadia "If he picks up on blood then we've got a real good lead Nad. This could the break we need. Let's hope to God that Doc comes back with some news"

A day later, after they had treble checked every single detail from every possible angle, Julia called Maria; she had important news for her. Before closing the Motorola hand phone, she added "It's time for Matt to be in on this now"

CHAPTER 5: THE ARRIVAL

Dubai, UAE

Matts taxi from Dubai International Airport followed the main drag across the Garhoud Bridge before weaving through the ultra-modern carriageways along Sheikh Zayeed Road. Matt noted that they seemed to be following all the signs that mentioned Jebel Ali and Abu Dhabi and as the driver stuck like glue to the speed limit of 80 kph they felt the wind of a land Cruiser with its black tinted windows that passed them so fast it rocked the sturdy Volvo.

"Nice" said Matt sarcastically at the virtual lunatic driving.

"Yes Sah," said the driver "Always they are the same like this Sir, they drive very fast. Speed cameras no problem for them, They don't pay, not like me. If I break the limit I must pay - not the company - see? Three hundred Dirhams (90$) it's very huge amount Sah"

Passing through the tunnel of 21st century tower blocks, White, blue, green and gold monuments to the spearhead of Dubai's Architecture, the Manhattan of the Middle East. To the left the Burj Lakes and the Burj Dubai, the world's tallest building they soon took the turn from the main Sheikh Zayed Road into the Jumairah Suburbs of Dubai, home to the famous Burj al Arab Hotel and its famous sail shaped profile visible above every rooftop.

Taking the road running parallel to the beach the driver quickly worked his way to the given address, a large detached villa painted a bright white with tinted blueish windows. It spoke of opulence, almost oozed the word.

"This is it Sir" the driver seemed pleased to announce as he blew the horn. Looking through the wrought iron side gate a small brown hand waved, and the electric double garage doors opened showing the way into a spacious parking area. Already there was the vintage Jaguar E type and a new white BMW 4 wheel.

"Looks like Stu is doing well for himself" flashed through Matts mind as the Filipina girl beamed a smile and welcomed him.

"This way Surr" the Manila accent came across loud and clear, bringing a flash of memories back to Matt of his days in the Far East so many years before, and he followed as the petite girl led him into the house.

Matt looked as he followed her, moving in through the large modern Oak doorway into a hallway and reception area that was Border line ridiculously large and then onwards through the pristine white Villa eventually arriving at the back door that lead out to the garden area. Standing in the doorway Matt looked down towards the large kidney shaped pool and saw the three men.

"Well, well, well……if the Devil could cast his net!"

"Hey Matt, welcome to Dubai" Stuart called from the pool and made his way to the edge. Tommy raised his glass of Bloody Mary and Sarge smiled as Matt strolled down and firmly shook everyone's hand.

Tommy poured a drink from the pitcher and handed it to Matt "Red Breakfast mate, it's a Friday ritual here. Cheers" and the men sat and chatted, after another couple of red-hot Bloody Mary's they laughed and joked. Matt felt good to be in the Company of his old friends, he had lived with them before, served with them, shared all the ups and downs that their lifestyle brought to them all. He felt at home. Eventually the conversation settled down, Stuart said what the men were all thinking.

"We were sorry to hear your news Matt……really sorry."

Politely Matt replied almost on auto pilot he had heard it so many times now "Yes, thanks Stuart" as the shook hands again.

Stuart leaned back in his wooden garden chair and looked across the large table at Matt. The men were silent "And now Matt? You're here to do something about things?" again Matt nodded, the guys were no fools and it was pretty obvious that Matt wouldn't have come all this way, especially at this time, just for fun. Stuart continued "If there's anything we can do to help, we're in, OK?"

"To be honest I do need help, any help is welcome, but I need local on the ground help. But, having said that, it's just with a few logistics - this one is mine. My personal job"

Sitting back, appraising the situation Stuart knew he was right; Matt's arrival in Dubai has something to do with retribution for his son's death. And he knew how Matt thought because they had discussed it and assumed that Matt was going to use Dubai somehow as a jumping off point to track Thomas' executioner down in Iraq or some surrounding country.

They both sat at the table, neither saying a word. Matt had made his position clear, but the English Lord still wanted to know exactly what Matt was up to and how he could help.

This time, the Lord's old trick of saying nothing and waiting for the other man to speak first actually worked on Matt.

Matt cracked. "OK, I could use a little help finding an individual in Dubai. And I admit that I need help taking that individual to a secluded location where he can be questioned for perhaps as many as three days". He did not tell his friend, however, that he planned to murder this individual. Matt made it seem that all he was after was information.

No one was fooled, they knew exactly what Matt would do if he laid hands on anyone, absolutely anyone, associated with his only son's murder. He flicked a glance at Tommy and knew he was thinking the same thing.

Stuart needed to know and asked "Matt, I have to ask. Is this official business or purely…private?"

Matt didn't hesitate, he might hold information back when needs be, but he sure as hell wouldn't tell a direct lie to his Comrade. "It's personal Stu. It's something I need…. no,…it's something I *have* to do. You know what I mean, no need to explain it is there?"

"No…not at all, we just needed to know that's all" Stuart was comfortable with killing anyone that deserved killing, officially or not it didn't faze him at all, and he continued.

"So Matt, what do you need to know?"

Matt was keen to get moving, he wanted to get straight in, the faster the better. "There is a man here, a local called Usman al Ghazall. He's been under suspicion for quite some time by the Brits initially, they were watching him for suspected links in recruitment of young Muslims in the UK, but he came out relatively clean, they could never pin anything on him. Besides, apparently he is a big fish and it would rock the relationship of the UK with the UAE. It's all about British exports and money too, that was his real protection at the time. The Brits really don't want to upset one of their best customers in trade.

Since then the CIA picked up on him the Brits passed over what intelligence they had. Now we are pretty sure that this guy is doing arms for cash dealing for Al-Qaeda, probably from some mickey mouse east Russian source. Then he's making a fortune out of the cash, buying in Gold and Gems and probably doubling his money from a chain of stores he's got in the Gold Market here"

"The Souk, the Gold *Souk*" Stuart corrected him.

Matt continued "Yes, that's the one, Dubai City of Gold, the Gold Souk. …Anyways, he owns stores there; fronted under a junior partners name but legally he owns the stores. We got his holding confirmed; he's the 80% shareholder of a chain called Al Shattaf Gold and Gems LLC or whatever they call their Limited companies here"

Tommy coughed, almost choked on his drink as Stuart looked sideways at him, Sarges eyes rolled skywards and he fidgeted a little uncomfortably.

"On the records, Al Shattaf's son was done by some of your mob, an SAS ambush, six months ago as they crossed into Iraq, near Tikrit. It was believed that the kid was financed by Usman, even encouraged to go there. Of course, there's no proof of it. But, either way, it's a direct link to Usman by Al Shattaf and his son. Usman knows who is behind the murder squad that's operating in Iraq, he's financing them because it's his son that's the big brave head honcho in the gang"

"Our people here have picked up on the Ghazzal family and it's known that Samer was a school friend of Usman's son, Khalid, who by the way dropped out of sight from here at the exact same time as his friend Samer a year and a half back.

The three sat and listened while Matt explained the whole sequence of events including his sons beheading, the emails, Maria's terrible nervous breakdown and finally the fact that his son went down fighting and bit his executioner. Summing up Matt concluded.

"Maria and her friends got the proof…. DNA from the Usman family was found….it means Thomas bit a member of the Usman family – he bit his executioner. "

He paused.

"He bit Khaled al Ghazzal…..Usman's son killed my son. That's the bottom line. That's what I am here to put right"

Tommy looked at Stuart. A *"what do we do now Boss sort of look."* Stuart flicked his eyes towards the rear upstairs of the house where his private office overlooked the pool and garden.

"Fetch your *thing* Tommy. You know the combination" (to the house safe)

For once, Tommy face was serious," Be right back" and he left the table.

Matt noticed it, Sarges face confirmed it, they *knew* something. He pushed things now, continuing in a very clear and quiet tone "This is the guy that financed my son's killers. And for sure he's financing other killings and assassinations. I intend to stop it and I intend to get my revenge………….. It's as easy as that"

Matt was convinced, he could see Stuart listening to him but then noticed that he glanced to see if Tommy was returning. Stuart for once looked nervous *"What was going on? Ask direct – it's the only way"* went through Matt's mind.

He looked at Stuart and simply said "OK Stu. What is it?"

As if relieved Tommy was retuning now, walking down the steps towards the garden table Stuart recounted the story of their last mission in service, the ambush 40 kilometers south of Tikrit. When he had finished he nodded to Tommy who leaned forward and placed a diamond on the table in front of Matt. It was a perfect and beautifully cut stone and in the Dubai sunshine sparkled like a thousand laser beams.

Pointing at the stone "That was Samir al Shattaf's payment, his bribe money for us to get him home" Stuart said and continued "Young Samie was one that we slotted in the last job, a group of Al Qaida crossing into Iraq from Syria about 20 miles North of Mosul.

"Well well" said Matt knowing fully that the link, the suspicions were growing stronger and stronger by the minute. Now he knew he had come to the right place.

Stuart paused and glanced at Tommy and Sarge, the look in return was "It's up to you Boss" which Stuart read in a millisecond before continuing

"The reason we know it was Samer al Shattaf's diamond is because he told Tommy about it just before he died" Again Stuart paused for the realization in Matt's face and Stuart nodded "Yes, we were the group that caught them. Twelve in all, eleven dead one slipped through"

"But definitely wounded" Sarge quickly added in.

"Now" said Stuart as if he was kicking into gear "Sarge knows for sure that he hit the runner and we also got his name from the two survivors before they pegged it." He paused and eyed Matt before giving him the best part.

"The good thing is we also got a blood sample and it will definitely be on the records at Cheltenham" Leaning forward he looked Matt in the eyes "The name was Khaled al Ghazzal "

Matt's questions were fast and furious. Did they know of Usman? Do you know this man? How can I get at him? On and on the questions came, Matt hardly believing his luck that within hours Langley would get definite confirmation of the killers' identity.

"Yes, they knew and yes I know of him" started the Lord. And as he elaborated, he slid the local newspaper, The Kaleej Times across the table to Matt. "There he is Matt, front page photo shaking hands with the local royalty. He's the tall one second from the right".

Sure enough, there was a picture of old hooknose and an underlying caption describing whom he was meeting and why. The headline of the accompanying story read "Al Ghazzal Properties Breaks Ground on Massive Building Project". The story read that, as members of the royal family were in attendance, Usman Al Ghazzal lifted the first shovel of sand to inaugurate the building of a major condominium project featuring a water's edge view of Dubai's Palm Islands not far from the exclusive Jumeirah Beach area. The project was to be financed using private investments.

Step by step the picture emerged. If Usman al Ghazzal wasn't financing the murder squad Matt would be amazed. Either way, he deserved bringing down for the financing of terror. Usman was now a marked man and little did he know, as he sat in the sumptuous lounge of his floating Gin Palace just four miles away eying another pretty girl's delicate mouth, that Matt had just passed sentence upon him worse than death.

"How can I get to him? Any ideas?" Matt's questions wouldn't abate, he had the scent of his quarry now and the guys knew and agreed that it would be an unstoppable hunt.

"Not sure what's the best angle for that Matt. Let's think it through carefully. But one thing for sure, Dubai isn't the best place to operate, much safer outside the UAE. Dubai is a, well….. not exactly a village but a small town. I know it's a huge sprawling City to look at, but the jungle drums work it like a much smaller place. Every other local, or rather it suggested everyone in three, are involved one way or another with the CID. They don't miss a thing."

Stuart thought briefly then continued.

"You wanted to come to Dubai and milk this guy for information – and then you wanted to *slot* him." Stuart paused as the vision went through his mind "Well, there's nothing wrong with that, but, I think that Dubai is the wrong venue for a kidnapping — murders simply don't happen easily here. If you implement your plan here and they find out, they'll hunt you down. And if your trail leads back to America, they may even ask their friends in the American navy — who, by the way moor and fuel their boats just down the coast from here with the permission of the Sheik — to have you back, causing an international incident. I suggest that you find a way to take action against Al Ghazzal somewhere outside of the

Emirates. Some place where he is better exposed. And some place where you can get away with eliminating him, no questions asked."

Tommy poured another round of Red Breakfasts.

Looking at his watch Stuart added "As for how to get to him, well, someone will be joining us soon who might be able to help on that. They're joining us for lunch here, and don't worry, they're on board and you will be able to be open with them. Part of our team so to speak"

The discussions continued, mostly about Al Ghazzal, how money could easily be doubled and trebled almost overnight in the tsunami of Dubai's property boom. Estimates of just how much Ghazzal would be worth. Every aspect that they knew and some that they could only forecast about the man and his lifestyle, beliefs and hypocrisy and greed were chatted through.

Unspoken, they all knew is that this was totally unofficial business, a private vendetta on Matts part and all agreed it was the right thing to do too.

As the two maids passed between them all, setting the garden table for lunch. Stuart and Matt decided to take a dip in the pool.

"Mabel, show Mr. Matt to his room so he can get changed, then help Agnes with the table please" Stuart spoke with the polite fair but assertive tone of someone brought up to deal with servants. Matt noted what old-fashioned names all good Filipinas seemed to have. A throwback to the Catholic Missionaries that still coursed through the Philippines to this day.

Ten minutes later Matt and Stuart were chatting in the bath temperature water of the luxurious Jumairah home pool.

"Matt, you don't know the half of it. Tucked away in there" Stuart pointed at the top half of the Burj al Arab that could be seen towering arrogantly over the tall garden wall that faced the coast." In the world's only seven-star hotel, that costs an arm and a leg for a single night. Irish ex IRA conmen openly scam the taxpayers of the United Kingdom and they've been living in there for the past four months. That" Jabbing his finger towards the monolith "Is their fucking *office!*"

Stuart couldn't help but show the hatred that he had for the IRA and he didn't care to hide it either.

"Across town at the Kremlin, that's the top, swank Russian restaurant, the head of the Chechenia mob directs his foreign operations. Everyone comes here, everyone is welcome as long as they basically don't shit on their own doorstep, at least not their holiday home, Dubai doorstep that is. Terrorists, swindlers, embezzlers, drug lords, tax dodgers, pimps and prostitutes can come and go as they please — as long as they haven't broken any of the local laws. It's wrong, its hypocrisy, its obscene but it's the way it is. The U.S. alone has had the last thirty odd requests for extradition turned down. The Paddy's in the Burj are creaming more than a Million Pounds a week, that's One point Eight Million US$ *every single week* from blatant VAT Tax scams. They're laughing about it, - and there's absolutely nothing the Brits can do. That's the way this place works, everyone is welcome, just don't do the dirty deeds here and spend a lot of cash and your safe."

Stuart needed to educate Matt about the place, the people, the last thing he wanted was for Matt to be sucked in by the veneer and it was an extremely well-polished veneer that Dubai presented to visitors.

"Look, let me explain Matt, all that glitters is definitely not gold here, except maybe the stuff you see in the Souk. Yes, Dubai is a fantastic place, tax free, safe, cosmopolitan, modern. In fact, all in all probably the best City on the Planet earth you could choose to live in. But, there is the other side, the hypocrisy, the get rich quick attitudes, the greed, the very blind eye that can be turned. It's important for you to know about that side too.

"I'm all ears, fire away" said Matt "The more I know the better" even the smallest insignificant detail just might have an important clue or indication later in Matt's scheme of things, so he wanted to hear it all, warts and all.

"Last week, some Indian laborer here, probably hadn't had his leg over in two years, anyway, he flashed at a local woman. He got 2 months jail, 1,000 dirhams fine and deportation at the end of it. OK, that's fair I suppose. Then, in the same court, a local kid, 24 yrs. old, was driving like the typical bully boy being superman in his 4 wheel and ploughed into the back of a British woman's car. Killed her outright, just through his vile arrogance and stupidity. He got three months jail and, and, you can bet your life he won't serve it. His dad will know someone who has a word with someone else, he will apologies and promise to be a good boy and then he will walk away. - Literally with murder.

Now and then they will catch the odd Indian or Pakistani trying to smuggle drugs in on a Dhow, the penalties are harsh, 3 or 4 years for a fingernail full of hashish but when an American record producer arrived here carrying a shit load of cocaine to a supermodels party in the Burj al Arab, he walked away free as a bird after two days. He was even seen smiling at the Judge, he knew he would walk away.

Stuart shook his head and almost laughed at the irony

"And the weird thing is that the system - it all seems to work"

As he spoke, the men's heads turned

"Hello guys" came from the two girls walking down the steps.

"Hey. Coffee – n- Cream!" called Tommy to the girls who laughed knowing his joke. Natalia tall dark leggy brunette and Lenna shorter, equally as curvy and a naturally contrasting blonde, had arrived.

"It isn't a catwalk you know!" Stuart joked as they approached down the steps, each in a silk sarong tied at their waist and split to the hip and each in the tiniest bikini tops imaginable. The waterproof make up hadn't been forgotten either. Stuart made a mental note that they had arrived probably 20 minutes earlier and had been in his bedroom to get changed into their bikinis to make their "entrance" like this.

They arrived at the steps of the pool and Stuart introduced Matt as an "Old Friend" to Natallia and then Lenna in turn. As Natallia shook his hand she eyed the scars on Matts shoulder and chest.

"I see ……. the same *business* as my lovely Stuart used to be in, yes?"

"Matt nodded "Yes, the same just retired – too old for it now" he joked.

A very charming and honest "Pleased to meet you Matt" came in return as Natallia leaned forwards to shake his hand, almost spilling out of the miniature thin material of the bikini top as she did so.

Lunch was served on the garden table after another 30 minutes by the two Filipinas; Matt wondered whether his old friend Stuart had any male staff. What was he running here, the Playboy mansion—Middle East? Natallia and Lenna came from the pool to join them and replaced their sarongs to sit at the table.

Tommy suggested "Can't you two eat your' s in the pool?" suggesting that he preferred the thong style bikinis to the sarongs. Everyone laughed - everyone was relaxed.

Matt made small talk with Natallia asking what had brought her to Dubai, he was impressed, Natallia was very open and forthcoming about herself. She ran through her history – including the breakdown of her marriage, her reasons for being in Dubai, her current profession, and a few of the details on how she met Stuart.

When she had explained the situation, Stuart stepped in and prompted her "Matt would like to know more about a certain Mr. Usman al Ghazzal, can you tell him about the man Nat?"

Both girls showed a distinct change in attitude at the mention of the name. Natallia was first to speak about Al Ghazzal. "Matt" she said, "You have no idea what kind of beast this man is. When he beat Millenna, one of our friends so badly, she's ruined, her face was pretty and now he made her so ugly…"

" *Gnusnoe Chudovistche!*" Lenna cursed in Russian "Fucking Vile Monster"

Natalia continued "We *know* him. On the outside, he appears to be a respectable, rich businessman. He is a successful real estate investor has lots of very big property developments over there" She pointed at the wall, but in the general direction of the coast "In JBR area.

"JBR?" quizzed Matt

"Jumairah Beach Residence" explained Stuart "Well at least that's what she (Natalia) calls it, but it's basically all the tower blocks and apartment towers that are being built down the beach towards the direction of Jebel Ali"

Natallia continued "Anyway, he also deals in Gold and has I don't know really, but maybe seven shops in the Gold Souk, one is very big, really big. But in reality, he drinks, does drugs, has a huge sexual appetite, he abuses women and servants, he's arrogant – and through his actions I can tell you he is a sick *saddiste*, sick. He is a total hypocrite."

"The worst way he could be hurt, the better" Natallia concluded "If Lecho, that's my…. Boss…. Didn't have so many business deals with Usman I would have asked him to help but when Usman beat Milena he didn't say a thing, so he must be owed lots of money by Usman or something"

"He must be selling Lecho something" Lenna threw in the comment "Ha ! Lecho will sell anything to anyone"

"Slow down, explain it slowly" Matt was amazed at the flood of information, this was better than he could ever have dreamed. Through the lunch and into the late afternoon Lenna and Natallia had no hang ups or embarrassment explaining just who they were and how they had become high class hookers. The lot was explained to Matt, even about them being used by Usman of several occasions too.

After the second bottle of Champagne for the girls was heading towards empty and the party was in full swing, everyone was more relaxed and Tommie's Red breakfasts had really done the intended job. Lenna said loudly "Lets toast, to taking everything that Usman has got, then let's show him to all his friends as a horrible bastard that he is…. then..then.." Her mind was racing through the pools of champagne ",,,,,,,," then cut his balls off" She turned to Tommy "That will kill him wont it Malenki (darling)?"

Tommy nodded "Well… it wouldn't do him much fuckin good Len?" making a mock move as if he were frightened of Lenna and her knife.

"Ohhh Don't worry Tommy darling… I won't cut your balls off. They're lovely little balls"

Sarge laughed loud.

"Thanks for the compliment Len, - really appreciate that" said Tommy glowering at Sarges laughter nodded towards him and added "So did that fat bastard!".

She was giggling now "…....then… rob his shop give me *allllllll* his diamonds" She was giggling now.

Tommy's red breakfasts had worked on him too. "Nah Len, we wouldn't just do *his* shop. We would do the whole fuckin Souk." Opening his arms in a big circle at the same time as knocking half a Bloody Mary over Sarges legs "Then they wouldn't have any money left to clean and no money for no more fuckin guns would they eh??"

What was perfectly clear to Tommy didn't deserve dwelling on "Ooop sorry Sarge, let me lick you clean" Tommy stuck his tongue out to which the Sarge politely replied "Fuck off you cunt"

At the table, Matt and Stuart were silent, looking at Tommy. And, as the realization of his comment sank in Matt said quietly… "My God, Tommy…… you could be right"

"I know I could!" Tommy was almost proud of his crystal-clear thought. He couldn't understand why no one else had ever thought of it; the whole thing was so obvious to Tommy.

"It's easy…Look, close Shindagha tunnel, seal off a couple of roads, throw a shit load of gas in the Souk, empty the shops and fuck off in a great big boat. Viola!" as he again opened his arm and made the "whole" gesture, this time rocking just that bit too far and disappearing backwards from the table.

The girls laughing, Sarges eyes rolling, Stuart looking down and shaking his head at Tommie's antics.

The voice, now from under the table could be heard "Rob the bastard………. Let's rob him blind. Let's leave him with nothing. That would hurt him – that would hurt him good – Rob all the fuckers……..Empty the fuckin washing machine, empty the fucking money launderette!!!"".

Matt turned and looked at Stuart, both thinking the same thing. Letting Tommy's words sink in.

"Empty the washing machine"

And then, all at once, everyone started to speak.

CHAPTER 6: THE PLAN

March, Dubai, UAE

After the Friday brunch that had predictably turned into an all-day drinking session. The next day everyone was in a more businesslike mood. Matt spent time with Stuart cruising around Dubai in the BMW four wheel giving Matt a bullet point run down on the history, geography, "what is where" and the location of various regions and landmarks of the City. Facts, figures, anecdotes and information of all sorts was fired across to Matt who soaked it in like blotting paper. By seven o'clock when they returned to the Villa in Jumairah Matt knew more about Dubai than a regular tourist would pick up in a lifetime of vacations there.

Natallia, Tommy and Sarge had joined in as usual for Dinner which had been delivered to the Villa and they were soon sitting round the table in the large dining room overlooking the garden and illuminated far "too blue to be real" swimming pool everyone enjoyed a classic Lebanese meal delivered by the nearest "automatic" Lebanese restaurant situated on Beach Road. Fresh salads that looked like a presentation at Harvest Festival, Houmus, Arayes, racks of delicate Lamb chops. All in all, over 28 different dishes made up the meal, so typically Lebanese in its presentation and style. The Kings of food in the Middle East are undoubtedly the Lebanese.

"Whichever way this can be done" Stuart explained "It's going to take money, that's a simple fact. - You can't make money without spending money. The fact is, we intend to severely hit the Al Qaeda "piggy" bank if you excuse my pun. And that will hurt them, set them back in arms supplies without any doubt. BUT, we are having to do the job off our own backs, so that means it's also fair to make a profit too"

"I've roughly worked through a few different scenarios, but again, essentially, whichever one we follow will need four basic stages. First the planning and investigation, the feasibility study if you like. Second the set-up of the foundation, getting everything in place at the right time, recruiting people, buying equipment, basically building our infrastructure of the project. Thirdly, the execution of it all, probably the cheapest part in financial terms but the most expensive part in personal terms, especially if it goes wrong, if you see what I mean. And finally, the escape and the backup plan or route for escape, let's not forget that one will need to be ready and in place……So first we must start with the fourth part.. How exactly, do we get away with it? The whole plan can only be based on that being on place."

Everyone was all ears, it was interesting for Natallia to hear what Stuart had to say, she had never actually been exposed to or fully understood how he worked before and this was fascinating.

For Tommy, Sarge and Matt they had expected it, they had seen his plans form and come to fruition on many occasions and they were looking forward to it for different reasons completely. They knew that Stuart could put something together and it would be sensible, logical and most of all, relatively as safe as possible for all concerned.

"So" Stuart continued "So first of all let's look at the last part, the escape. After all its no good going into anything unless we can get away with it"

"My way of thinking is that it has to be fast, it has to be as safe as possible. It has to put as much distance between us and the competition before they have time to react. That means one thing; the escape route has to be by air.

One approach would be to use aircraft capable of lifting a lot of men and cargo out of Dubai. The problem with that is we'll need a long runway, so that means Dubai airport and Dubai Airport just isn't an option.' Stuart paused then added "Unfortunately, I don't see helicopters as an option either, limited range and speed with these types of payloads would make them risky. Loading them would be cumbersome, too time consuming and besides everything else, we would need too many of them, so that options out straight away."

As Stuart was about to float another idea, Natallia raised her hand, like a school child asking permission to speak Stuart nodded as if giving approval "Stuart, call Lena. Oleg, her husband….."

Stuart smiled "Yes, I was coming to that" as he held a hand raised orchestrating Natalie to politely shut up.

"Natallia here" waving the same raised hand, now more gently in her direction "used to work at an establishment called the Ekranoplan Design Bureau for several years, in her *previous life*"

"Nine years, and it's called the *Eliseev* Design Bureau" Natallia was proud to make the correction.

Stuart continued "The Eliseev Design Bureau produced a selection of hybrid aircraft called Ekranoplans. In a nutshell, these were big beasts, some as large as 747s designed to carry lots of troops and equipment very quickly and very low level over water. NATO called them The Caspian Sea Monster when they eventually saw them with their spy satellites"

Stuart handed a selection of pictures across to the group. Pointing at one he explained" This one is called the A90, it's the perfect size for what we want, right size, right payload and hopefully the right price too"

"Their Design Bureau is based on the Sea of Azov, just North East of Crimea…That's where Nat and Lena come from and that's where Nat used to work and where Lena's husband Oleg is still a pilot"

"So…Let me explain more now about a friend we have here called Brad Johnstone" Stuart paused "You will meet him tomorrow Matt, he's a very close friend of ours – He met Lenna, Natallia and Lenna's husband when he was in Crimea doing some special sort of exchange training about fifteen years ago. We met him on special ops when he was on detachment to us as a pilot; he's "one of us" …. Anyway, these three, between them, could have our escape option – an A90 Ekranoplan. – This is what I will be looking at as closely as possible as our prime escape vehicle."

Moving on quickly Stuart then went on to the sale of the goods.

" Now…IF we succeed in depriving Usman of the trinkets he's selling day after day in his gold shops, we will then have achieved a significant blow, not just to this nasty piece of work Usman, but to terrorist funding too, which is important for sure but, and it's an important but again, we need to at least recapture our losses and they alone are going to be significant. There will be a lot of expense involved in just setting this operation up, let alone carrying it out. So, the question is. Who can we sell the gold to?"

Stuart looked around the table and asked

"Any ideas?"

Sarge threw in "How about we don't rush it, filter it out into the market anywhere in the world over a longer period"

This was dismissed, each man would need to take and hide the best part of half a ton of gold and jewelry each. Not feasible.

Matt was searching, who fences stolen goods in the States "How about the Mob? The Mafia?"

Stuart looked and he heard Natallia say very quietly "The mafia, …the Chechnya Mafia, they're even bigger and richer and of course they're already here"

Stuart wasn't convinced "we're talking a lot of money here Nat, I don't think some gangster from the back of beyond could take on a deal of this size"
She smiled "You don't think they make enough money from fighting Russia for a whole country? From selling arms and everything else they can lay their hands on all over the world? Usman makes deals, real deals with Lecho, what do you think Lecho might be selling Usman?"

They all paid attention now, this girl was well informed indeed.

"But can he afford it? I really mean this is a lot of money we are talking about – Look" said Stuart as he fetched a laptop computer from a corner table and opened up a link to
"That's per ton" said Tommy. "What its times twenty tons?"

Stuart smiled and said with a confidence "Oh it's worth a LOT Tommy…around the 200 Million mark! And that's not counting the stones"

The realization of just how big this could be started to sink in. There was silence at the table. Stuart had already worked through the math's and the ramifications of the potential venture

"So, the question still is, can Lecho Dudayev afford it?" Stuart asked the question and directed it at Natallia.

"Oh yes, definitely. Believe me he is extremely rich; he could buy the whole of the Gold Souk three times over if he wanted. It's incredible what he has taken out of Chechnya and Russia too. Oil, gas and robberies he even sold aircraft and all sorts of arms. He is rich, very very……….. very rich

"But for something like this you need to approach him carefully, probably its best if Matt is the one to talk to him. Maybe get Lecho to think he is someone from the American mafia or something like that."

"OK, we will work it out, how to impress Mr. Dudayev properly" said Stuart, nodding at both Matt and Natallia. "We'll need to get him signed up first as our fence, second to assist in the "kidnapping". Matt, I'm going to leave this to you to figure out how to persuade.

"OK then, back to finance. Tommy? We will need the diamond, OK with you?"

Tommy nodded, "Sure, why not? It didn't cost me anything in the first place did it?... Yeah, throw it in the pot!"

Sometimes Stuart was pleased that Tommy was quite mad. Stuart Bonham smiled, got up and left the room, only to return minutes later with a small, velvet jewelry box — the kind a jewelry store would place a ring in upon sale. When Stuart opened the box again Natallia and Matt, they both saw a large, brilliant, white diamond!

"What you're looking at" Stuart said, reading from a diamond appraisal "is a fifty carat, radiant, fair cut diamond. It's extremely high quality and the bottom line is that it has a retail value of about a million U$D — and a street value of probably five-hundred thousand dollars.

He noticed Tommy looking at the diamond and wondered if he was having second thoughts.

"You sure Tommy?"

Tommy smiled, "Yeah. I'm sure Boss…. besides Sarge prefers me in sapphires anyway"

"Great, OK, Tommy, Sarge, lets sort out the old boy's network shall we? Let's see who we can rope in to help us, we're going to need some good lads for all of this" the three left to sit in the private bar, the downstairs bedroom near the main door which had converted perfectly into a little pub, home from home.

Natallia and Matt strolled outside, looking at the reflection of the cobalt blue and silver lights firing from the pool. She spoke in a serious tone, there were things Matt needed to understand. "Matt…let me..errr explain more about myself and Lecho?"

Matt nodded.

"You see…when Lena and I first arrived here we got a job working for Lecho. He runs a place here called the Kremlin in Bur Dubai, it's a…cabaret show but with certain "extra" amusement for top clients if you know what I mean?"

Again, Matt nodded; he was too long in the tooth to be shocked and assured her "OK…carry on"

Natallia took a breath.

"OK..well I, well Lena and I, handle his top clients" She went on. "He's a powerful man, not just with the Mafia, I mean in himself. Can you imagine just what he had to be like to get to the top of the tree in Chechnya, in the early days? You need to understand, I know Lecho doesn't frighten you, but you *must* understand this Matt. *You* don't frighten Lecho either.

These are people that turned against the whole of the Russian Army and have been fighting them for years and remember, they're also Muslims. To them, the war for independence in Chechnya is a jihad but to the Russians it's all about oil and control, just like Iraq is for America and Britain."
Natallia was trying to be diplomatic, but it was coming out straight and direct after all. Her English was good but not good enough to veil some necessary direct statements that were needed for Matt's own good and hers too. She knew for a fact, that if Matt went in there too hard and Lecho felt even the slightest threat or even worse, any hint of insult or arrogance from Matt then Lecho's only reaction would be to ignore him. And that would only be because they were in Dubai, if it were anywhere in the ex-Soviet bloc, it would be a full scale and immediate attack from the Chechen.

It was crucial, Lecho must be handled properly. She continued; she knew that she had to get the point across.

"He is known to most people in Dubai as the owner of one of the most popular Russian restaurants in the city. But from there, he runs the entire Chechnya mafia. He keeps a very low profile in

Dubai, local law enforcement officers know that Lecho Dudayev is the head of the Chechenia mafia and that Dubai is his sort of office here. But they do nothing and will continue to do nothing about Dudayev as long as he keeps his nose clean".

"Matt, we'll need to approach him on two aspects of this project. First, because he runs the mafia in Chechnya, we're going to need him, he is rich enough believe me. He could buy all the gold in Dubai, I mean he has many Millions of Dollars from the war in Chechnya."

Natallia paused, Matt was listening, and hopefully she was getting through.

"Second, Lecho is the kind of man who can pull strings and get the marionettes to dance. For the right price I'm sure that he can find a way to deliver Al Ghazzal to a place of your choosing, outside Dubai, outside the Emirates. He can invite him someplace, trick him to come."

But really Matt wasn't listening and our "All due respect Natallia, but I think I know exactly how to deal with his sort and I don't much like having to lick his kind of ass, sorry" Matt seemed adamant, but so was Natallia and now she was starting to dislike his arrogance and selfish attitude, still, she quickly deiced, let's try to explain more, lets him see sense.

"Please, listen to what I am saying Matt. Can't you understand he *isn't* frightened of anybody. It doesn't matter is you have an army and he is alone; he is Chechen, he would fight you. Don't try to threaten him you will get absolutely nowhere. You have to make a deal with him. Understand? A deal, money, that's the only way."

Natallia felt like shaking her head, why has he got to be so aggressive? It won't work, not with a Chechen - never.

Matt didn't care, didn't respect the likes of Lecho. "Actually, now that I think about it, hitting him on his home turf might be exactly what we need to do to convince him that we are a real force to be reckoned with. We'll have him in a confined area; we'll be able to identify his protection; and we may be able to catch him off guard. Tell me more about this restaurant"

"*Pizdat*! (Idiot) Do you have a problem with your ears or your brain? You think I will help you to go in there so that you can try to threaten Lecho so that Me, Lenna and all our families in Ukraine are murdered? Do you?" She was angry, Matt was being inconsiderate, ignoring others safety and plight simple to be "Like a Cowboy" she thought. "He wants to be so arrogant, so can I" flashed through her mind.

"You've been here one day, and *you* want to tell *me* how you will handle these people? Since when did you know so much about this place? About the Chechen people? This morning? Since when did you have the right to put me and all of my friends and our families in danger?? .. Eh?"

"Whoa! She has a temper this one! And a backbone to match it" Matt thought to himself. She was also a woman, and to get a message across to a "mere" male it was habit to send it time and time again. In other words - to "nag".

"You might not like it Matt, but are wrong, totally wrong....Fuck! "And a foot was stamped!

".... and if you go into Lecho like this…it is arrogant….and selfish…you will be murdering us and getting absolutely nowhere yourself because of your arrogance."

She pointed over the wall as if to indicate where a place was "The war in Chechnya, do you know what they do? Do you? Hundreds of school children on their first day at school. – Can you imagine the poor little children, their very first day at school??? They were all killed, slaughtered like animals. Didn't you read about it? Ha, maybe not." She hit the nerve of the Americans not paying attention to any world events except those inside their own borders "Then just a few months after they had killed all the babies they attacked ordinary people sitting in their cars in the traffic going to work, attacked, shot dead. Over a 100 of them. All this and lots more. ……And the cinema in Moscow, same again.

She paused was she getting through?

"The Chechen mafia rules the Russian Mafia *that's* how strong they are, how vicious they are. They kill 10, 20 a 100 people or more at one time, it means nothing to them. Believe me, they are called mafia, but they are much more violent than any American mafia you are used to."

Again, she paused, seeing if the message had got through. At last Matt replied, this time more rationally, sensibly.

"Very well. So, what kind of deal would Mr. Lecho agree to Natallia? Give me the outline"

"Please????" Suggested Natallia.

Matt smiled; "OK I got the drift…. please?" Matt wasn't suitably chastised; he was suitably embarrassed.

"OK Matt" Natallia paused and regained her composure. "I will tell you everything you want to know, but you do this *my* way or not at all.... Deal?"

They sat at the garden table. Natallia described the Kremlin in great detail. "The restaurant is located in the Bur Dubai section of town in a hotel called the Churchills. It's a five-story building separated by parking lots and grounds from other buildings in the area. The entrance is set up such that people who are entering can be screened before they are seated. Lecho runs a security camera both at the restaurant and in select locations around the restaurant. He even has a security man sitting in a room full time off the kitchen looking for potential trouble. He usually takes a table by the far wall, where he can see everything and make sure everyone is doing what they're supposed to be doing. At times, he'll get up and walk around the restaurant, greeting customers and rubbing elbows with rich locals and visitors. That's a usual evening for him at the Kremlin".

Getting the picture Matt said "We need to let Lecho know, we need finance, we need him to use the diamond as collateral. So, let's figure out how to orchestrate that – your way, OK?"

"I can ask, to see if Lecho will meet and talk with you about it" said Natallia "Oh and Matt, I did mean it. And now we've got a deal, it's my way or its no way, understand?"

"Oh, you got your message across Natallia, loud and clear" Matt was under no illusions, Natallia would totally fuck this deal up to protect her family and friends if he didn't play it her way completely. Over the process of the next few days her methods started to make sense; he would eventually come to learn that she had been absolutely right.

At the bar in the converted bedroom the other three were chatting. The general consensus had been reached.

"Low tech is best, full stop. The less that can break down the better, the simpler the kit is the easier it is to replace or to fix" Stuart was saying what the other two already knew, but none the less he hammered it home.

Continuing his explanation "We need pickup trucks, all on rental, all easy to replace immediately if they break down. Mini diggers, again on rental so we rent 20% more than we need on standby just in case. Basically, this is going to be a smash and grab – as simple and crude as it sounds it's the fastest and most effective way of doing thing. It's a single chance, single hit and run"

"Were going to need about thirty hands" Tommy was confident on this one "Old boys' network, we will get that many easy, bet you fifty quid Boss!"

"If we go low tech we need speed and muscle as well as stamina for the heat. It has to be more mechanical and manual than high tech. But, whichever way we go, we're going to need strong, able-bodied, men with military skills" Stuart said to Matt. "And that means its class reunion time"

"That's right Tommy" said Stuart. "So, can you and Sarge take the action item to track down all of our old mates and arrange a reunion back in jolly old? And Matt, can you coordinate with Tommy and invite your buddies from the States too? I'd love to do it here and familiarize the men with the place, but if this this gets off the ground I don't want anyone ringing any bells here before the "kick off" so let's set it up for maybe around the beginning of May in England, I will let you know the details of exactly where and when.".

"Certainly" responded Matt, chuckling, and Tommy, too, acknowledged the request. Most, but not all, of Matt's former platoon had retired. But one or two were still in the military. All would be invited — but those still in the service would not be invited to participate apart from help with certain logistics.

Stuart nodded "phase two, Tommy — that's us" said the Lord. "Now for the unknowns. It could cost a lot of money for the aircraft. Again, I need to have time on this one. So, let me speak to Brad first before we go much further"

At one a.m., the group decided to call it a night. The next day Stuart and Tommy would have to firm up their plan, work out the number of men needed to pull-off the job, figure out what supplies and munitions would be needed to do the job. As for Natallia she would make arrangements for Matt to meet Lecho. And she would visit her old friend Lenna to look into the feasibility of getting Oleg, Lenna's husband, to pilot his magical plane into and out of Dubai.

CHAPTER 7: ALL ABOARD

Dubai, UAE

The next day was predictable bright and sunny with traffic jams crawling in reverse from Garhoud bridge due to a minor accident between an Indian woman having taken her kids to Dubai English Speaking School, or DESS as its better known in Bur Dubai, had promptly driven into the back of a pickup truck carrying Masafi, the local bottled water. The ensuing wet mess created a grid lock of over 7 kilometers from Garhoud straight back to Sheikh Zyed Road tunnel of tower blocks. Everything was normal.

After a few coffees and a flick through the newspapers in the garden, Natallia left to go upstairs and get ready for her mid-morning Brunch with Lenna. Stuart and Matt alternated taking showers in their rooms and quickly checked for any important emails in Stuarts private office on the first floor of the spacious Villa.

Spacious was actually an understatement, the villa had it been in Europe would have been measured in the tens of millions of Dollars. In Dubai, it couldn't be bought, Villas were only for rent, payable one year in advance and this seven-bedroom mini palace cost a full 100,000$ a year to borrow from its owner.

Stuart however, found it reasonable to pay such an amount. His businesses throughout the region were flourishing. Mine clearance and private security companies in Iraq and Afghanistan were doing well. They were relatively new, given that the conflicts in the respective countries were not "quite" over yet, being an understatement, mine clearance and personnel security companies would have no shortage of business for some time to come. The villa in Dubai served as an office, a tax-free hideaway, a stopover hotel and a conference facility for his various business deals and business associates. All in all, it paid off to have your own little palace in Dubai.

Looking smart, classy and sexy at the same time, Natallia trotted into the Office and kissed Stuart on the cheek "See you later *Radnay*, (darling) I meet Lenna now, bye" turning to Matt and waving politely "See you later Matt" as she clattered down the marble stairs and along the hallway to the front door. The noise of the heels on the marble echoed, sounding her exact location as she made her way eventually to the front door and into a hot busy Jumairah side street. - Natalia had a very busy day ahead of her.

Stuart quickly pressed in the numbers on the phone and spoke to his friend Brad and in his best Queens English greeted him.

"Good morning Bradley Old chap, how the fuck are you?"

"Hum dee fuckin diddeley" came back. That was Brads version of the Arabic "A hum de lah" *I am fine*
"Great" said Stuart "We need to meet, you around tonight?" and the time was set.

Next Stuart called Hertz the Avis car and truck rentals and made appointments to meet them later in the morning. He deliberately avoided other so-called reputable car rental companies who were nothing more than a cheap front cover for Pakistanis who buy the name to hold the franchise in the Emirate. He had almost lost a good friend in a car crash on a vehicle rented to him from a "Thrifty Car Rental" earlier that year because they cut back on expanses and rented cars to tourists with no airbags. Stuart knew all too well that everything had to be treble checked with companies in Dubai, the mix of cultures and the craving to get rich quick opened every possible scam to the end user spending his hard-earned cash. From fake Rolex watches to Chevrolets downgraded by greedy Pakistani Managers of Thrifty Car Hire who were happy to let people die for an extra 100$ in their pockets. Any quick cheap trick was possible here and everything had to be checked inside out and upside down.

Meeting up with Lena was always a pleasure for Natallia. They were sisters, confidants, friends and had even been lovers when Lecho had commanded it.

"Now Oleg...." Natallia started

"Why Oleg? "Lenna interrupted wondering why Natallia needed to speak to her ex-husband.

"They need an Aeroplan, to escape, I told them about the Ekranoplan. This is why I thought of Oleg.... Do you think Oleg would be interested in this?" said Natallia.

"Let's see" mused Lenna. "Oleg is a flyer who can't fly his precious aero planes anymore because the Bureau is broke. Its killing him, you know flying is his life, that's why he started going downhill in the first place. Believe me, if it means he can fly Oleg is mad enough to do this for free! "Then she continued "He's still with the Design Bureau but they're not doing anything with his darling Ekranoplans. They're still there but that's about it. Probably they will never fly those things anymore. He says his job is to watch planes rust, and fill out reports on any new rust spots he finds"

Lenna pulled her mobile phone from her bag.

"Let's ask him" as she stated to scroll through the memory for Oleg's number.

"Noooooo" said Natallia, preventing Lenna from dialing. "We can't do this over the phone. It could be traced back to us. We have to be careful. …Tell me, is Oleg still in touch with Brad??"

"Of course," Lenna said. "Why?".

"Stuarts meeting Brad later, he wants him involved if he's interested" Nat informed her

"Wow that's great, all friends together "bubbled Lenna.

Stuart and Tommy sat together "Okay Tommy doing this manually. But we're talking about moving twenty plus tons of gold as quickly as possible. How long do you think it would take for one man to move roughly a ton of gold and jewelry?" asked Stuart.

Tommy thought for a minute, and then said, "come with me". Tommy led Stuart to his car, and they took a short, fifteen-minute ride down Sheik Zayeed road over to the Al Marooj Rotana Hotel — a hotel complex. Descending to the lower level, Tommy took Stuart to the weight room, which was empty, as usual, this time of day. "I've got a deal with the manager" said Tommy. "He lets me come in here and work out during the early afternoon when nobody is around. And well he should considering how much support I'm giving him with my bar bill" he laughed.

Handing Stuart his watch, Tommy pressed the chronometer and proceeded to pick up loose weights and move them down a tight twenty-meter hallway out to the pool area. In fifteen minutes, he had moved a ton of weights out the door.

"Very impressive" said Stuart. "But remember, the men will have to pack all of this loose jewelry and gold into loose bins or something before they can move it out the door. That's going to take time too".

"Okay, so we give them all a bunch of handcarts and bins then" said Tommy. "They can then quickly wield the loot out the door where we can have a front-end loader waiting to lift the booty into waiting trucks. Low tech, simple — at the front end we give each man five minutes to lose the tear gas and clear the stores and markets; we give them twenty
five minutes to load a ton; and we give 'em five minutes to drive to the dock where we have seaplane waiting for us. We give 'em five minutes to load and split — total elapsed time would be" he paused "forty minutes to do the deed".

"That's ten minutes too long" said Stuart. "We'll have to find ways to do it quicker…"

Tommy agreed.

By the end of the afternoon the Caterpillar brand mini diggers were deemed perfect by both men. The 2 Ton Japanese Low Loaders for vehicle recovery were almost perfect, except they might need an extra winch fitted, so were the 5 Ton Mercedes vans, huge and reliable beasts, Tommy loved them all and at the same time as he was thinking about the days progress on the other end of Sheikh Zayed road in Bur Dubai, Natasha was walking into the lion's den of the Kremlin feeling decidedly nervous.

It was now 4 O'clock in the afternoon. The staff at the Kremlin were doing all the necessary things to prepare a top-class restaurant and cabaret for yet another night's work. A Muscovite dance troop leader, also called Natalie, was running her girls through a rehearsal of a new routine called "Valenki - My Shoes" a classic Russian folk dance that was to be upgraded to a spectacular sequence of nostalgia for any future Russian clientele at the Kremlin.

The manageress was supervising some table that needed moved together to join for a 20-seat birthday party for a Mr. Al Salya who was to celebrate his 54th birthday and the extortion of his legally enslaved labor locked in his Sharjah factory for cheap and carcinogenic construction materials.

Everything was normal

And as normal, Lecho was in his office pawing through books of accounts, not just from the Kremlin, but from his home base activities in Chechnya too. Knocking on his office door, Natasha took a deep breath for composure and entered.

Looking over his desk the raw boned an intimidating figure, squat and less than six feet tall eyed Natalia as she entered. Not a word was spoken by him; it was a female's job to pay respect, not his.

"Privyet Mr. Lecho Sir"

He didn't acknowledge, still not a word, he simply nodded towards one of the smaller and deliberately lower visitors' seats on the opposite side of his desk.

Lecho liked Natallia, she didn't talk back but there again no one did. She was good at her job and did as she was told and never came back with excuses. Lecho's chosen "customers" had brought him good reports of her performances in her "job" all in all, he was happy with her but that, in no way at all, would save her if she ever displeased or betrayed him.

In return, she drew fairly large compensation for her efforts at making others happy with the services that she provided — and Lecho, almost totally out of character, rewarded her fairly generously for her efforts. He didn't need her earnings, for Lecho, controlling a group of women, bullying some of them, and humiliating others was what turned him on.

No one ever messed with Lecho, he had no compunction about beating a woman to within an inch of her life or even further if money was involved.

She sat and looked, trying to assess his mood, praying it was a good one.

"We have been missing you my long, lost Natallia. Where were you last night" Lecho asked in pure Russian and he smiled.

"*Thank God for that*" shot through Natallia's mind, he wasn't in one of his notorious bad moods this afternoon.

Natallia was prepared for the question. He would want to know how much money she had made for him in her absence. "I was with an American" she responded meekly, yet honestly. She then handed him an envelope with two-thousand U$D in it.

"Not bad Natallia" he said as he pocketed two thousand — handing eight hundred back to her as "salary".

"And I think there could be something very interesting for you Sir" now Natalia was in full actress mode and making sure Lecho saw her excitement with the news she had.

Lecho looked, now with a direct eye contact, it was habit.

"Such as?" the look was piercing, making Natalia quickly think at the speed of light *"this was going to be hard, stay in role, don't fuck up, don't freeze, he's watching for it"*

Totally in role, as the dedicated honest and reliable worker for a good and caring boss dutifully passed the news "There's something else about this American I must tell you"

The eyes didn't blink "Then tell me" and leaning forward menacingly added "Talk to me".

Holding back the nerves Natalia continued

"Lecho, he …. The American….told me… he has a diamond that he want's looking to sell, he showed it to me. Its *huge.*" She exaggerated with hand gestures..

" He was asking if I knew anyone in the business. I said no. He said the diamond is of unusual brilliance, and that it's over forty carats. He said the retail value is over one million dollars. I said nothing about you, but if you wish, I can arrange for you to meet this American. I didn't know what to do or say, so I came to tell you as soon as I could, he kept me there until late this morning".

Lecho thought carefully about what Natallia had just told him. She had never, ever, approached him with a proposition such as this. Was this some kind of setup? Or was she just trying to bring him some new business — perhaps to ingratiate herself to him, to curry favor? Of course, he'd be interested in diamond that size. Who wouldn't be? Clearly it was stolen, or the guy wouldn't be trying to sell it via a prostitute. And with all of those oil-wealthy Saudi's visiting town all the time, he was sure he'd have no problem selling the diamond. In fact, he had a few in mind right now that may be willing to pay perhaps eight hundred thousand for a ring that may only cost him four.

Finally, he reasoned "Who better to ask than a high class, expensive whore to find a contact for buying a hot diamond. It made sense"

"Stand here" he commanded as if she were a dog, pointing at the floor, positioning her within arm's reach. As she assumed the position, her heart beating wildly, she waited for Lecho to strike her which he did, a full force stinging blow to her ass. She gasped, he smiled.

"Good girl, why don't you invite this. American you say? To dinner here, - Thursday night."

He gripped her waist and turned her to face him as he sat in his leather-bound chair and reached forwards, as he reached up and slid her skirt to her waist then stuffed the twelve-hundred dollars he had just taken from her down into the front of her black G string.

"Good work, Natallia" he said. "Now kneel down"

"All Aussies are quite mad" said Stuart as he, Tommy, Sarge and Matt headed out to the cargo side of Dubai airport to try and find Bradley Johnstone. "Only this one is madder than most" he said with a smile. He had just left a message on Bradley's answering machine and had been greeted by a message consisting of a number of animal noises followed by "leave a message" in heavily accented Australian.

Bradley Johnstone's aviation company, Ozzair, was housed in a hangar in the Northern side of Dubai International Airport. It was ten at night when the group pulled up to security gate and asked for "Captain Johnstone – Ozzair Hangar nine".

"He is backside Sah" said the Indian security Tommy smiled, he loved the way they used the phrase "backside "instead of "behind" the building, which is really what the guard meant!

Stuart was used to the terminology too "Excellent, then is there any chance you could get a message to Captain Johnstone in the *backside* and tell him that Stuart is here?"

Not catching Stuarts joke the guard replied seriously "Yes S*ah*, straight away one minute - I send somebody in to find him".

Stuart explained to Matt, "Really Brad is the sort of catalyst here. We knew him from days gone by. He was a special Ops pilot for the Aussie SAS. Those days we worked a lot with them. Later he turned up in Iraq and we did quite a quite a bit there too, but he's always been sort of based in the UAE more or less, his parents used to live here, and he spend a lot of time growing up here too. "Anyways, cut a long story short, he was the guy who first invited me here years ago. We've known each other ages, he's one of the boys"

Brad, on occasion, had taken Stuart with him on trips to off the beaten track places such as Nepal, Uzbekistan, and even the Ivory Coast.

A guard returned several minutes later — with Brad in tow.

"Whoa, The Lordship himself! To what do I owe this pleasure mate?" said the muscular square jawed Australian as he approached the window of Stuarts BMW to shake his hand. Accentuating the English upper-class act Stuart replied "Bradley, we were in the neighborhood and heard that there was a Beer tap somewhere about. Could you direct us? There's a good chap."

Soon Brad was leading the group into the hangar toward the back where he had built his own little English pub as they walked and chatted he introduced himself to Matt.

After dishing out the "tinnies" of beer all round, the conversation shifted quickly "So, What brings all of you special forces boys to my pub?" said Brad. "Coincidence? Free beer or …. something else?"

Stuart wasn't surprised that Brad had picked up that there was a secondary agenda for this meeting and led straight into it "Brad, we've got an operation underway and we have need of your skills. And you're going to like this one. It involves a major bit of larceny and we all get very, very rich in the end. Oh…and it involves aeroplanes!".

Taking the piss now Brad threw in "Oh Fuckin *Good - Oh* Mate, you know I like aeroplanes"

"No. Seriously Brad, we've got a plan in the making and we need you on board, the flying side is an important part of it." Stuart replied.

Now more serious Brad paid attention and asked" Okidoki, what's it all about then?"

Natalia said that you know about the Ekranoplans, the stuff that Lenna's husband used to fly. She said you had flown them too. Is that right?"

"Too right, they're fuckin incredible things. I flew them with Lenna's husband, Oleg, he was their Chief test Pilot, great Guy."

Brad paused, thinking back through some strong memories he had had there.

"You rate them?" meaning the Ekranoplan, "Was it any good?" Stuart needed to know if these unique designs were actually as good as Natalia had said.

Brad started to explain "Well…. They're sixties technology, the planes are old hat now of course but really were built like brick shithouses,"

Turning to Matt, Tommy explained quietly "Brick shithouse…..That's Australian for *strong*"

"…you just can't break them and if you do, you can usually fix it with a hammer! I loved them and…. they could lift anything you put inside them. I remember once I asked a Ruskey Officer, How many soldiers can you get in one of these and he laughed, just said - depends how big they are! – what he meant was, if you can get them in, them it will carry them….incredible machines" almost as an afterthought as he came back from memory lane Brad added towards Stuart "…..Why are you asking?"

Stuart didn't mess around "We think we've found a way to rob the gold Souk of over four hundred and eighty million dollars' worth of merchandise. And we need you to help us fly it out of Dubai.

That's it plain and simple and we wondered if the Ekranoplan would be the tool for the job".
Brad was quiet now and looked around the room at the men's faces as the realization came to him
"Fuck......your serious arnt ya?"

Stuart nodded.

Immediately Brad asked for more details, so Stuart asked if he could use his computer and pulled a map of Dubai showing where the gold Souk is, and then tracing a route from the souk to the point of departure only 250 meters away on the shoreline near Port Al Hamriya.

"At Port Al Hamriya, I would want you to be waiting for us"

"'Hang on, your worship" said Brad "How much gold are you planning on taking?"

"Oh, only about twenty tons, maybe thirty if we can manage it" said Stuart, waiting for Bradley to come to the obvious conclusion.

"Stu, I'm an Aussie, not very clever at sums you know...."

Stuart knew Brad was "ripping the piss" (being a bit sarcastic) in an Aussie way.

"So, what might, say 25 tons of the yellow shiny stuff be worth mate? Just approximate you know.....to within the nearest few zillion dollars?"
"On the World market or at our sale price?" Now Stuart taunted him back.

"Oh, perhaps our *sale* price would be sufficient your Holiness?"

"Two hundred and Seventy-Five Million U.S. Dollars for a quick cash sale at half the market value……approximately…. But we're working on a safe 200 Million…don't want to be greedy do we!?" Now Stuart was showing he was on the ball.

Tommy had watched the conversation progress and he also knew that Brad was no fool. He would need motivation, a reason to be involved with this and it would need more than just money as the catalyst. Tommy knew all too well that in his line of work, the best didn't do it just for money.

"Listen mate" Tommy said to Brad, for once in a serious tone "There's a real reason for doing this Brad; it isn't just about the money". Looking at Matt, Tommy then turned to Brad and told him the story about the brutal execution of Matt's son and many others too. Matt then moved in and explained about the finance and it being funneled directly to the murder squad operated out of Dubai and is using the gold Souk to launder Al Qaeda money. Motivation was what Brad was looking for and when Tommy and Matt had finished, Brad signed-on. And Matt thanked him. Stuart spoke next. "Brad, we're going to need you to make a trip to the Ukraine to assess the condition of any Ekranoplans that they might have left there. We're also going to need you to negotiate how we can get one in good working order and just how much it will cost".

"My pleasure Mate, but you do understand it's no use me going there alone don't you? No fucker speaks English, we are talking deep Russia right out in the sticks mate, there's not even a road sign in English and where I need to get to is about a day's drive from Simferopol, way over the other side of Crimea then up on the coast of the Sea of Azov. Definite I will need help, an interpreter" smiled Brad "Now, whose round is it?"

"Ok" said Stuart "Best if Natalia goes with you, she knows everything about this too, she's on board"

Brad laughed "No problem your Eminence, I don't mind taking Nat away for a few weeks!"

Even Stuart laughed at Brads irreverence knowing full well about his and Natalia's relationship, however strange it might seem, an English Lord and a Ukrainian hooker, *whatever lights your fire* was the unsaid consensus. And passing the fresh cold tins of lager round from the fridge, it was decided that Brad would go back to his old stamping grounds in Crimea with Natalia as his assistant, "That would be perfect" Brad said, fully aware that Natalia used to work there, "At the design Bureau and she knows the Director Simonov very well too, plus without any doubt they would have Oleg to help."

Brad added" For sure Oleg will know exactly what the real story is, that will stop Simonov from giving us bullshit. First let me email Oleg and see if they still have the any left there, most likely they've cut them up for scrap or have built 200 dachas out of them by now, either way let's check first"

Stuart was happy to confirm that according to Lenna, they hadn't done that yet but he also wasn't reassured much when Brad told him that he had seen perfectly good working order aircraft stripped of crucial parts, grounding them forever just for the collection of scrap metal or crucial wiring from their innards that raise no more than 10 dollars on the market. Definitely he needed to check the aircraft; as he explained "Even if they're in one piece they could still be scrap by now"

He continued "Understand Stuart, once these boyos hit the vodka anything can happen. I've seen watchmen rip out central wiring looms of aircraft to sell for two bottles of the cat piss Vodka. Completely wrote off the aircraft because a new wiring loom has to be made from zero, there are none left in stock. So, imagine it, if they scrap an aircraft for two bottles of booze, anything is possible"

Stuart was worried, but he also had faith in Brad

"Well, best get there and put the fence around one eh? "Stuart suggested "No time to lose."

CHAPTER 8: THE OFFER

Two days later on Thursday night, at 10.30 pm and the night life is just starting to come alive in the City as Matt pulled up outside Churchills Hotel for the Valet Parking service to take over. Barely a four-star hotel it did its best to increase standards in Bur Dubai but being one of the oldest hotels there and had long since been overtaken by the mega emporiums.

Immediately an Indian doorman in his finest silk Rajahs uniform opened the car door for Natalia as she swung her long - long legs out into the hot and humid night air. Its 10.30 pm and the night life is just starting to come alive in the City. Almost uncontrollably the Indian glanced down at them and without him knowing Natasha smiled gentle, satisfied smile. In her blue velvet cocktail dress, slinky heels with her hair tied back in a more Spanish look than any Spaniard could carry. The bright red lipstick and pale make up exaggerated the look and took it to the "ultimate" level.

They smiled and most certainly looked the part of a perfect Dubai nightlife couple as they moved through the hotel lobby towards the elevator. Stepping into what must be the oldest and slowest lift in the City to eventually crawl its way up to the dizzy height of the top floor, the fifth floor. Matt glanced at himself in the mirrored wall of the lift, checking he looked the part. The Rodeo Drive suit, Gucci handmade shoes and the metal and gold Rolex Oyster completed the perfect impression. Matt looked the part, the serious player, there to do the business. As the lift took its time Matt complained

"Hell, how can you live here all the year round? In New York it's bad enough but wow never as hot as this"

Natalia laughed and then teased" Oh, you get used to anything if you experience it enough. Didn't you know that Matt?"

"Besides, once you get into the restaurant you won't be so hot, they keep the air conditioning there so cold that it feels like Russia. Even the waitresses wear extra underwear it's so cold"

They laughed; they knew the lift was bugged.

He glanced at Natalia and she smiled back. "Damn, she's cool this one. Not a flicker of nerves" he thought to himself. The lift doors opened, and the hallway was Mother Russia itself. Brown wood walls, huge mural paintings across the walls depicting the snow-covered Motherland and to the left, the antique wooden door that lead into the restaurant itself.
Matt eased the door open and then felt it pulled open from inside. There to greet any guest arriving was the regular doorman for Troika. Nothing like the muscle-bound steroid poppers in the West, this man, middle aged, raw boned and not too tall didn't smile and nodded at Natalia as he spoke a quiet, "Dobradien" while at the same time carefully measuring Matt. This one was a real pro and infinitely more lethal than any weightlifting pony tailed wrestler could ever hope to be.

Matt smiled and the Russian guard didn't. Palm upturned he motioned them to enter. Nat took the initiative and confidently walked inside, glanced over her shoulder, like a mother hen leading her chick and then continued towards a table where a two man were sitting with two girls. As they approached the girls stood up and left the table with the man. The three of them slinking away without even being told. Two waitresses scurried to clear the glasses and hardly used ashtrays on the table. Suddenly Matt felt like a VIP.

Lecho remained the only one left at the table, his back to the wall, he could view almost the entire room. He eyed Matt very calmly and said a quiet "Hello" as Matt shook his hand. He didn't stand as Matt offered his hand. He also made a mental note that the handshake was soft, almost sly but more importantly he noted that Lecho made no attempt to stand up when he had extended his hand. Lecho waved towards the chair opposite and again, in a soft voice "Please.."

Matt smiled and sat. Natalia ordered Matts drink, waitresses scurried, they settled at the table.

"I'm very pleased to meet you Sir, you have a strong reputation" Matt was using words, choosing them carefully, knowing that Lecho's English was a long long way from perfect. Natallia seated at Lecho's side, re confirmed Matts words in immediate and perfect Russian.

Lecho was unmoved; no sign of anything on his face at all and in an accent so thick it could almost be exaggerated with his deep Russian voice " *Sank* you *Meesterh.*" he smiled now, quite sickly, acted smile.."It *is* Meesterh????" and turned his head sideways as he looked at Matt.

"Oh, I think at this stage Matt is enough don't you Mr. Lecho?"

Lecho smiled more now and said in Russian for Natalia's ears only "His name is probably a fucking lie anyway" Nat smiled and didn't need to translate

Lecho also smiled, and turning to Matt started the conversation "And so, *Mister* Matt, I received your message" referring to the diamond as he patted his breast pocket to indicate that he had it in his possession "What exactly do you wish to speak to me about?"

Matt saw Lecho's eye flick towards his gold Rolex and thought to himself "*Yes you bastard, it's real*"

There was no need to dance round handbags, Lecho was a player, an experienced pro and at this stage he was treating Matt as one too.

"Of course, I have a proposition sir, a lucrative proposition" Nat emphasized and translated the word lucrative putting extra importance to it. She knew better than anyone just how greedy Lecho was. Greed to a degree it was almost a mental problem with him.

Dachodnay, lucrative, the word hit the early warning greed sensors that coursed through Lecho's blood.

"Lucrative? How so Mister? What would you call lucrative?" Lecho wanted to know.

Matt leant forward and looked at Lecho straight in the eyes. "Very"..he paused, Lecho still looked him back in the eyes "and Matt nodded his head towards Natalia but kept his eyes fixed to Lecho's "She should go"

Lech smirked, almost insulted that Matt might think he didn't know how to own and terrorize his servants. "You don't worry *Mr. Matt*, this one" he smirked "This one*," it"* will be silent"

"Very well" Matt paused as if deliberately taking the measure of Lecho and then gave him a number that wiped the super cool face clean.

"…Around 450 Million US dollars lucrative Mr. Lecho……. Most probably more"

Lecho, now showing at least a small amount of etiquette towards Matt, raised a hand as if to excuse him while he spoke to Natalia almost whispered quietly in Russian……"You DO realize what will happen if you breathe a single word of this don't you pretty girl?" For the first time Natalia looked genuinely concerned and she had every right to be, she had just had her life threatened by a multiple murderer. Matt didn't miss a thing, he noticed but he didn't show it, he had expected it." Yes of course, please don't worry, never one word from me, never"

Unconcerned at Natalia's assurance he turned back to Matt.

"And now, most important, what is my share?"

Lecho's greed had surfaced in full flow, Matt thought to himself, in flashes almost, that Lecho wasn't asking "What do I do, What do I put in or what is my role…..only "what is MY share." Isn't greed a wonderful thing? All these flashed through Matts mind.

Matt started to explain step by step. Firstly, he started using the "Royal We" indicating to Lecho that he was part of an organization and not a legal one at that. Lecho took this for granted.

Next came the need for security and secrecy, again Lecho was all for that part but for sure, he was interested to know just what exactly Matt needed from him.

"First Lecho" The *Misters* had been dropped now "Let me tell you what "we" need from your side"

In the Ukraine we need help fixing bureaucracy to export some equipment. Believe it or not, nothing illegal, but we need to bring a transport aircraft out and want the paperwork done super quick, no hold ups, no interference from the tax police and no red tape. We will also need total approval by the Civil Aviation Authority that the aircraft has passed all tests and is airworthy for international use"

Lecho nodded and acknowledged "Niet. No problem. But let me tell you this is much easier from Russia than Ukraine but no problem, what else?"

"The aircraft will need some modification made to it, again, nothing too technical or too big but we need it done and need it done fast and proper and on time. We need someone to make sure it's done as fast as possible with no 5 day vodka breaks so we need to put this message across to the people we are dealing with there."

Lecho laughed, so, Matt knew a little about Soviet drinking binges and how they brought everything to a stop from the Kremlin down once they kicked off.

"OK, again, it is not a problem" but now Lecho was starting to think that this was too good to be true, where's the sting? Is this a con trick? If it is Natalia says goodbye to her face.

"Now Mister Matt, now you get to the point or have you come here to speak to me about bringing some airplane from some Ukrainian shit hole?" Lecho threw *the mister* in again to show he was getting suspicious.

Matt didn't rise to the bait; he showed him just enough backbone not to insult him but not to be intimidated either.

"We want you to buy 25 to 30 tons of Gold Bullion *Mister* Lecho at half the Market Rate at 11 Million Dollars per ton instead of 22. That will give you a return of about 350 Million US once you've recycled it onto the world market. That's enough to *buy* you a Country *Mister* Lecho, enough to make you a President." Matt paused.

"We also want the little present in your pocket converted into 500,000 $ hard untraceable cash, for out of pocket expenses shall we say?"

The greed gene was now at full bore racing through Lecho's mind in nana seconds. 350 Million, how long to recycle the gold? Where can it be sold fast? What's the highest price possible? Who to? Where? And as fast as the questions shot into his brain, so did the answers.

He didn't want to show it, but he couldn't help it "And when would this be done?"

Matt looked around, noticed the Guard was still watching him but now a little more casually than before. Also, that two other men on stools at the bar with their backs towards Matt were watching too, through the mirror where the bottles of alcohol behind the bar were hanging.

Matt placed a printout of a map on the table in front of Lecho. It was just A4 size and showed the plains of Western Uzbekistan and his forefinger circled a region to the east of the Caspian showing a large salt lake "The delivery shall be made to you here in late July this The exact deliver location is yet to be decided, it as a logistical problem that will be fixed, however, this is the general area we will hand over to you. From this point onwards everything will be your total responsibility" All the time at Lecho's side Natasha quietly translating every single word into Russian just in case Lecho had missed anything.

Lecho paused "And if it isn't delivered?"

Matt smiled, tempted to say *"what a stupid question"* but didn't, instead he told Lecho calmly

"If the delivery *isn't* made Mr. Lecho, then me and my team will either be dead or captured; will have lost our 150 million shares. You will have lost your investment and so
will we "looking at Lecho's breast pocket to remind him of the value already in it." If it isn't delivered as promised then no one will be more disappointed than me I can assure you, seeing that I will be the one that is dead and not you"

That was it, Lecho loved the prospect of someone else standing a chance of dying while he stood a chance of winning, raised his glass to make a toast on the venture with Matt and at the same time poured a sense of relief into everyone who was watching the meeting.

They drank and Lecho came back at Matt straight away "You understand that my out of pocket expenses will be far higher than this" as he patted the breast pocket on his coat "I cannot pay you so much for it. Maximum this is worth is 200,000 – maximum."

Matt raised his glass" That's might be true Sir, given that it (the diamond) isn't exactly, shall we say, legal, but there again, you won't end up dead if it fails, will you? And you are taking 50% of the profits too"

Lecho nodded, then laughed as he thought to himself "Worth a try anyway"

As if by remote control, the band increased its volume, the cabaret dancers started their show, the table filled with food and booze, girls joined them and charmed Matt. Even the sour faced Lecho seemed to be having a good night.

The night was closing but Brad wanted one more thing. As the men stood to leave, taking the opportunity as Natalia was gathering her bag from the table Matt gently held Lecho's arm and said quietly. "There is something else, a small side deal, just between us two"
"Ahh, at last" thought Lecho, this was real music to his ear; he had found a fellow in greed!

Motioning Natalia to stay at the table and he led Matt into the area reserved of the restaurant staff to eat, discretely hidden away to the left of the bar out of sight from the main area. The two men sitting at the bar started to move off their chairs, the move had caught them unprepared. Lecho made no effort to hide the fact that they had been surveying Matt since the moment he had walked in two hours before and told them to "Stay"

They got to the area, didn't bother to sit, Lecho looked at Matt and said quite simply.

"What?"

For ten minutes Matt spoke softly to him and afterwards Lecho didn't need to waste any time thinking about his answer.

"Agreed"

They shook hands and Matt noticed this time the handshake was firm. Natalia noticed that Lecho was smiling, not acting, but an almost genuine smile.

Once inside the car Natalia looked at Matt and asked, "What was that about? What's the secret Matt? He looked happy, that's not normal, what did you talk to him about?"

"Oh, don't worry Nat, I explained to Lecho that I would need you full time from now on, Told him I need you to help me to fix all the dealings in the Ukraine etcetera etcetera. He wasn't too impressed, asked why you, so I told him I was screwing you inside out!"

He went for it. "So, it means you're out of there full time now. Not a bad night really was it?"

Nat was satisfied, happy with everything, but little did she know just what the extra sideline deal had included a lot more other than her freedom from The Kremlin.

CHAPTER 19: BACK IN THE USSR

Crimea

After the Malaysian Airlines flights that had taken them to Istanbul and Aerosvit flight on to Simferopol in Crimea, Brad and Natalia finally cleared passport control. The sour faced customs officers having been far more interested in Natalia than Brad hoping to set unpaid tax demands against her as in their eyes, any Ukrainian female that works in the middle east is without any doubt, a high paid hooker and has more than enough money to pay them off.

Stepping out of the passport control area they could see Oleg waiting for them. Brad noticed that he looked gaunt, thinner than ever, he had gone downhill. Giving Natalia the customary kiss on each cheek, Igor looked at Brad and with a genuine beaming smile gave him the sincere, brotherly Russian bear hug. His comrade had returned, Oleg was glad to see him, and it showed.

Oleg ushered the couple out to the car park and soon they are heading out across the Crimean countryside, due east towards the Sea of Azov in the microbus that had been sent to meet them by Oleg and Natalia's old boss Siminov, the Director of the Ekranoplan base 50 kilometers out of Theodosia on the remote south west coast of the shallow sea.

In the back of the bus, Oleg light his cigarette, looked at Brad and asked

"So, Brad, there is some flying to do?"

Brad beamed; he knew the one passion they both shared above anything else was the love of aviation.

"Yes Mate, some *real* flying" Glancing at the driver sitting in the front, hunched over the steering wheel in his almost compulsory brown leather three quarter length leather jacket, Brad hesitated to speak, Natalia saw him look at the driver cautiously and stepped in

"Brad, it's OK, I know this man, he was one of our drivers when we were all together on the project" looking towards the driver" He's OK and doesn't speak a word of English"

Brad relaxed at that, turned to his old flying partner and looked him in the eyes

" Oleg, I know things have been shit for you since the changes" Brad knew only too well of his friends suffering, not only financially but with the whole decline of the Soviet system which meant Oleg's flying career had come to an awful full stop "But there's a chance for it all to change for us now, for everyone. I have a lot to tell you and I need to know you are on board otherwise none of this will work"

Igor looked at Brad and joked "You mean flying and getting paid? Oichin Kharashol! (very nice) What else could I want?"

Brad started at the beginning, outlined the whole plan to his old friend, there was no use in hiding anything from him at all and he knew full well that if he tried to Igor was certainly more than intelligent enough to see it straight away.

Oleg paused, just two seconds and said "Its good, OK I am on for it"

Brad was taken back a little, he knew Oleg intimately. After the flight training system, they had been through together they wouldn't be alive now if they didn't know each other inside out and he knew that with Oleg, there was always just one more question. Always questions to be asked just in case any little item had been missed, and often with the kind of flying that they had done together, a tiny insignificant point could lead to death.

"And that's it my friend? Not a single *qvestion*? "Using the Russian pronunciation of the word as it was a standing joke that Oleg always raised a finger and said "*Qvestion*"
Oleg looked at Brad and answered him straight "Look at me Brad, look where I am, what I am doing. You know what we had here before, jobs, research, pensions, food, law, order.......... Now look at it, just look at it. There is nothing left, it's all gone, ruined for years to come. My future is to sit on my ass and drink Vodka, and I mean homemade shit Vodka at that! You think I will turn down money PLUS being able to fly again? No Brad, this time there's absolutely no *qvestions* my friend. Let's do it, whatever it is. Better that I am dead than to stay in this shit for the rest of my life"

Brad nodded and looked through the side window of the microbus as they passed through a tiny cluster of semi derelict hand built peasant wooden houses, outside one stood an old couple she holding a small basket of berries, he was holding out two small fishes by their tails, showing them to the microbus as it bumped past on the potholed road in the hope that they could sell them.

"Yes mate, I understand" Brad said quietly knowing full well his friend's passion for flying and how much he must miss it now it was removed from his life completely.

Two hours later the van was pulling into the long private road that separated the Design Bureau from the so-called main route that ran along the western coast of the Sea of Azov. After a sadistic 15 minutes of bumping along the cratered road the research facility came
into view at long last. Its dilapidated iron gates and guard post now unmanned they eased their way inside and parked. Oleg instructed in Ukrainian to the driver, warning him not to drink as they would be leaving back for Kokdebil, a small seaside town on the south coast of Crimea in about two hours or so.

"*Me* not to drink. And you having your fucking party with Simonov??" The driver knew full well that no way would Brad, and company be going in to meet his director, a well-known and dedicated drunkard, without the Vodka and pickled tomatoes he was so fond of.

"Either way" Oleg warned him raising to his old officer and Chief test Pilot status "No drinking or no fucking pay!" The raised fingers rubbed together showing the money sign seemed to complete the message well.

Natalia lead the way and both men automatically watched her wonderful ass as she climbing the wide dusty and worn concrete stairs inside the empty Office Block, then along the equally empty corridor towards the Directors Office at the end Brad had time to think just how much the place had gone downhill from the hustle and bustle of just a few years earlier. Now it was dying and by the look of it, especially with a rampant alcoholic running the show, would continue to die, just like Oleg had predicted.

A quick knock on the dark brown door before turning the handle, which was about to fall off rather than work, Natalia led the men inside the huge conference room to an equally huge conference desk. On the wall was still the massive imitation painting of Sergei Eliseev, founder and designer of the original and revolutionary Ekranoplans.

Director Simonov stood up, his frame, like a bear rising from behind his massive desk he came over to them. His face had got redder with the years, Vodka was setting into him and Simonov was welcoming it to stay "Brad, tsarevich good, good, Da, good to see you" and then the bear hug that Brad tried so hard to emulate but needed another 20 kilos of muscle to even equal it.

Soon, assistants had appeared from nowhere in the silent office block. Turning to his underling who had appeared from nowhere in the labyrinth of empty offices Simonov shouted "Go to my office and get the best Vodka, the…. Not the cheap shit"
"But *this is* your Office Director" the assistant answered and that was more than enough for Simonov to launch into a tirade of insults, how dare he talk to him in that manner with a guest present!

The bears face went redder as he roared in Russian "Don't you fucking speak to me like that you dirty little bastard. Fuck off. OUT! Out Out!" an ashtray just missing the assistants head as he disappeared through the door.

"Pizdet" (idiot) Simonov muttered as he leant down and opened the swinging door of his ancient desk out of sight of Brad and Oleg as he pushed through half a dozen empties to grab the best bottle at the back.

"Here. Good. Now we drink hello Da?"

Vodka was on the table and so were the salted and sour black bread, Pickled Cucumbers and Tomatoes, the whole works, it was party time, or at least an excuse for Simonov to drink even more.

Brad knew for a fact, that no matter how politely he might ask, no matter what excuse he could possibly come up with that nothing and absolutely nothing was going to divert the meeting away from alcohol. He could have said *"No sorry Director Simonov, I have to fly a 12-hour route carrying 500 blind orphans to hospital"* the answer would have been "Drink tsarevich!"

Simonov took glee in pouring his beloved silky liquid. It was almost a religious act as far as he was concerned and had Brad turned it down, it would have been sacrilege to the Bear.

The small glass disappearing in his oversized fist, Simonov stood to make a toast. His toasts were notoriously long and the more he drank the longer and more emotional they got. Sometimes it was fun to drink with Simonov, provided you didn't laugh at his toasts.

Sincerity on his face now "To welcome one of our birds' home to our nest. Brad welcome back "and Simonov offered his glass.

The toasts went on, some sincere, some witty and from Brad plain outright Australian crude "Up yer arse" was actually his favorite and translated the Russians loved it. They had a very similar irreverent sense of humor.

Before toast number four, it was time to talk business and Brad leant forward to speak man to man and face to red face with the glowing, happy Bear. Being more relaxed now Brad called him by his Russian Orthodox Christian Name.

"Alexei Alexeievich, I am here on business"

His red face looking drunk but his brain nowhere near it Simonov lowered his eyes and replied precisely and to the point "Yes Brad of course I know this, Oleg told me and for the sake of everyone here I hope it is profitable too. I am sure that Oleg has also told you of the situation here. It is very bad. Very bad indeed"

Brad nodded "Yes of course, now here is my offer. In Dubai we have been approached by the Government to operate a freight service. It's a guaranteed contract that can be secured for at least a three-year period. What they want is a scheduled run between Dubai, Abu Dhabi, Doha, Bahrain, Dhahran and Kuwait City and then back. Basically, it's a Gulf delivery service on four days a week basis. Empty or full they will guarantee us a set payment. My company has submitted a quotation to the Government. From a friend of mine inside the Department responsible we know that we will win the contract if we have estimated the right prices for the overhaul and modifications to the A90"

Of course, all of this was complete bullshit, but Brad didn't have any conscience of serving it to Simonov by the dish full. What he needed was for Simonov to be enthusiastic enough to get everything done that he needed, and to get it done on time. Either way, whatever the Ekranoplan was going to be used for, Simonov and his Design Bureau was going to be quids in so what did it matter what the real use was?

"And you need our A90 for this?" was the obvious question from the Bear.

"Yes, and with some modifications too which will need to be done extremely quickly" pushing the Bear a list of requirements for works to be carried out starting with:

1. Removal of upper gun turret and all hydraulics or extra weight components linked solely to the turret.
2. Extensions to wingtips. A) removal of wingtip ventral fins and B) replacement with tips as per attached drawing reference BJ 001
3. Observation windows in tail cone, including access tube from rear bulkhead number 3
4. Extra fuel tanks to wings and bladder tanks.
5. A fuel jettison system venting from both sides of the mid fuselage just aft of the wing root,
6. Installation of afterburner igniters, fuel rings and exhaust nozzle control systems into the existing turbo fan exhaust ducts,
7. Radio Altimeters need to be changed to western Models in Feet and Millibars of pressure instead of the Russia meters and Hectopascals
8. Garmin 830 Global Navigation System to be installed on the top of the cockpit cowling in the centre.
9. Western jack plugs and Dave Clark intercoms system as a back up to the GNS intercom to be fitted.
10. Six separate pairs of in and out intercom jack points needed here, here and here etc.
11. Transponder model Gramin with Mode Charlie. With following modifications.
12. Air Conditioning units
13. APU Auxiliary Power Unit to be fitted connected to (see attached list…)
14. Two extra water pumps with independent power systems.

The list went on and on. Almost forty alterations in all, even down to the electrical systems, getting rid of heavy outdated Russian avionics and replacing them with compact state of the art Western satellite aids, dumping wet Russian batteries and replacing them with ultra-lightweight western equivalents, every kilo counted. Even modification to the previously sealed off inlets to the afterburner systems for the two-nose mounted Kuznetsov NK-8-4K turbofans. If everything was carried out as requested, it would mean that the Ekranoplan would be almost three and a half tons lighter and fly 2000 feet higher while carrying an extra 800 kilos. More importantly, the range would be doubled even when carrying more weight. Brad had done his homework well; very well indeed.

Also required would be some wheeled Bins, containers to fit inside the aircraft hold, they must be extremely strong, but light. Russian titanium was cheap, in fact they couldn't give it away following international trading rules set out by the European Community and America basically rubbishing ex-Soviet titanium by implementing nothing more than a bureaucratic scam. Drawings were already done and ready to form part of the deal.

The requests for modifications and changes almost made perfect sense to Simonov bearing in mind what Brad had told him the aircraft was to be used for. The bullshit tasted even sweeter when Brad made the financial offers and the very sweetest part of it all was that there would be an advance payment, money on the table to mobilize, to breathe life into the dying Aircraft Workshops. This was the best news since Sputnik for the Russia Bear and the Vodka glasses were filled without any delay and the pickled cucumbers weren't left out of the ceremony either.

The following day work started in earnest and after making sure everything was under way and under control by Oleg, Brad returned to the UAE with the news that everything was now *"go"*.

CHAPTER 10: TIMELINE

Dubai, UAE

Upon his arrival back in Dubai, Brad Johnstone made a beeline straight to Stuart's home. He was elated that his deal had gone so well — and also pleasantly surprised at the condition of the Ekranoplan. But he did have reservations about the payload weight, altitude, and distance the plane could travel.

Greeted at the door by the petite Filipina, Brad was led to Stuart's bar where he helped himself to a cold tin while waiting for Stuart to appear.

Walking in, still drying his hair from the shower Stuart apologies as he entered the room "Sorry you had to wait Brad"

Looking at Stuart, Brad glanced down at his watch "Its fuckin lunchtime Mate. - What? You just got up?"

Stuart laughed "As if! No, I've been in the Gym, need to be on good form for the job you know"

"Congrats, mate" said Brad shaking Stuart's hand. "Help yourself to a tinny - it's good for your balls and good for your brains".

"I think I will" said Stuart, ripping the top of a large ice cold can of beer "So, how was the Ukraine?"

"It was good, very good" Brad was pleased to say "the plane is in better condition than I had ever imagined. The Director, Simonov made us really welcome, the bloke wants to do a deal badly, they're dead on their feet there mate. Haven't got a penny to bless themselves with, nobody has had salary for over a year, they're desperate for the deal and to earn money".

Right to the point Stuart asked, "How much?"

"Relax mate" smiled Brad. "We got the plane on our terms. This is the plan. First people need to be brought back to work, they won't go for free, all they've received over the last year plus how long is bullshit and promises of salaries. Now basically they're on strike. So first the Design Bureau need to pay them something. This is the only way to get the Ekranoplan back to life. It needs a complete full overhaul from tip to toe and the only way to do it is to use the certified and licensed staff and they are the ones on strike. So, step one, we've got to pay them."

Stuart nodded as Brad continued "That's phase one, actually get the people we need working again. Next is the modifications we need. Most of them are fairly straight forward; you know ripping anything out that isn't needed to reduce weight, for example. I had a quick work out just looking at the 60s designed Soviet Radio and Navigation systems, if we rip all this out, including a massive internal Radar system, and then replace it with new Western stuff which is better and far more accurate. Basically, we take out One and a quarter ton of outdated crap and replace it with three Kilos of American Garmin Global Navigation Systems.

"So, phase one it the overhaul of the aircraft itself, phase two is removal of outdated equipment and other stuff that isn't needed and the replacement of new stuff that's lighter and better. Then phases three are the modifications we need making to the aircraft. Extra fuel tanks, the wheelie bin rails and bins themselves plus a few other things I might need to help us do the flight itself."

"After all of that is done, then there needs to be the test flights and the paperwork. Namely the Certificate of Airworthiness and the registration of the Aircraft itself so we can fly it internationally and legally."

"Then putting certain stuff back in that we are going to need. We'll be giving the director one hundred thousand U.S. as a "service fee" for representing our cause to his superiors; one hundred thousand to fuel the plane and bring it up to snuff; and another one hundred thousand as a down payment toward the purchase price. The director was quite reasonable — it was almost as though the director was in a hurry to get rid of it."

"Brad, you got a good deal" smiled Stuart. "Excellent!"

Stuart was now scribbling down a few notes, questions but he let Brad continue.

"From the financial angle this is the deal. My Company, Ozzair will offer to buy the Ekranoplan on a lease purchase option. It's not too complicated, basically we deposit 50,000$ into the account of a new Ukrainian Company called *Ekranocraft* which is owned by Simonov and his nephew."

Stuart jumped in "Nephew?"

"Yeh" Brad smiled "His nephew is shit hot, a good guy and well respected by the workers. One of the new style lads there who can understand how do a deal and get it
done. Also, Oleg knows him well and trusts him. He is important to us for the simple reason that as sure as God made little apples; once Simonov sees any money he's going to be hitting the Vodka like no tomorrow. We know it and the workers know it too. He doesn't command their respect, but his nephew does. Hence we

need him as Simonov's partner. Plan is, the Vodka will keep Simonov out of the way and the project will be pushed through day and night by Oleg and the nephew."

"OK carry on sorry" Stuart apologies for the interruption.

"Right, where was I?" Brad rewound his brain "Lease – Purchase. This is how it works. The value of the aircraft is set at 1 Million US $, that's agreed. The Overhaul will cost an estimated 40,000 $, that's a Ukrainian estimate which will actually mean in reality about 70,000$ by the time it's done, so we allow 80,000$. This overhaul cost has to be paid 50% up front and 50% on completion. If they've screwed up their estimates, which I guarantee they will have done, then we don't want delays by them running out of steam with finance, so we allow $80,000"

Brad explained "Listen mate, these boys are top, I really do mean top technicians and engineers but when it comes to the math's of working costs out, forget it, they're fucking useless, always the same, so we have to be prepared to accommodate them on this…err…weak point.. To make sure we don't get delayed. After all, if there is no Ekranoplan then there's no project is there?"

"OK I understand" Stuart agreed, preempt any potential delays, if you can predict them and then make allowances for them, *common sense.*

"OK, then after the aircraft is certified to fly, that means an official certificate of Airworthiness needs to be provided by the Civil Aviation Authority and the Aircraft is Registered, again by the CAA then its ready to go. As part of the lease Purchase we have three years to pay back the 1 million in quarterly payments fixed at 83,333 $ per quarter. However, the cost of the overhaul is actually their responsibility, so we deduct the money its cost us from the first quarterly payment. OK?"

"Excellent, Stuart raised his eyebrows" In fact, bloody marvelous "That put us loads in hand on cash flow. Cheers!"

"There are other costs to add to it mate, also we will need help from Matt's Chechnyan friend too"

"Such as?" Asked Stuart.

"First we found out that the Ukrainians are getting really difficult about registering aircraft. You see, they want to, actually applied to join the European Community. Part of that means they have to operate the same systems inside the Ukraine as they are operated in Europe. This applies to all sorts of things from human rights through to agriculture, laws, you name it. Anyway, it means that their CAA is also under scrutiny and the one thing that Europe and America don't need is any form of competition to their aviation industries, so, to cut a long story short, they are screwing down on just what the Ukrainians can and can't say is an airworthy aircraft. It's all to do with money – nothing to do with what's right or fair. A second point is that the Ekranoplan was a Soviet design, and the Russians say, actually quite rightly, that it was a Russian design and not Ukrainian. Only Simonov secret little bureau was situated in the Ukraine as a sort of satellite operation to the main core of the program which was essentially Russian. Therefore, the aircraft needs to be certified and registered with Russia and not Ukraine."

"The bureaucrats strike again" Stuart flicked in.

"Yes, and believe me, Russian bureaucracy is one huge fuckin nightmare mate. For you or me to get through it would be impossible, but for Natalia's friend? Easy" we need him to arrange

the Russian CAA to issue the paperwork so we can legally fly."
Brad took a single piece of folded paper from his shirt pocket
"This is what we need registered and certified"

Glancing down at it, Stuart saw the various technical descriptions, type of category the aircraft needed to be on, all in detail and assured Brad.

"OK, I will see what can be done"

Brad explained the importance of the paperwork; he needed Stuart to know it was crucial
"Stu, understand, there's a phrase in aviation. *When the weight of paperwork exceeds the weight of the aircraft is when the aircraft is legally allowed to fly.* If we don't get the registration and certification done, we won't be allowed to fly into the UAE"

"Okidoki, then it's time to get cracking. When can the aircraft be ready and be delivered here?"

Right to the point Brad informed him "Three months from the day that they receive the first $50,000"

"Good, give me the details. I need three days, max. Then if it's on it's definitely on and the money will be sent straight away." Stuart wasn't messing around, but he needed to work through the plans thoroughly now that he knew the aircraft was a definite option.

After Brad had left and with deliberately only two small cans of cold beer inside him which had a zero effect on his thinking, Stuart went upstairs in the massive sprawling Villa, through the upstairs living room with kits spread of comfortable sofas and hi fi equipment. Put on some David Gillmoor and unlocked the door to his private office, a small anti room at the end of the living room.

Here he could work, could think. He could use a computer but for this part he wanted to see a bigger picture and started writing with his markers of various colours onto the large plastic whiteboard on the wall.

A list running downwards was already on the board

TIMESCALE	End of third week of Ramadan
FINANCE	In Progress
AIRCRAFT	Ekranoplan A90 - In Progress
DIVERSIONS	Planned. Burj al Arab, Jebel Ali Power Station, Road = Chaos
PERSONNEL	In Progress
REMOVAL OF GOODS	Planned
ESCAPE	To be agreed – definitely Uzbekistan or near
CONTINGENCY OPTIONS	Alternative escape route to Afghanistan
SALE	Lecho Dudayev

Each heading had a sub list, the plan spread like fingers of oil on still water and with each addition, looked more and more possible to pull off.

Stuart sat in his leather Captains Chair and gazed at the board full of lists and notes in front of him, his mind working through things and he said to himself "OK first things first. ......*When*.

"When" has to be the start and has to be fixed.

Consider his plan. Almost all of the gold Souk stores are owned by Indians and boom time for them would be Ramadan, the Holy Month of giving. Stores would be stocked full in preparation for celebrating the end of Ramadan. Hence, it was highly likely that every store would full to the brim and many of the shops would have their safes open in order to bring goods out for display, or to replenish stock during an extra busy period. Hitting the stores during prime evening hours might even enable the teams to get direct access to the safes without having to blow them. Team members could heave tear gas simultaneously into all of the stores, and then fire gas canisters each down the main alley ways to clear the crowd and keep the police or even military away. The overhead canopy, used to protect shoppers from the strong, hot sun during the day, would serve two purposes. It would block people in the surrounding area from actually seeing what was going on at the souk — and it would actually serve to trap the gas in the Souk area — ensuring that only police and militia responding with gas masks could enter. And, it is very unlikely that the police will come prepared with gas masks. And best of all, there would be no collateral damage. Yes, this plan could definitely work. He now had the prospect of removing twenty tons of gold and jewelry from the Souk in less than two hours.

When? He looked at the calendar and remembered a phrase his Mother told him many years before as they sat in the family manor in Worcestershire in the early hours as his father lay in bed dying. He saw the picture so vividly to this day as he remembered sitting at the foot of the bed in the grand room. And before the sixteen-year-old Right Honourable Stuart Henry Bonham inherited the title of Lord Bonham of Martley Bishop upon his Father's death he asked his Mother if "Father would be alright?"

He could remember hiss Mothers face as she told him. "No Stuart, I don't think he will." As she looked through the window into the dark English Winter night and then to the boy "The darkest hour is just before dawn dear. This is your Fathers darkest hour now"

The words echoed, darkest hour is just before dawn, Eide al Fatah is dawn, the ending of Ramadan – before dawn, it has to be before dawn. The "night" *is* Ramadan – thirty days long; ten days from the end will be the lowest ebb, *that's* when it needs to be. There – July 22nd, 10 days before Eide al Fatah.

Working through the time of day was a lot easier. Shops opened at Iftar, the breaking of the fast, the time of day, the zero-hour Iftar will be at approximately 6.20 p.m. Zero hour 6.30 pm or 18.30 hrs. in Stuart's terms.

It ran clearly through Stuarts mind now "Iftar is the lowest point for them, lowest sugar levels in the blood after a day of fasting, lowest glucose, worst decisions made, grid locks everywhere as they hurry home to break the fast. That's the darkest hour of the day at the weakest point of the month." The date was fixed.

Stuart looked at his notes on the white board, wrote beside **TIMESCALE 18.30hrs 22/07** and drew-up a precise schedule of execution for the robbery of Dubai's famous gold souk.

Who, what, when, where, how, what if, contingency plan here, alternative there – everything started to appear on the board as he updated it.

TIMESCALE	**18.30 hrs. 22/07**
FINANCE	Stone, Personnel, Others, Balance 820,000
AURCRAFT	Underway
PERSONNEL	25 UK, 9 US, 5 SOV, 1 Ozzie

EQUIPMENT	(see list)
REMOVAL OF GOODS	Yet to be confirmed
ESCAPE	Option A Direct Flight
CONTINGENCY OPTIONS	Option B dissolve and disperse
SALE	In Place
ORDINANCE	C4, Tear Gas, Kalashnikovs, Flash bangs, Smoke canisters (black or blue) ECMs (electronic jammers for mobile phones)

He thought it through in the smallest details, human psychology, natural reactions, the environment, the weather, the everyday predictable habits, people's reactions and emotions to given circumstances, the systems in place with the various emergency services. The effects all of these factors would have on the plan and how they could be used to an advantage. Steadily and surely the "how" was taking shape on the board with an important underlying theme:

Stuart noted underneath the "How" question. *Minimum harm - Maximum chaos.*

Over the next three days a solid plan had taken shape. Action lists were drawn up for Sarge, Tommy, Matt, Brad, Natallia, Lenna and Stuart too. All had their various tasks to complete and times to achieve them by. These were nonnegotiable, unchangeable. Everything was planned for that set time on that set day.

CHAPTER 11: THE REUNION

Worcestershire, England

E-mails, phone calls and various messages were sent out through the old boy's network to old and trusted comrades in arms inviting them to a weekend at Lord Stuart Henry Bonham's ancestral home in Worcestershire, England. One month later, men had arrived from various parts of the world for this weekend reunion. Some from their new jobs guarding oil rigs in Libya, some having taken leave from their jobs in various American Airlines where they worked as international sky marshals, some from private security firms in Iraq and Afghanistan; others bored with guarding racehorses in Dubai itself arrived too. All in all, there were 53 men. Between Major Bonham and Captain Donnelley all men were known and trusted.

One month later, all had arrived, in ones and twos and had settled into the 600-year-old Oak beamed Elizabethan Manor in the ridiculously green Worcestershire valley overlooking the meandering River Severn that eventually finds its way to the Bristol Channel that separates Wales from England. The Elizabethan Manor had only ten bedrooms, so a large tent had been erected near the stable to accommodate the overflow. Not a single man objected to the tent, in fact, most seemed to prefer camping in the lush Worcestershire countryside.

The Lord had chosen this particular meeting point simply due to seclusion and privacy. Even in the 21st Century the Lords Manor and its grounds commanded a certain amount of respect and the 300-year-old high stone wall that ran for almost six miles around its perimeter helped a lot too. From the west side high on the ridge near Martley the Border county of Herefordshire could be seen in its lush green glory as it spread itself towards the Black Mountains of Wales. A little to the North, the Market Town of Bromyard surrounded by its Cider Apple Orchards and to the East, the County of Worcestershire and the longest river in the British Isles, The River Severn beyond which were the flat plains of the Midlands, the very Heart of England.

"Afternoon Gentleman." Lord Bonham announced from the stage he had had set up in the Grand Hall which resembled a museum more than a home. All of the men were seated at tables, their lunch had finished, everything had been cleared away under the supervision of Tommy. All men had helped; there were no staff, no servants and no one in the sprawling grounds surrounding the manor House, this was a very private meeting.

Of this cadre, six remained on active duty, all the rest had retired from the armed forces. All but two of the men had maintained their special operations physiques as if by an unbreakable habit more so than desire

"Gentlemen, firstly I would like to thank you for attending our…little reunion here. If I can perhaps introduce some of our American colleagues here, all of whom are experienced in their field and known to several of us here, particularly Tommy, Sarge and myself had the pleasure of working with our friends here in Central America. Glancing quickly Stuart knew that there were others in the room who had worked in the same jungles hand in hand with their American counterparts.

"Very well. As expected, the need for absolute discretion is expected and assured, as usual "So nicely put" thought Tommy as he translated it to *"No one breaths a fuckin word of their meetings to anyone, ever"*

Stuart paused and cleared his throat, the next part needed to be delicate "Unfortunately, as some of you are already aware Captain Donnelly lost his son in action in Iraq five months ago. Sadly, he was executed as is their…..disgusting habit" Stuart didn't need to elaborate, all present were fully aware of the usual scenario that would have befallen the Captains Son, and all were well aware of the anger he must hold inside himself against them. Many of the men present knew the feeling of having lost a friend to the same fate.

"Today I'd like to talk with you about how some of you can help, shall we say, to *balance the books* a little. Matt, Tommy, and I have some highly confidential information that we'd like to share with you. And after you hear it, we want you to consider volunteering for the venture we have in mind".

Still no words were spoken amongst the crowd.

Stuart looked over to each table in turn and each man nodded his assent.

"Alright then" said Stuart, "This is the situation. In Iraq, we know that there is a particular cell that is led by a young man, from Dubai. He is also financed from Dubai, as are many of his associates. To explain finance, we actually mean to a figure exceeding 10 to 15 Million US Dollars per year. A serious logistics support for insurgents, recruitments and training camps alike. In a nutshell, what we have found is a major financial backer, their supply routes of cash and the source of their prime execution squad. In particular, we know the key figures involved. Who the money man is and who the leader and certain members of the execution squad are too? We believe that the right approach is to destroy the system that funds the terrorists, cut their food chain and then as a very tasty cherry on top, eliminate the brave execution squad itself."

Again, Stuart paused, that was the introduction in a nutshell, now for the explanation.

"To destroy the financier, and turn off the flow of money, we need in effect, to take the money from them. Very simple, it's called theft" The men laughed, they liked that idea "To do so will mean a little larceny on the soil of a foreign, sovereign Middle Eastern country. We must essentially rob their *bank*. Only this bank is a market — a market filled with gold, silver, and jewels. Our financier is using this market to launder Al Qaeda money. We plan to take all of his holdings in this market and then, having accomplished that part of the venture, we will deal with the terrorist cell immediately, the two sections of the plan are consecutive but in very fast sequence, within possibly 48 hours of each other".

And now Stuart thought, best to tell them straight.

"So, gentlemen. The *venture* "he emphasized the word "and I refer to it as a venture because it is not, repeat not an officially sanctioned mission – it is purely a private venture and it is, most definitely, not legal. Having said that Gentlemen, as with any sensible, illegal venture, it is also extremely lucrative." The men laughed.

Stepping back. Stuart concluded, "Gentleman, Captain Donnelley will now say a few words"

Matt, on cue, joined the Lord, looked around the room at the serious faces and paused before addressing the professionals seated in front of him

Matt stood and cleared his throat…looked around the room and then began "My feelings said to me…, you now… just kill this man….do it all by yourself. The natural feeling, I am sure you can understand." He looked, he saw agreement, then continued" But Stuart has convinced me that killing this man would not help prevent other soldiers and civilians from being killed and desecrated in the same manner. The Al Qaeda money would find another way to Iraq and the murders will carry on too. This Al Qaeda money must be confiscated and so, we have a plan — a very good plan. And for those of you who choose to participate in our project, as a change for once, there will be a large reward at the end."

Matt paused and continued "Gentlemen I make no excuse and I am not here to give you bullshit. I intend to kill the bastard that murdered my son and the fact is I would happily do it for free. The money is a bonus and…in the long run, it might stop some murders at least for a while……*Think* about it"

Lord Bonham then stepped forward. "We're going to take a one hour break now. Talk amongst yourselves. We do not want you to feel compelled to join our group. If you choose to come on this mission, I will require three months of your time. If you choose not to come due to family matters, a commitment to the military or to your jobs — or whatever, then that is perfectly understandable. I want you to follow your will, not mine or Captain Donnelly`s. For those who choose not to participate, there is the Admiral Rodney just down the road, an excellent pub and the bill is on me. For those of you who are interested in signing on, phase two of this briefing will begin one hour from now, right here"

Many questions arose at the tables as men spoke in whispered tones. We're they too old for this kind of duty? Were they willing to take the risk? If caught in a foreign, Middle Eastern country robbing a market, what would the penalty be? How much money are they talking about? But all of these concerns were overridden by the proposal on the table — the proposal to do something to make right the desecration of Matt's son. The ex-special forces troops were insulted, enraged, and ready to do something about it.

When the hour had passed, the volunteers reassembled. They had all talked amongst themselves and weighed the pros and cons of following their former commanders on a new, non-sanctioned mission. There evolved three classes of men amongst the group: those who were completely retired with little to do and simply bored with their new civilian lives; those who had taken jobs in the private security firms operating all over the Middle East; and those who still had commitments to the military. The twenty-seven men who were retired and living on pensions all signed up. Hell, a chance for some excitement and a chance to make a few extra bob — why not? The men who had jobs in the private sector — jobs they worked hard to get and keep through these rotten economic times — all also signed on

Counting thirty-six men stood in for the second briefing. As the group assembled, Matt went to each individual and thanked him personally.

"Gentlemen" said Stuart, "Welcome aboard. Your help and your skills will be greatly appreciated. Now I will tell you what we've been up to. Our target is the Gold Souk in Dubai. Our friend the Al Qaeda financier launders drug money through this market. He takes Al Qaeda cash, dumps it into the purchase of gold and precious stones, skims the profits, and sends the money to selected terrorist organizations throughout the Middle East. He's smart — although the Dubai housing market has been raging out of control and he could be making a killing in real estate, he holds only about a quarter of his investment money in land and buildings. The remaining three-quarters has been invested in gold and diamonds — both of which have surpassed the real estate boom in financial yield over the past five years.

We know the actual stores with whom he does business. Our plan is to strip those stores of all of their inventory in a very short period of time — and to fly out of Dubai with approximately twenty plus tons of gold and jewelry".

A roar went up from the men. "Twenty tons, Boss? What's that worth?" said a man from Bristol. "Bobby, that's worth approximately four hundred and forty million dollars, we are working on a safe estimate of 200 million for a quick sale" declared Lord Bonham.

Again, another roar went up from the men.

"Now don't get your knickers in a twist ladies" said Tommy. "There will be costs involved, and the sale price has to be low, to get rid of the stuff quickly. Those costs could be forty percent or fifty percent of its overall value. Still, we're talking approximately eight million dollars per man on this mission when all is said and done".

The crowd hushed, taking it in. Eight million dollars. Never in their wildest dreams…
Stuart stepped forward. "The plan is both simple and complex. Gold heists are very rare, primarily because the metal is so heavy. Gold is hard to transport and usually very heavily protected. And we're talking about carrying twenty tons of it away. That's a bit heavier than your usual Bergen *(backpack)* We will need to move it about half a kilometer away to a waiting seaplane — a Russian

seaplane capable of carrying thirty tons of goods and people at under-the-radar level out of Dubai".

"Our target date to conduct this exercise is July 22nd. This will be in the middle of the third week in Ramadan, when we believe that the army and police will be staffed minimally on that day — simplifying our job. We should meet minimum resistance" said Matt.

"We will commence training here within two weeks, then you will move on to Dubai." Stuart said. "I will purchase your tickets and arrange for your food and lodging. We will be staying in various parts of the town with one central HQ and a backup location for a secondary HQ as and if needed. Your arrival dates will be varied, spread over a ten-day period as not to draw attention to our …endeavor".

"Once you arrive in Dubai, Matt, Tommy, Sarge or I will take you on a tour of the gold Souk. You will each be assigned a set list of gold stores to "relieve". Pay close attention to how that store is laid out. Also, upon entering the store, see if you can spot the safe. Usually they're unlocked during opening hours and we want the contents from them along with the rest of the inventory. When you hit your store, **do not** let them lock their safes. The safes will hold the most expensive stones and that means big extra profits. A single stone can be worth five kilos of Gold – Think about it – worth a lot more money and much easier to carry".

"After two minutes in the store, you are done. Two minutes per shop and that's it. Clean the safe into a bag we'll provide to you and get out the door."

"You will be there as tourists and businessmen. In the event of a call off or if the plan goes tits up, there will be an initial evasion plan and a secondary less attractive evacuation plan for each of you to choose as you see fit. The first is that simply you disappear, go back to being on vacation in your hotel or go back to following you cover doing business deals, then slowly filter out of the place after 7 to 14 days. The second is that you will each be given job offers by my Company operating in Afghanistan and you will fly there and re group at my HQ there.

However, I do not intend to fail. This venture is planned to succeed.

Gentlemen, thank you for joining. Detailed briefing shall begin at 0700 tomorrow, again in here"

CHAPTER 12: THE BRIEFINGS

Worcestershire, England

The next morning in the Great Hall again Stuart took the stage.

"Morning Gentlemen, no hangovers I hope?"

Stuart knew full well that there wouldn't be, these men were professionals.

"I would like to introduce Captain Brad Johnstone. He is a long-term resident in Dubai and will give you the run down, even though a lot of you already know about the rules and regulations there, Brad will run through it with you now. Also, Brad is in charge of the aviation side of events, so the two sections, Local Rules and anything Aviation related are his baby"

Brad had no problem in stepping forward and doing his stuff and kicked off with an expected

"G-day gentlemen. Nice to see ya all chipper and dandy "and yes, Brad was taking the piss out of the pommes! all in good heart.

"First, the basic do`s and don'ts, who's who of the place.
Do not get into any fights here. If you can't avoid a situation try to cool it, If that fails simply run away and if that fails and you have to become involved DO NOT repeat DO NOT call the police or wait for the police if someone else has called them. Quite simply, disappear.

You will all be here on tourist visas, even those of you under the cover of being there on business will be officially on a tourist and not a business visa. This means that essentially the police will not wish to involve you in any proceedings at all if they can avoid it. That's because its bad PR, bad for tourism. Be polite, be cool, smile and accept a bollocking, that's normally the worst you will get. This doesn't just apply to any fracas you might be involved in, but everything else from a traffic accident, speeding pull over and so on.

Most of the Police in Dubai are imported from poorer Arabic states such as Syria or Jordan and quite a low percentage speaks English. This will actually help you as mainly they can't be bothered with getting an interpreter and they're also under pretty strict guidelines to look after the tourists here.

Meantime avoid the typical "meat shops", "whore joints"; you never know who is on the lookout from the authorities there and as a matter of interest, its rumored that one in three of every local is linked to the CID in some form. – Plenty of eyes are around – ALWAYS remember that.

Lots of the CID are also imported from Pakistan, so ***do not*** be mistaken that all CID are local Arabs.

Now, let's give you some more background on the actual place and the policies there. First understand that it's UAE Inc. Think of it as a booming business rather than a Country. As the TV advert says, what's going on there really is the Greatest Show on Earth; it's a colossal expansion program beyond anyone's dreams.

The investment here has reached critical mass. If they try to stop the expansion and say "No more construction or development from midnight tonight" - it would still take five years to stop the boom in business. Basically, it's a financial supertanker going flat out, it CAN'T be stopped overnight even when the "bubble bursts" which for sure it will one day – the place will still be "rich pickings" as far as the Gold Souk is concerned.

Bear in mind, 50 years ago it wasn't even a state, 40 years ago they were cutting each other's throats for pole position in each Emirate, 30 Years ago there was a boom and 20 years ago the place went through a depression. They have been on the roller coaster of growth, not just in financial terms but in a sort of coming of age, a maturity so to speak, and now…now.. the up curve is incredible, they are aiming for the stars Gentleman, and they are going to get there too! This place is going to be THE place on the planet earth. Already it's an Icon in the region, the Middle East but what they've got planned doesn't stop at that. They intend, and will be, the best Country in the World to live in, to invest in.

But first, let's go back and look more at the history of the place. The old hands, some are still alive now. The locals who have made it into the super league of wealth. Some started by immigrating here from Iran and other Gulf states, trading in Mother of Pearl, walking 3 days to post a letter and having to wait 3 months for a response from London. Another who worked as a bell boy in the only hotel with a lift, taught himself English and listened to the conversations of the English businessmen when they took the lift. He picked up enough information to become one of the largest landowners in Great Britain now. The boy that walked 3 days to post a letter now owns the controlling share of Mercedes. Another who trusted an Indian that said he could manage to smuggle precious gems here from Sri Lanka, borrowed the money to bank roll him. They are still partners today and own a fleet of supertankers plus several household name companies in Europe.

But in the recession, I mentioned, 20 years ago, there was also an accidental change in the structure. You see, from historical trading links, this place was the crossroads between the Iranian Empire,

Asia and near Europe and all of the locals would speak Arabic, Hindi, Urdu and then lastly English. This means that communications with Indians and Pakistanis was easier for them and when the recession came, after having 20 years of technology drip fed into the system here from Europe, it was a cost cutting exercise to get rid of the expensive Brits and replace them with Indians and Pakistanis in middle management – much cheaper and easier to communicate with.

Now don't fall asleep lads, this all comes together in the end and will show you *just* why this whole idea can be workable.

So…….. we are now at a point in the mid-80s, the place started to stabilize, the systems are in place, but due to the recession the progress and development doesn't necessarily take a major turn for the better and things start to stall. However, other changes kicked in at around the same time and in the Royal family, there were gentle power shifts and the 3rd youngest son of the Ruler started to have more and more influence. Now he is Clever, yes, with a Capitol "C"

Deep thinking, cool, calculated and precise. A natural pro, groomed in politics and schooled in literature and economics, i.e. the perfect man for the job of taking this Country into the 21st Century and putting it on the World platform as THE Icon, as THE best.

So, in the mid to late 80s the power shift started to have its effects. Investments were made in forward planning. Global infrastructure linking the Country to the rest of the world, foresight and forward thinking. Professionals from Europe were brought in again, business consultants, business developers, planners and last but not least…. the spin doctors and these…*these* are the ones who have really opened the door for you here Gentlemen!

So, stay with me on this, we now have a Country that is rooted in trading everything but manufactures nothing, its cash rich but has nothing to sell except *itself* as a place to be, a place to live and if you think about it, what makes a place attractive to the successful westerners?

First, no tax, no demands to pay the government for something they don't provide. So, the place is a tax haven.

Next is sunshine? Plenty of that for sure, even the horrible 50 degrees plus, with 99% humidity appeals to the average European better than months of grey wet rain.

No crime. Live in a crime free environment. That's a major plus too; after all, people with money in the rest of the world are *the* targets for crime so why not move here and live openly and safely with your wealth?

On top of all this, throw in the world first 7-star hotels, unlimited choice of restaurants, even pubs, go out and eat or drink in 365 different places a year. Where else could you do that in the world?

The place caters for everything, every taste in food, almost every sport, even indoor snow skiing, every single taste in nightlife and lifestyle too. Strict rules about morals? Well walk into York's at Chimney Corner or the Cyclone club and see a thousand hookers from virtually any country on Earth working there seven nights a week!

In effect, they're building paradise and they're selling it at a premium to all and any who want it and as natural traders, they don't care where the money comes from to pay for it.

By far, the majority of buyers here are genuine people who are attracted to the place for all the reasons I've mentioned earlier but there IS another element, the bad boys, they go there too.
In this place you have every single element of international crime. Mafias elements from the US, so called Mafia or rather the extortionists from the ex-Soviet Union, even Triads are getting their part of the action from the Chinese hookers here. At the extreme, the IRA has opened up shop here and is happily beavering away running huge UK tax swindles from Dubai too.

Now, all of these elements are there and in fact are operating from there too. But the place is also their money laundering holiday home, none of them will push the limits, at least not too far, in other words, none of them intend to shit on their own doorstep and lose their lifestyle. The Government knows it, turns a very very blind eye and in turn lets them bring even more wealth into the Country so, everyone is happy.

When the Americans ask for people to be extradited, out of the last 16 requests none have been upheld, the Brits want to nail the IRA, even have their MI6 onto them there but they get zero help from the UAE Government, so the IRA is laughing. The International community cries foul about the money laundering so laws are put in place, riddled with so many loopholes to ensure the cash keeps streaming in. Hell, the only time they've ever cracked down was when some Pakistanis tried to sell nuclear bombs there and even then they didn't nail the Chechnya's who were behind it all!

So, the bad boys have their run in Dubai, but they behave; operate *from* Dubai rather than *in* Dubai. Everyone is happy, safe and getting richer by the day.

Its paradise… paradise on earth where there is never any bad news. That's what the spin doctors make sure of, no bad news ever. No murder, no extortion, no terrorism, no rape, no burglary and no robbery.

Get it? NO robbery, no matter how BIG.

Gentlemen, the little escapade we are talking about would be very bad PR for Paradise. After we do it, after we pull it off, I believe they will pretend it will never have really happened.

Think about it…The Gold souk is one of the main tourist attractions; everyone that visits Dubai buys gold there. It's in every holiday brochure, been on every TV station promoting Dubai.

Almost every jewelers shop there is owned by none locals, either Iranian immigrants, Pakistanis, to a lesser degree Sri Lankans but the majority is Indian ownership. So, if they are robbed who losses? Not the Locals at all, in fact, by admitting the event would be their real loss. So why admit something if it has been no loss to you? Why damage their own image for the sake of immigrants who are in their country earning themselves a fortune out of it? The locals owe these people nothing and THAT'S why they won't put themselves out for them.

Then on the other hand, just how much of the stuff that they sell is already stolen, or is a means of money laundering? How much would the shop owners even admit that they had lost?

So, Gentlemen, now you can see just how helpful the plans for Paradise and the input of the spin doctors can actually be to us.

Well, that's the very basic background of it all. Now Stuart will tell you the plan…
Without any delay, Stuart took his turn.

"I know many of you are jotting down notes and questions, we will leave them all for a question and answer session later. For now, here is the plan and the time frame.

First the plan." Stuart turned to the large map behind him showing the peninsular that contained the City of Dubai cut in two by "the creek" that separates North from South, Bur Dubai in the south and Deira Side in the North.

The entire Gold Souk at the tip of the Northern, Deira side where it is linked by Shindagaha tunnel to Bur Dubai and its road layout which so obviously begged to be a perimeter sealing off the peninsular itself. Last but not least, the beach that was so accommodatingly close to the Souk itself was a natural cherry on top of the rich cake.

Pointing at the map Stuart explained "Our plan is to seal both sides of Shindagaha tunnel here and here. The aircraft will take a potion offshore and then be called in to a position here" again tapping the map.

Two hours later the men knew the outline of the plan, two days later every question had been answered.

"You will all be issued side arms. We will only need RPGs for initially smoking the Souk up" added Tommy. "So, we will also be clearing the souk using tear gas which we will lob in with the RPGs from here and here" pointing to positions on the public parking area that separates the Souk from the beach. "As was said before, timing will be critical during this engagement. We will practice here at the estate, work out timings and pick up on any potential glitches and attend to them. It isn't ideal but it's the best we have for privacy. At present, we have twenty-seven men for this mission. We may add just a few more" Stuart said. "Twenty-

One of you working in three-man teams shall be assigned five stores per team. The remaining men will be working security. These men will be used to create three key bottlenecks which will effectively seal off the area for a while, plus there will be a number of "distractions" around the city that occur simultaneously. After the bottle necks are fixed these men shall give back up to the Souk Teams to help flush out all of the tourists and Souk employees as well as to guard our perimeter".

"With respect to payment" said Tommy, "we will distribute that payment equally amongst you".

Tommy, Matt and Stuart paused for a minute to let all of the information that they had just relayed to sink in. "Are there any questions?" asked Matt.

Many questions were asked over the next half of the day until eventually they all congregated at the bar to celebrate the forthcoming "adventure", but none breathed a word of it out loud.

As the men chatted over a quiet pint or three in the Admiral Rodney pub while Stuart had pulled up in the Short Stay Parking at Birmingham International Airport in the heart of the Midlands, forty miles to the North East.

Walking inside he glanced at the arrivals board EK 039 from Dubai estimated 19.35 "Good, he thought to himself, that's about on time" as he took up a stool at the nearest café and waited for his arrival. With just hand baggage Collin Peters emerged from the automatic air side doors before anyone else from the flight and spotted Stuart, making a bee line for him. They shook hands with Collin looking pleased with himself "Hiya Boss, all well?"

"Fine thanks Collin, and with you?" Stuart enquired.

"It's good, all sorted" Colin confirmed as they stepped out into the already dark and damp Midlands night and walked towards the car Park. Once ion the car and on their way, easing out in to slow moving traffic on the M42 that surrounds the mass of Birmingham City they chatted in detail.

Collin was Stuarts Junior Partner in FieldEx which was essentially a company operating in Afghanistan for mine clearance. The money was good and there was no shortage of work. Under various Overseas Aid Grants the Afghani Government could afford to employ specialists like FieldEx to clear areas of the sophisticated western mines that had been strewn, almost at random thought the Country. The company, by the very nature of its business also worked closely with all the International agencies and ground forces deployed in the different areas. In other words, Field Ex was licensed to buy almost anything it needed, legally for its own security.

Stuart continued "OK, what did you get sorted mate?"
"Got the lot, some of its even better than I thought as well." He started counting out on his fingers" Pistols, (type make etc.) Holsters, belts fitted with extra pouches on three of them just like you asked, I managed to get the American gas masks, much better and the spare filters are included too. All the AK47s and ammunition, absolutely masses of CS is kicking round, I got plenty but just let me know if you need more, RPGs, Digital timers.

I've got black smoke canisters, they were quite difficult to get, I only managed thirty and I don't think I can get more without rocking a boat. If you wanted red, yellow or even green it would have been easier. They use that more for recognition and rescue, easy to get in canisters, but black was a bloody nightmare to find."

"Perfect" said Stuart "Now, for delivery to Dubai? Anything sorted?" Stuart was now indicating to move into the fast lane; easing past the night rush of traffic so he could move to the M5 that would take them south to Worcester.

"Yep but DHL were a bit expensive, so I got it arranged by the UN" Collin started to laugh.

"The U.N.? United Nations?"

"Yep, that's the one!" Collin said, very pleased with himself "We can, let's say, arrange that their flights to Dubai are our delivery flights. The UN can't be searched; they carry whatever they want in or out of anywhere. "Collin paused "Course, you can't come it too blatant, but some of the Russian crews that they've got operating for them freelance are
on our side, if you catch my drift? They will bring whatever we want into Dubai. Or out come to that – it just costs a few bob that's all"

"Excellent, OK set all this up with Tommy, he will arrange and coordinate with you to meet your Ruskies as they bring the stuff in. Well done Col" Stuart was pleased

"Now, are we making any money there?"

Again, Collin was happy "Yes, and we've been paid too. I put a quote in for a field clearance up in Kandahar Province. Its top turnover job and they've agreed to a 50% mobilization payment. We are up 800,000 $ now and the job doesn't start for a month. Also, I know the American Major up there, he's a good guy, if we want he can delay the start another month, maybe two if we want, it will give you the cash to play with"

"Perfect. Perfect" Stuart was pleased "Now, First stop is the Admiral Rodney for some home brewed, there's a bunch of the lads there for a get together."

"Fine by me" said Collin, never one to kick a drink into touch.

As Stuart was making his way off the Motorway and through the country lanes of the dark late winter night Matt and his compatriots were still at work. Sitting in the library of the Manor House the floorboards creaked at Matt walked across to the blackboard placed in the corner.

The eight Americans were sat round listening intently to their former platoon Commander. The tallest there, a naturally fair-haired Californian, lean and tall, very tall, was calmly absorbing every word of Matt's explanation.

"Your call sign is Beachboys….. 1 to 8," it raised an approving laugh "Pointing at the now retired six feet six-inch Captain "You being Beachboy One. Your mission is twofold and first off, most important that you let me explain why"

Matt paused.

"You're all aware what happened to my Boy and I've got no intention of giving you guys any crap on this one"

He looked round, he saw the look in their eyes, any one of this cadre would happily end the life of Thomas`s murderers with their bare hands and he knew that his old team would go for this with a vengeance, they had seen far more than one boy like Thomas suffer the same sickening end.

"So, to just make things very plain to you people now. The reason I am doing this is solely to bring me time in the same room as my son's murderers. That's my motive. My sole reason. I want to be honest with you about this."

The men nodded, one said "That's appreciated Sir, don't worry, we're with ya"

"OK.... thanks.... now.... the two-fold part of your mission. I think you're gonna enjoy this bit.

Matt continued, passing round several pictures taken inside and outside the Burj al Arab Hotel.

"You might have heard about this place, it's pretty cool. You're going on an all-expenses paid vacation to the Burj as phase one of your detailing. Your cover will be *Madisions Oil and Drilling Inc* and you will be in Dubai on a fact-finding tour as part of a heavy investment proposed in the Gas Fields of Kazakhstan. Part of your investigations will be the proposal of setting up your own Power supply for the fields. That is how you will visit Jebel Ali Power station, 20 miles out of Dubai. Your brief is to plant between 2 and six timed explosive devices that must not be detected or discovered. If they are, the whole mission shall be in jeopardy. At the same time, throughout your stay in the Burj,
You shall, at your leisure gentlemen" Matt smiled "Install in each of your rooms another pre timed device and a smoke canister. If you can access any further rooms by fish or foul, you shall install the same devices there too. The more, the merrier"

Matt knew this was all too easy for the guys. Where were the jungles, the snakes, the sandstorms and booby traps? This wasn't a challenge for their skills.

"OK, enough of the Apple Pie gentlemen. "Matt paused before continuing.

"You won't be part of the hit on the Souk at all – This is your job"

Matt peeled back a large sheet of paper and showed a blown-up Map of the region encompassing the whole of Iran, the Gulf the Caspian and Western Afghanistan. He pointed at a place where the three Borders of Turkmenistan, Uzbekistan and Kazakhstan meet, an inverted "T" of the join of the three Countries Borders was the exact point.

"Here is your destination." He peeled back the map now revealing a much closer blown up map of the Lake

This Lake, known under various names from the various Countries is our point of delivery for the goods. You are our advance party and reconnaissance; you are to achieve the following objectives:

1. Unseen, you shall survey this lake, in this particular region, in its North North East sector. We need an accurate report on its depth at the time of our arrival and of any potential obstacles. It's a salt lake and in July, it will be at its lowest ebb, sometimes it has been known to dry up completely at other times it runs a depth of between 15 to 25 feet. Either way, this is where we intend to land, with or without water. Our pilots if necessary shall sacrifice the aircraft and belly land if needs be. The worst scenario is if the lake is at a level that's too shallow for a flying boat to land, and too deep for a land craft to land. A water depth of between 2 feet and 6 feet being the most dangerous. And of course, the deeper the better after that. Hence, we need to know before we land.

2. Here on the shore, we except to rendezvous with up to fifty Chechnyan's. They are our Customer. However, they are also Muslim supporters for what they want to be known as an Independent Chechnya. Therefore, we must assume that they *may*, I repeat may, turn hostile upon our arrival. Sensible we have assumed that they won't turn against us, simply because it isn't in their interests, but…. let's not be caught napping eh. Now, in the aircraft, especially if the water levels are between the critical levels I've just mentioned, we will be sitting ducks, excuse the pun, and you will be our lifeline. Observation points are suggested here, here and here but of course I shall let you decide the best on the ground and work in with whatever you chose.
3. The third major issue for your information at this stage, you will need to know this part for it to add up….. I shall be with the Chechnyan's as their "guest" The plan is that I shall offer myself to be their guest as a form of security deposit for two things. Firstly, they are helping to finance this whole venture, let's say, major shareholders but secondly, most importantly for me, and I want you to know this. Is that my deal is…?

We deliver the goods; they hand over Thomas murderers to me. - That's why."

So, in a nutshell, you do all the set-up work to create all the havoc and confusion we need for Stuart and his guys to hit the Souk itself. As he does that you will already be set up in Uzbekistan ready to come in like the 5th Cavalry if the Brits are attacked once they arrive at the lake. Without you there it could mean a suicide for them delivering themselves and the gold in a single wrapper"

The room was silent. Matt spoke quietly "Any questions?"

There were hundreds……..

CHAPTER 13: "ROMEO THIRTEEN" LIVES

Crimea, Sea of Azov

The cash that Brad had transferred to the Design Bureau had breathed life into it, brought its workers back, gave them their first salaries in 18 months. They now had a meaning and purpose again and they loved it. The first 50,000 $ was like a cardiac jump start to the heart of the workshops.

On his previous visit it had taken only a week for director Simonov to agree a full and complete deal with Brad and everything had started to swing into operation almost immediately or rather, three days after Simonov had sobered up from his celebration drinking binge.

The whole project, in essence involved the complete overhaul of the Ekranoplan plus many modifications. Every one of which had to be investigated thoroughly, some even had to be designed from scratch such as the titanium wheely bins, reinforcing the deck of the cargo hold, fuselage fuel tanks for extra range, pumping systems for cross feeding the fuel, even the miniature rail tracks that were to run in two lines for the full length of the fuselage.

Removing the fully armed gunners' turret behind the cockpit and replacing it with a hatchway, gutting the radar dome housing the heavy and almost useless internal radar systems, both of these modifications saved a huge amount of weight that could now be exchanged for extra fuel to be carried and hence, extra range. Everything that could be stripped out that was superfluous to the aircrafts peace time role and could save weight was taken out and dumped. The old, heavy Soviet wet cell batteries went and were replaced with small light and more powerful Western gel cell types. All in all, the Ekranoplan slimmed down by almost six tons at the end of its diet. Oleg's baby would grow with long legs!

Director Simonov had every reason to celebrate the deal. It had not only saved his Bureau but also rescued it from closure all together by the sale of the A90 Orlyonok Ekranoplan to Bradley Johnstone's company, OZZAIR. Only two weeks earlier news had come from Moscow about the closing of the facility. His superiors were going to allow him to scrap the planes for a pittance but now instead, he paid them the negligible amount and had sold the A90 to starlight for a relative fortune. Now the bear could really enjoy his Vodka and with good reason too.

By the time Brad had returned to check on progress under Oleg's constant supervision the ownership of the Ekranoplans had already passed to the director Simonov and his nephew through a dummy company that served as a front for their interests. Engineers and maintenance staff had begun work even before this under the strict supervision of his friend Alexie who was probably the best aero engineer in the world and the only man trusted by both Oleg and Brad to see to every minute detail.

Batteries, rubber hoses, gaskets, fluids, belts of all shapes and sizes were found to replace parts that were either "missing" or that had dried out during the Ekranoplan fifteen-year respite. Spare generators, modulators, gyroscopes, and electronic parts were removed from the salvage Ekranoplan and stored in the cargo hold of the Ekranoplan that was being restored. Crews worked day and night on the A90, fixing the hydraulics by replacing dried rubber hoses and gaskets, bleeding systems and checking fluid levels. Mice nests were removed from some wiring closets and power systems were tested for spikes, while wiring plants were inspected for possible shorts. Fuel was pumped into the Ekranoplan tanks —

and due to the tanks being emptied before storage, no holes were found — and no crud remained in the tanks to foul the new gas. And Oleg Kulbaba was there every step of the way, ensuring that repairs were done properly to his new baby. And every time Alexie shook his head – they did it again.

After just five weeks, the formerly super-secret A90 Ekranoplan was ready to make her public debut after a fifteen-year slumber. To the cheers of seventy-two technicians, engineers, and maintenance workers, Oleg, and a crew of five brave souls, fired the A90 up on a cold, minus 21 degrees Celsius day on the Sea of Azov. and took her for a short run around the Caspian Sea. She traveled five hundred miles that day about five to ten meters above sea level without a hiccup. She also managed to scare the hell out of several sailboat and motorboat captains.

Two days later Oleg with Alexei looking over his shoulder on every flight took the A90 out for a different, but equally crucial test. The ability of the A90 to climb to a height of eight thousand feet needed to be tested. Slowly, the A90 ocean beast easily made her way up to a thousand feet, then two thousand, six, then eight — as Oleg watched his fuel gauge descending almost as rapidly as the plane was rising. "She's going to be a real thirsty girl" he thought, as he let the plane descend. The Ekranoplan was going to need a lot of fuel to make it over the mountains of Iran.

The next day, complete with a full cargo hold of two soviet army trucks filled with a variety of scrap metal making them an all up weight of 28 tons Oleg and Alexie again took his baby up to 8,000 feet. This time slower in climb she was still willing. Next to 9,000 which seemed the limit. Heading into wind above the Sea of Azov at 9,300 feet the controls were sluggish almost with no effect. Balancing the aircraft on what seemed like rudder alone it stalled and dropped a right wing slightly over 9300 feet. Pushing the yolk forward, full power still on and opposite rudder to the yaw Oleg regained flight after no more than 800 feet had been lost. Excellent.

Two weeks later Oleg knew every single performance characteristic of his new, slim line baby. He had worked through every flight regime, even spin recovery. He knew his new girl inside out. Now it was time for Brad to come back and get familiar with her too.

On the 4th. Of April, the Russian Civil Aviation Authority arrived to ensure that the aircraft could pass all tests required to make it airworthy for international use. They didn't go outside from the warmth of Simonov`s Office. They were pleased to issue both the certificate of Airworthiness and the Official Documents of Registration without as much as looking at the aircraft. It was a forgone conclusion the paperwork had been paid for, the choice was to accept the payment or accept a second visit from serious Russian Mafiosi linked to Lecho. Without and problem, an official traveled the 4 hrs. on Aeroflot and another 4 hours by car to bounce his way to the Ekranoplan Design Bureau and successfully deliver the necessary international paperwork. Glancing at the dates on the document, Friday 13th of March, before the Ekranoplan had even been test flown!

He smiled as he noticed the paperwork was issued on the thirteenth of that Month. The Registration of the Aircraft issued was coincidentally R.A.018123, meaning R.A the abbreviation for "Russia" followed by the numbers 01813 which added together they equaled thirteen - in total and legally the Radio callsign was an abbreviated version of the full registration, making it R or Romeo One Three.

The next day a bright green heart with an equally bright yellow thirteen was painted on the nose of the Ekranoplan. His baby had a name, "*Romeo Thirteen*".

While Oleg struggled to make the Ekranoplan airworthy and seaworthy, Brad had negotiated permissions from the UAE to bring the aircraft into its airspace as the first step, next the overfly permission which were needed. Surprisingly Iran was very helpful, since the Iraq war their over flight take up had increased almost 300% and business was business after all.

In the end, OZZAIR was forced to spend Six Thousand dollars for the permission. And Brad set off for Crimea for a full week of flying with Oleg in the aircraft for refamiliarization and to press out any weak points that the overhauled giant may still have hiding in its systems. In particular they carried out flights testing the service ceiling of the aircraft at different weights and were happy that after Alexie's week of extra work almost 10,000 feet could be maintained with a previously normal upload of fuel. This would help them a lot with the ferry flight to Dubai over Iran's high ground. Using simple navigation, it was easily worked out that the Ekranoplans would burn off sufficient weight in fuel by the time it reached the Iranian coast to climb to its maximum 10,000 feet and with the flight plan approved, just a few dog legs in the route in central Iran meant that the transition from Caspian Blue to Persian Gulf Blue should be relatively simple.

After a week everyone was happy and finally entered the flight plan Brad that would take them to Dubai via Iran. The next day nine hours after leaving a still and frosty Design Bureau mooring on the Sea of Azov the Ekranoplan was being vectored by Dubai Radar for a touchdown 1 mile from the Port of Hamriyah in the northern Emirates.

Oleg and Alexei had supervised the modification of the ekranoplans fuel system to allow fuel to be pumped from inside the plane. The ekranoplan was to carry five thousand gallons of extra fuel for the trip – more than enough to get the plane from the Ukraine to Dubai.

On June 14th, the Ekranoplan said goodbye to its former home on the base. Following a dawn take off from the Sea of Azov almost seven hours late they had already burned three-fourths of their fuel and Oleg wanted to be sure to have the tanks full as he cleared Iranian air space. Meanwhile, the A90 was performing like a champ — not even a hiccup of a problem.

As they exited Iranian airspace into their last leg across the Persian Gulf the Iranian fighter quartet followed them fifteen miles out into the Persian Gulf. The fighter pilots had enjoyed watching the Ekranoplan fly by, it was a real aviator's curiosity. But with their fuel running low, it was time to return home to Bandar Abbas.

The eventless flight ended with a landing in the Arabian Gulf, followed by the Ekranoplan taxiing itself up to its new dock at Port Al Hamriya. On hand to watch the arrival of the plane were several members of the local Royal Family with their usual entourage of hangers on and yes men. Members of the press were also there, and the aircraft made page three the next day in both the Khaleej Times and the "7 Days" free newspaper. The Ekranoplan had made a big splash.

The following day the Kaleej Times had a front-page article announcing the arrival of Dubai's newest tourist attraction — the Russian-built Ekranoplan. Bradley Johnstone had provided a press release describing what the Ekranoplan was, why it had come to Dubai, and even a timetable when it would be ready to open to the public. He had scheduled the opening for July the 29th, the day after Id al Fitr. Hopefully they would be long gone by then. Until then, however, the Ekranoplan would be "under repair" — ensuring that the plane would be ship-shape for its public debut.

CHAPTER 14: COME TOGETHER

Dubai, UAE

Sitting around the twelve-place solid wood garden table beside the pool in the comfortable Dubai night air, Matt looked across at the towering Burj al Arab just a mile distant. He smiled

Matt laughed quietly "My guys must be loving it there"

"Yes, they certainly should do. That's the best hotel in the World bar none. Money no expense" Stuart replied then added "Pity they can't throw those Irish wankers from the helipad while they're at it"

Tommy chirped in. "Nah, that's our job Boss, we can always come back for them later"

"OK then, down to business" Stuart said and looked in Matts direction. "First the Beachboys. All OK?"

"Yes. All confirmed OK" Matt was pleased to note "They are *Madisions Oil*, Chief young buck executives. Here on a fact-finding tour, for oil well developments in Azerbaijan where they intend to set up their own infrastructure and need power for the oil fields. All planned, including a visit Jebel Ali Power Station on the 26th of the month, booked into the Burj for a full three weeks all bonafide first class confirmed"

Turning Stuart asked "OK, Brad, aviation things?"

"Yep sure, I reckon we can crack the problem about getting a flight plan entered. There's a Pommie flight controller at Ras al Kheima Airport. His name's Jason. I was teaching him how to fly. Reckons he's a natural top gun" Brad said with more than a hint of sarcasm seeing as he had attended the real top gun flight school at Miramar many years earlier whereas the Pommie Private Pilot *wannabe* hadn't - and never would.

Brad continued "Anyways….. he's the typical *up his own ass great white hunter pommie*, been here a year and knows it all. You know the sort, all beer gut and ego - no balls or brains. Bottom line is we need a flight plan entered, that's the only way we can get into Iran legally, without it they will get very anti and without it we will have to go low level all the way. That actually isn't so bad, but if they've got anything up there, looking down, like one of their F16s we won't even hear the bang. So, we need this wanker to enter the flight plan for us. I've invited him down for a drink or six on a Thursday night thrash. We're meeting up at the Alamo Pub and Nat and Lenna will be there, by accident of course. Plan is three weeks from now, tops; I reckon he will be ripe to do anything that Lenna asks!"

The men laughed "Poor fucker" said Tommy "Lamb to the slaughter"

Stuart nodded again "That's good, and if it doesn't work?"

"Well "said Brad "*If* it doesn't work I will be amazed. He's absolutely ideal material, perfect for Lenna to nail. But, *if* it doesn't work and push comes to shove we will go low level balls out all the way – no choice"

Tommy did it again. "What about his Missus? This wanker's missus"

Brad looked at Tommy "OK Tommy, what about her?"

"Well" said Tommy "I bet she does her shopping at Tescos every Saturday morning, you know, pulls up there in her nice Mazda hatchback, pours the kids into a trolley and pushes them round the aisles in the supermarket while they listen to that music, Chris de Burgh Lady in Red while she buys all the cornflakes and sliced ham, you know the kind in the sealed packets that they make out of recycled rubber…oh, and those biscuits and cheesy dip things that the kids like.."

"Stop!" said Stuart shaking his head.

"Anyway" said Tommy "Just thought it was simple really. Get Lenna to look through his wallet while he's washing his cock after she's finished with him. Send our mates round to 27, Wiltshire Close, Croydon post code EC99 1QW2 and half – bet that's where they live – and some of our mates can take her piccys while she's shopping"

There was silence round the table again

"Then, if he doesn't play ball, we blackmail him – Bobs yer uncle, simple!" Tommy clapped his hands and leaned back.

Stuart turned to Brad, they were both silent with a look that said Tommy was totally mad, but as usual absolutely spot on with his assessment. It was a few seconds before Brad suggested "Errr..I`ll let Lenna know OK mate?"

"OK" Stuart stepped in getting back to business. He always liked to have a backup solution for every single aspect, Brad and now Tommy had already seen to it that more than one was in place.

"Good, now Logistics" Stuart explained "Our Contracting Company is now legally registered and open at long last, the bureaucracy here is incredible, but it's now open and we now own GSE Limited Liability Company registered in the free zone at Dubai Airport Free Trade Zone which means that we didn't need to use a local Arabic partner at all. Tommy, what about the *tools*?"

Tommy was ready with his appraisal "The mini diggers are on hold with the supplier, also got a six month guarantee on them" Tommy laughed knowing that they were only needed for three hours in total and continued as he placed brochures on the table" these are the machines, Japanese, bloody good kit. We can collect them any time after we pay the balance. Next the pick-ups, they're not new but they're very good, two Mazda 1-ton pick-ups. Again, we couldn't legally buy them until the Company was open because of registration crap with Dubai traffic Police but now we have the Company; it can be done in a day. Very easy. As for the low loaders and the 5-ton Mercedes vans, I've done a deal for a three-month rental that will sort out all the transport we need to deliver the diggers to the Souk Car Park and include the other three vans for different teams. They are minibuses, also on a three 3-month deal. The mini diggers and transport are covered"

Tommy turned up another piece of paper. "Sarge is in Sharjah. There's a metal working company there that we have found. He told them that we've got a contract to supply the Police in Iraq with 2,000 tire busters, so they're making these for us" Tommy showed a drawing of the treble X shape pieces of metal, sharpened to points on each tip, designed to be strewn onto a road at random and pierce the thickness tire.

"They'll be ready in a week, we've checked the progress and the quality, it's surprising, bloody good for a bunch of pakis in a back street, you should see it, like something from history, a real dump, but they're working like the clappers and turning out some good stuff"

Now it was Stuarts turn

"Very well. Now for everything else we need. The majority is here now. We had a problem with the night vision goggles but that was just flat batteries, so it was easy enough to sort out. We are just waiting for the last delivery now and expect everything to be in place by the end of the week. The Beach boys have already taken their stuff into the Burj and its being placed step by step. So far they have 8 devices in place and are hopeful of at least another 8 by the end of their stay"

Looking round the table Stuart concluded

"OK so far so good. Now "actions. – First, Brad, let me know how things go with your "top gun" boyo. Tommy you and Sarge, get everything cracking with the transport, I will give you the cheque to clear all the payments off but don't pay the Pakistanis until you have inspected the stuff to make sure everything has been done."

Stopping, he turned to Matt

"Matt, we need to talk"

Brad and Tommy decided that the best thing to do was to down a few pints in the Dhow and Anchor pub, situated on the ground floor of the Jumairah Beach Hotel and looking out directly onto the Burj al Arab. Also, it was best to leave Stuart and Matt to discuss things in private.

Once in private, Stuart came to the point "So Matt, I don't need to know the how bit, just the where and when parts?"

Matt responded to Stuarts sensible questions. "Where, will be in Uzbekistan" he took the map on the large coffee table and pointed at the lake on the southern boundary of Uzbekistan that forms the Border with Turkmenistan and pointed "Here"

The area is remote; we can deliver to this place more or less undisturbed. If all goes well it will take several days to value the goods and agree the final pay out from Lecho. There will be lots of different stuff, not just gold, each item is going to have to be valued and added into the final list. It could take days. So, this is the *where* part"

"When… well it has to be during the period of the handover, it has to be then"

"And just how do you intend to get them both there at the right time Matt? That isn't simple to do you know" added Stuart

"I know, but I want you to trust me on that one. OK Stu?"

Stuart quickly thought it through; he didn't like having a secret factor no matter how personal it was to Matt he had to consider everyone else's safety too.

"OK Matt, I will run with you on it, but I have to know what the plan is, and it can't under any circumstances, jeopardize the men. OK?"

"OK Fair deal" said Matt. "This is the plan…………"

The following day, Matt had contacted Lecho and had been invited to meet that night at The Kremlin. When he arrived at the Club, the smile from the raw-boned doorman was civil, almost warm and he was shown to Lecho's table in the restaurant. Standing to greet him Lecho also looked happy to see Matt.

Quickly they were descended upon by a host of waitresses fluttering around to prepare drinks that Lecho was ordering to be brought over and then almost as quickly as they appeared the staff were gone. Standing at a safe distance and waiting for Lecho's hand to be raised so that they could be at his table in minimum time.

Almost ignoring them Lecho spoke.

"I hope for this meeting Matt, that you will enjoy our Russian cabaret". A wave of the hand and the singers finished their Russian duet and the dancing girls raced to get ready, they were to start early tonight whether they wanted to or not. Matt had to be impressed when six of the longest pairs of legs in Russia accentuated by a feather headdress another 18 inches tall kicked and strutted their way through "New York, New York" in a top-class act.

As the dancers left the central floor the singers picked up their act again. Lecho turned and then looked over Matts shoulder to see that no one is close. And no one had dared to come close, he had made it obvious this is private meeting.

Smiling in a sort of quizzical way, he could smell a deal, Lecho simply opened his hands and asked simply and quietly…. "What?"

Matt paused then started his explanation "I can confirm now, what I mentioned in private when we met……I want to buy something from you. …Something special." Lecho was now grinning and joked "Do not tell me you want little boys my friend!"

Raising a smile at this Matt thought quietly to himself that he must be getting closer to Lecho now that he is comfortable enough to share a joke

" Ahhh, you guessed!" both men laughed and then Matt continued

"I want two people brought to a certain place, shall we say, to pay some debts to me and my……….. Shall we say, *Senior Partners*" Matt took the opportunity to push the message deeper that someone serious, indicating the American Government, was behind this concept.

Now Lecho smiled broadly, now it was murder and profit, plus he could at last be earning the one thing he never thought he could have – respectability with a Government. What a wonderful night he was having.

"*Only* two my friend?" Lecho was really enjoying this.

Matt nodded and Lecho asked

"OK who are they and where would you like them to be delivered? All this will affect the price of course"

Matt smoothed the way into the conversation, knowing full well that the only way to *Mr. Greedy's* heart was via his wallet "Oh you know them Mister Lecho and for what I am going to offer will more than compensate any potential short-term losses you might incur."

That part done Matt cut to the chase

"Your business associate, Mr. Usman Al Ghazzal has a son. We both know who they are and what they do so let's not mix words."

Lecho was taken aback; he had no idea at all that Matt was so well informed. And Matt just had to fix this portion of the deal. The Ghazzal's were the sole reason why he was here at all. Lecho could see it clearly now, definitely Matt was working for the Americans, how else could he know all of this?

"I want them Lecho and I will pay for them. Your offer is ten percent of the bullion extra, for free"

Lecho's head whizzed 25-ton haul, 2.5 tons is 10% resale value 55 Million US$. He paused, didn't want to seem too anxious to agree and besides, how did this Matt fellow know so much?

Lecho didn't like how well informed Matt was, immediately he suspected Natallia and then dismissed it, she had no idea at all about Usman's son and that led him equally fast to the conclusion that Matt must be linked to the US Government – only they could have that kind of information "You have too much knowledge of things my friend. This I do not like...."

Matt knew it was time to make his play.

"Yes, I do Lecho, I do know a *lot* and to be honest so do the ...and so do the *people I represent*. So, let me speak very ..." now Matt glanced around quickly "very straight about this." Matt was in full poker mode, now there was no option but to play his game all the way.

"You know full well that with your pressure from the war in Chechnya, the Russians in their new democracy will soon start to get fed up with the financial costs even though the human one doesn't matter to them. With the right help, the right backing, you know that Chechnya can become an independent state very soon. All you need is the right influence from the international community at the right time, plus enough money in your hands to force the issues through. Then who else would be more suitable to be the first President of the independent Chechen people, other than the richest Chechneyan in the world Mister Lecho?"

Matts earlier throw away comment about having enough money to buy a Country came back and rang the jackpot bell in Lecho's greed account.

"But to get there Mister Lecho, *all parties* concerned need to feed from the same table. For me to be *allowed* (again inferring that someone very big and very powerful was turning a very blind eye) to carry put this operation certain conditions have been demanded. They must be met otherwise we will not be allowed to deliver. Do I need to paint any more of the picture?"

His mind racing now "So that's it" Lecho realized "This is an American backed job. It's the CIA who's behind it and they've got all the backing they want from the President himself most likely too. Control of world oil is what it's all about anyway, and they want Chechnya for that. If I don't go with it they will find someone who will. Losing Usman al Ghazal will be inconvenient but not for long, there are lots of al Ghazzal's."

Joining the same poker mode automatically Lecho was quick to start his play "Very well. It is an interesting offer Mr. Matt, but I want a security, how do I know you won't double cross me? You think I am stupid to risk for no reason? I will want half in advance"

"No advance" Matt was playing it ALL the way, now he was cock was decidedly on the block.

"There will not be any advance. The security you will be given is simple Lecho"

Lecho looked, questioning.

"Your security is Me. I will deliver myself to you at the given place. If we break our promise and fail to deliver, then" Matt paused "Well, then Mr. Lecho I would be paying a lot, indeed wouldn't I?"

Lecho nodded, he would have preferred money, but murder can be fun too, that is if he couldn't sell Matt back for cash when the time was right. Either way he will make a profit and really, what else mattered?

Five long seconds passed before Lecho made his comment "I will… er, think about this Matt. I am not so sure. After all, I do have a quite good trading relationship with Mr. Usman and his associates which does promise to continue for a very long time doesn't it?"

Matt resented Lecho's comment inferring that America would be bogged down in on going situations much worse than any Vietnam and for much longer than the World could dream. Either way Matt didn't bite and for sure Lecho was playing it out for even more money. But now Matt was all out, this had to be settled.

"Well…how long things last? Let`s not debate this for now. Just let me make a few very clear points. Firstly, you and I know that there will be another Usman along soon, he will be replaced. Secondly, if your goods (meaning arms and explosives) are still available at the right price then your present customers will still continue to deal with you I am sure." Matt resented Lecho more for the supply of his enemy's arms than anything else, but he needed Lecho too and to spend just two minutes alone with his son's killers he was prepared to kiss the devil himself. "Thirdly, you have to sell a hell of a lot of guns to make 55 Million in profit in one day don't you?"

Eying Lecho's body talk, it was all or nothing now Matt continued "Its 10% extra. On the table for two, very replaceable, pieces of shit. It's a straight yes or no and it's needed now Lecho"

Matt tried to hide the emotion but Lecho saw it. Lecho also got the emergency bell ringing too, Matt was serious, Lecho's mind was racing between his natural feelings of greed and suspicion. The thought flashed through his mind, the passion in Matts voice had provoked it - could he be serious enough to close the whole deal if this wasn't added into it? A nano second later "Screw the Ghazzal's" was the final flash before Lecho agreed to the deal with a very brief

"Ok, it is yes" and smiled as he added "You will have your two very expensive pieces of shit!".

Relieved but able to hide his emotions this time Matt pushed straight into the practicalities.

"They are both to be delivered to Uzbekistan within two days either side of July22nd. After the goods have been delivered to you and the deal is satisfactorily concluded you will tell me where they are being kept and I shall then kill them both. In return for this you will take 10% extra of the haul, be it 10% of less – either way you get 10% extra of whatever we have. You will also receive, at a later date, certain…. shall we say, diplomatic support, in your fight for independence in Chechnya. At this point you will not provide any further support or sales for the enemies of the United States of America"

"It is good. OK we have a deal. And do I take it this is strictly private? That your associates here do not be a part of it?" Lecho predicted pretty accurately and he knew it as Matt smiled.

"Very accurate Mr. Lecho you are correct, no one else knows of this…. extra deal"

The men leaned forwards, half standing, shaking hands firmly across the table and the staff sighed a silent relief.

Lecho drank Vodka and Matt a good Scotch on the rocks as they watched the dancers go through a passionate choreography to Roxanne sung by Pavarotti.

Leaning forwards Lecho brought Matt closer to him, almost laughing; there was something he wanted to tell Matt that obviously amused him immensely.

"You know Usman has been to Uzbekistan several times before?"

Lecho continued "Well, it wasn't for the hunting you know. At least not for the game birds. It was for" Instinctively Lecho looked around again as he did the staff looked the other way automatically

"It was for something very special that he likes……." and Lecho whispered into Matt's ear.

After explaining Lecho continued "So Matt, I think I can guarantee one of them easily but as for the other – the son. That's far more difficult"

"Ahh" now Matt was smiling "Now I think I might just be able to help you with that Lecho"

"Good, then it **will** be done. Now we eat!" and with a wave of his hand the flock of waitresses returned.

As Lecho and Matt now relaxed with each other and enjoyed the world Class show that the girls of The Kremlin had worked so hard to perfect, Brad was finishing his first pint of stone-cold Lager in the Alamo Pub at Dubai Marine Hotel on the other side of town. He looked around the bar with the imitation Mexican décor and there was still no sign of his newfound friend Jason.

He slipped the mobile phone from his waistband and sent an SMS to Lenna "*not here yet. Will SMS u when 2 come in*" and a minute later one came back "*ok no prob am ready*" as he was reading it the Indian barman leaned forward to him "Same again Mr. Brad?" but before he could answer a noisy voice from over Brads shoulder demanded.

"Make that two young man – and be quick about it!" The great white hunter had arrived.

Ignoring Jason's ignorance to the barman Brad lunged straight into the hail fellow well met sequence, massaging Jason's over inflated ego with "Hello mate, great you made it at last, traffic a nightmare?"

Jason was noisy; he spoke loud, too loud as if he were the constant performer and entertainer. Most definitely *he* thought the sound of his own voice was entertaining so why shouldn't everyone else too?

"Ahh well you know how it is Brad, fucking Jinglies (Indians) and Rag Heads (Arabs), think they can drive…" as he waxed lyrical about camels and bullock drawn carts being more suitable for them.

The beer flowed and Brad smiled. Moving the subject onto Jason's exceptional flying skills and totally agreeing with him that as soon as he had attained his private Pilot's License he would most certainly be on his way towards a Captaincy in Emirates Airlines with Jason's natural aptitude for flying, it could only be a question of time Brad assured him as he thought to himself *"Fuck me, I'm full of shit at times"* and smiled. Still, if it got the flight plan entered so that Brad could at least be legally allowed into Iranian airspace, who cared and another two pints of lager was passed across from the barman as Brad sent *"Am ready, come now"* on his SMS to Lenna, waiting on the car park outside.

Three minutes later Brad noticed Jason glance over his shoulder, obviously something had caught the fat boy's attention as he felt a gentle poke in the ribs and turned to see Lenna and Natasha as usual looking absolutely stunning even though they had dressed down, giving a very casual effect. The last thing they wanted to look like were hookers tonight.

"Hey Brad, how are you" turning and following with the obligatory European kisses to both cheeks, Brad introduced Lenna as an Art shop manageress and Natasha as a beautician. Jason suddenly became the Chief of Operations at Ras al Kheima International Airport and he loved it.

Two more pints later, Jason's ego was at warp factor twelve as they all set off to hear some live music at the Rattlesnake Bar in the grounds of the Metropolitan Hotel on Sheikh Zayed Road with Brad in the front of the taxi and Jason more than happy to be sandwiched between the two lovelies in the back. "hahahha a rose between two thorns" was his self-centered joke. They all laughed but not at his quip, they laughed at him. Tommy's words were ringing true thought Brad to himself, *"More like a Lamb to the fucking slaughter!"*

Finding the table in the Rattlesnake was easy, it had been reserved by Brad a day earlier and they soon settled to enjoy a meal as they watched the extremely good Filipino band doing their stuff. Lenna sitting beside Jason, hanging on to his every word. Brad looked sideways to Natasha who smiled back at him and said, "Yes – its normal" and took a sip from her glass as she winked at Brad.

"Fuck! Brad" thought to himself. "I don't know about a lamb to the slaughter, this is more like a cobra hypnotizing a rat!"

The band left for their break, now the Cobra finally decided to "strike"

"Come on Jason, let's dance" and the fat 30-year-old knocked his beer over in the rush to get towards the dance floor. Lenna saw it and smiled. Three dances later and after the six pints of beer now slopping in his gut, the Adonis Jason was kind enough to press his erection against Lenna's virginal mound. Just very slightly she pressed back, and the top guns ego went into a vertical climb.

"mmmm you're a bad boy" Lenna giggled and teased "A *big* bad boy" as she held his hand and led her newfound puppy dog to the table. Him *thinking* that she meant his manhood, she *knowing* that she meant his sagging beer belly. Both of them smiled to themselves - but for completely different reasons.

Brad whispered to Natasha "Looks like Lenna's has just filed our flight plan!" and ten minutes later Jason was pleased to take the taxi to the Arabian Courtyard to spend the most fantastic night of his life.

On the other side of town, having finished his meeting with his new found friend, Matt called Maria on the pre-paid mobile that they had both set up for their private chats "Honey, this is what I want you to do and I need you to do it fast......."

CHAPTER 15: THE EVE

Dubai, UAE

By the 1st of July, on the first day of Ramadan everything was in place.

Brad was working Daily with his crew, attending to the Ekranoplan, making sure every single system was checked and re checked, everything fully operative. They had been over things so many times, that they were now down to actually polishing and cleaning the Monster aircraft.

Even the Green Heart and the Yellow "13" had been repainted in brighter colours. They all loved the badge; it somehow gave the aircraft life.

In Jumairah, turning his chair away from his computer and towards the window Stuart eyed the Burj al Arab and looked at the curved line of its beautiful impression of a sail in full flight. High intensity lights flicked down the right hand seam of the building at night and accentuated its curve and as he looked at it, Stuart could see in his mind's eye, the 41 smoke canisters attached with old but extremely reliable preset Video recorder timers silently awaiting the end of their 23 days of rest in the ceiling cavities of the various suites guest bathrooms.

He smiled as he thought about the Beach Boys stay at the fabulous Burj. Between eight of them they had all insisted on Junior suites on that side of the building facing the smaller Jumairah Beach Hotel. Within the first 5 days each had complained, politely requested or even once sweet talked a gorgeous Indian receptionist to change them to new rooms. A few of them even moved twice, several others decided it would be fun to take a larger suite and doubled up thereby giving them access to other kinds of suites but always on that same side of the structure.

As a thankful sweet cherry on top of the sumptuous cake of their stay in the World's best hotel. Three of the younger Beach Boys had spent several unexpected but very welcome nights in other guest's suites.

All in all, 41 smoke containers were lying in wait for their command which had already been placed into their Siamese twin timers who were all singing the same song 17:53:21:07 in perfect harmony.

Flicking his mind 9 miles further down the same coast to Jebel Ali Power Station, Stuart could see the more sinister big brothers of the Burj devices. Three of them sat at the jugular vein of the Stations output to whole Emirate of Dubai, but this time each of the three big brothers Siamese twin was 4 kilos of Semtex High Explosive. One would do the job, three would completely ensure that there would be no Power for several days and in the middle of high summer with temperatures, humidity and soon to be tempers running at overload levels, the effect could only be maximum on the grid locked society. His mind's eye flicked to confusion, some panic, grid lock, tempers running short, arguments, queues at petrol stations, accidents at traffic lights, frustration and ultimately, exactly what the team needed to succeed; total, perfect chaos.

The big brothers were silently singing their song 18:05:22:07

With the help of Brad, a friend flying for Emirates had kindly brought a package from New York given to him by Maria who had flew into JFK solely to pass it on by hand. It was far too precious to trust to a courier mail company. Matt had looked through it over and over again, everything was absolutely perfect, better than perfect; the documents in the pack were real, authentic and original. Slipping the DVD of Lenna and Usman into the same heavy A4 folder he set off for his meeting with Lecho.

In Ramadan the Kremlin was closed. This time when matt entered, even at 2.00 o'clock in the afternoon there were people working. Decorators, new lighting systems, refurbishment in the kitchens going on too. Lecho was overseeing everything, making sure not to miss a trick as usual and his presence there just made everyone nervous, it didn't help.

Matt was shown into the Kremlin only after knocking the locked door, for sure they could see him on CCV, but this didn't worry Matt at all, by now, the commitment was total on all sides.

Once inside Lecho smiled, he was glad to see Matt and ushered into the haven of his office. Quickly, an ever-present manageress started to take an order from Lecho for beer and food to beer brought in. He had decided that it wasn't Ramadan inside the Kremlin.

Matt looked across Lecho's Runway sized desk and began the conversation.

"I think this will help you to attract the Visitors we need as part of the deal" and slid the envelope across to Lecho. He lost no time in leafing through it, starting with the top sheet, a Birth certificate for Shawn Mathew Donnelly, next some Education Certificates, Next a driving License, next a genuine (care of Marie and friends) US Marines ID card even an old but apparently original photograph, showing a face of the newly recruited Shawn Donnelly in his first Marines dress Uniform.

Lecho looked down at it and then looked at matt "And what is this? How can it help?"

Matt explained, slowly and clearly so that Lecho wouldn't miss the importance.

"Eighteen months ago, a Marine called Tomas Mathew Light was captured in Baghdad following an ambush on their Humvee. Within less than 15 minutes of his capture he had been beheaded and it had been recorded on film. Later it was released openly on the internet but before that, it was sent to Tomas Donnelly's parents."

Lecho, even as no stranger to murder leant back, he didn't like it. "Continue please" he said quietly. Now his eyes were scrutinizing Matt.

"The boy's Mother suffered a nervous breakdown and spent three months in hospital. Tomas was their only son. She will probably never recover fully from this event"

Matt nodded towards the file in Lecho's hands, the same murder squad has beheaded a further 17 victims, one of which was a young Iraqi woman, a Muslim and a reporter working for Al Arabia News TV, here on Sheikh Zayed Road. She was stripped naked, sexually humiliated and then skinned alive prior to her beheading. Again, the video was released."

Lecho kept an even straighter face now. He had seen the video, one of his men had shown him and he had been disgusted by it too. He nodded "please, continue..Matt"

"This squad has passed far beyond what is war, far beyond anything that can be in the name of any religion. And they are being financed largely by Usman and they are being led by his Son."

He held back now, waiting for everything to sink in properly then continued.

"The file in front of you is of the brother of the murdered Tomas Donnelly, the first beheading by the Iraqi murder squad. I know that you can contact al Ghazzal and I also know you can get a message directly to his son. This is the bait to bring him to Uzbekistan. You will "sell" Tomas Donnelly's brother to him. You can say that he was captured while on attachment to a civilian aide unit to Grozny as part of a UN force protecting a Medicines sans Frontiers hospital that's being set up there"

Lecho was impressed that Matt knew of it. For the last month, that had actually been
happening, the hospital was a gift from the EU had been assisted by the United Nations for protection.

"You ask for money for this hostage, but in return the young Ghazzal can get to make his video with your help in the seclusion of your set up in Uzbekistan. I am gambling that the taste he has for killing will be too much for him to resist, especially as you can point out the propaganda effect of him killing two brothers from the same family captured in two different parts of the world"

"As for his father, if your present plan doesn't work, this DVD can be your back up, your lever, if…and only IF you have to use it"

Lecho turned to his side and placed the DVD into his computer. After a short session of mouse movements and clicks, Lecho started to laugh. He didn't bother switching it off or diverting the screen as the Manageress entered to serve the beer and Pelmeni, the Russian dumplings with sour cream, local Arabic style sandwiches, to them each.

"My…. well…. You seem to be very well connected my dear Matt…I see you have Lenna at your beck and call too now!"

"Lecho had taken the information in.
"Good, I will use this" he gently shook the file in his hand "And Matt, I want you to know that if you do not kill this man, then I will." His face was serious, Lecho didn't bluff.

"But believe me, I won't need this to get his father there" and he passed the DVD back to Matt.

Slipping the disc into his light coat pocket Matt concluded.

"As for our deal Lecho. I am free to leave now at any time you say"

Matt offered himself as a hostage, a guarantee as promised.

Lecho's had been watching him carefully.

"Very well, I will let you know when, perhaps about one week from now"

Matt stood and for the first time, felt a genuine, firm handshake from Lecho before turning to leave the room. As he did so Lecho clasped his hands and placed them beneath his chin and pondered.

"How it must feel to lose your only son like that. The man is a hostage, willing to be a hostage because he's got nothing else to lose……….."

Lecho knew now that Matt was Tomas Donnelly father.

Tommy and Sarge were also checking, double checking everything in the secure warehouse they had managed to rent in Al Qooze, just across Sheikh Zayed Road from Jumairah. Everything was in place and ready. Five Ton Mercedes Vans Japanese Pickup trucks, Ford Low Loaders now with extra winches fitted, tire poppers, all the ordinance that had been so thoughtfully and carefully delivered by the Russians working for the United Nations. Everything was in place, checked and counted.

Looking at Sarge as he was working his way down the clip board and quietly counting the same number of CS Gas containers for at least the eight-time Tommy said

"Let's have a piss up"

Sarge turned sideways, "A piss up?"

"What part don't you understand Sarge? I`ll explain it?" Tommy asked.

"Nah, your OK, I can work it out Tit. OK, let's have a piss

CHAPTER 16: TAKE THE MONEY AND RUN

July 22, Dubai, UAE, The Souk, The Beach, Uzbekistan

Two weeks later, with Matt having already departed for Tashkent in Uzbekistan eight days previous; in the 7-bedroom villa in Jumairah checks had been going on since before dawn on that day, the 22nd. of July. The first Day of the 4th week of Ramadan.

Stuart, Tommy and Sarge were happy that all was AOK, all was ready. For months now they had been preparing, for week after weekday after day over and over again they had been training and rehearsing everything. When they had gone over everything, they went through it again just in case. When they knew everything inside out, they ran through it again just in case and when it got boring, they did it again, just once more to make sure.

Looking at his watch he knew that the ECMs, the electronic jammers, were being delivered at that very minute. As with all preset devices there is always the risk of discovery. With the Burj and the Power Station this simply had to be agreed and actioned and put down as being an "acceptable risk", there was no choice the whole plan needed the diversion that would bring every single Emergency resource to a focal point, the flagship of the Emirate, the Burj al Arab. It also needed the break down in infrastructure that a total blackout could bring and so, the Power station became an acceptable risk too. But the third wave could be done more safely and held away from discovery completely.

The seven rented cars were each searching for the optimum parking spaces nearest to their preassigned targets. Inside the trunk of each car was a powerful ECM that once activated would blot out any and every mobile telephone transmission. These clever devices had been developed as a matter of great necessity by the British Bomb Disposal crews in the early days of the IRA terrorist campaigns in mainland Britain when Irish terrorists had taken a turn at setting off bombs by remote control as they watched Bomb Disposal teams trying to deactivate the bombs that they had planted. Using various devices that could range from anything that sent a remote control message such as garage door controls, even the old TV handsets through to the newest but cumbersome mobile telephones of the period, or the best yet, model aircraft radio controls, the terrorist lying in wait could ensure the death of the British Soldiers sent to investigate the Bomb. ECMs basically take any and every transmission, screw it up and throw it back at the sender and "anything" within a 100 meter radius equates to a massive amount of damage to communications in a crowded City, even more so when they have been placed at each side of Dubai Police HQ and each of the Deira Side Police Stations. The seven timers were counting down to the appointed time preset at 17:56.

Everyone was programmed to be in position 30 minutes before zero hour, 6.00 p.m.(18:00 hrs.) at night and at 4.30 p.m. (16:30 hrs.) Stuart sent and SMS message to the "pay as you go" rented telephones of his 10 teams of 4 "Rock-n-Roll" It was a Game On situation. As he sent it he pondered, wondered about Matt.

"If this is a screw up we are all, totally, completely and absolutely fucked. But that poor bugger will be even worse off".
....

By 5.30 pm (17:30 hrs.) The Ramadan rush hour had already started with a vengeance, people who had eaten and drank nothing all day were heading home for Iftar Feast literally meaning "The breaking of the fast" (*Breakfast*) They were thirsty, hungry and anxious to get home and added to all this, their blood sugar content was way down following the crippling summer heat. Full roads, a mix of different nationalities all desperate to get home in a rush hour that was invented in hell and so many of them driving almost as borderline drunks due to the lack of glucose. Just as Stuart had predicted the nightly madness of the sometimes suicidal Iftar races had begun.

The teams had positioned themselves, the majority spread basically along the shoreline between the Hyatt Hotel and the east side entrance of the Shindagha Tunnel that runs underneath the mouth of the creek that separates East Deira Side from West, Bur Dubai. Others were at and near the traffic intersection near the Hyatt regency and Galadarri Galleria and another crucial team were parked outside the 4-star Highlander Hotel overlooking the intersection that is the last stop between Bur Dubai and the entrance 2 Kilometers away from the Shindagha Tunnel.

On the sprawling car parks that make up the majority of the area between the Souk and the Beach two large Mercedes vans were being carefully parked; nose into the curbed area of the parking bay, rear to the open roadway that links the car Parks together. Inside each were three brand new, but tried and tested, Caterpillar D440 mini diggers. Small, Powerful and reliable with their hydraulic shovels sticking upwards, like open hands begging to be filled. Less than a mile away at the Car Park outside the Hyatt Regency hotel two more vehicles were parked and waiting. The Ford Transit heavy duty low loaders, normally used for winching broken cars onto their strong, low, flat backs to carry them home, were now full of brand new shiny oblong aluminum containers. Almost unnoticed were the two powerful winches that were tucked in behind the driver's cab. All along the beach front, the team members, split into 1s,2s and at most 4 in a group were very deliberately non-descript, unnoticeable.

On the beach front, exactly halfway between the Hyatt and the tunnel Stuart turned to face the sea. He felt a gentle and almost 100% humid breeze on his face. Perfect, an onshore breeze just as his science teacher in school had taught him so many years before. "Land heats up quicker than water, water cools down slower than land, hot air rises, therefore at night the hot air rises from the sea and the air from the land rushes towards the sea. At dusk, following a 50 plus degree day, the land temperature was still raging higher than the sea and the wind would blow towards it and that means, to Stuart, that so will the tear gas. Perfect. Looking at his mobile phone he pressed "send" and out went the final mass SMS to the teams "Go, go,go 1800"

Instantaneously four Mazda Titan dump trucks packed with the strange loose tire spikes started their work. One pulling out from the Highlander Hotel to turn right towards the Shindagha Tunnel heading towards the gold souk, another crossing the key interchange that links Deira with other outer suburbs of east or Deira side Dubai. The two others working their way in a cut off direction from the Creek itself and into the heart of Deira.

The Mazda pickup truck allocated for the run "inbound "to the Souk from the Highlander Hotel had delayed its turn at the lights, letting the previous traffic move ahead before pulling out in order to let the traffic in front get about two hundred yards ahead. Horns blared behind them as impatient Dubai drivers tried to squeeze by — but to no avail. Then, suddenly, the truck sped up, and about fifty yards before the tunnel, members of the team started heaving shovels full of tire spikes onto the highway.

The impatient Dubai drivers also sped up, racing to recover whatever time they perceived that they had lost. At fifty yards before the tunnel the steady pop-pop-pop of tires could be heard as the nail spikes bit into truck, automobile and even motorcycle tires.

In the mile that separates the intersection at the Highlander Hotel and the west side entrance to the tunnel enough cars were halted to make sure that the only thing that reached the tunnel itself was the Mazda pickup truck itself. Ultimately eighty-eight cars blocked the carriageway a good half mile before the tunnel entrance itself.

On the outbound side, the other vehicles met with almost the same result. This time at the interchange overlooked by the Hyatt Regency Hotel, a mile from the east bound entrance to the tunnel. An instant gridlock of on this side with fifty-seven cars and trucks completing the mêlée. After having exhausted their supplies of spikes, the cartons the formerly had held the nail spikes were ejected overboard.

The first RPG launched CS gas was shot towards the Gold Souk from the beach at 18.00 plus half a second from just over 200 Meters away on the edge of the Car Park areas between the Souk and the beachfront. Hitting the roadway in front of the main entrance to and smoking at full force it bounced then hit the revolving doorway at the main building of the North facing Souk. An Indian rushing out to see what was happening pushed the door so hard to run through it, he helped to flick the canister to the inside of the building. In a rapid-fire quick succession 14 more RPG launched CS grenades hurtled towards the façade of the Souk. Bouncing, ricocheting, some slamming into the concrete pillars between windows and bouncing back into the road, two even went straight through the strong plate glass windows of jeweler's shops. Such was the onslaught, over 18 hits in first thirty seconds from Zero Hour, no one would ever have believed that this barrage was laid down by only two of the team members. They were having fun, doing what they do best and within 60 seconds the face of the City of Gold was lathered in a swirling white fog firing a panic into the Indian shop keepers and workers alike.

At Zero hour plus not more than 2 minutes the CS Gas was already starting its amazing effect of shock and panic. A loudspeaker from a White Datsun Van bellowed out "Gas Leak Gas Leak, evacuate immediately, everyone go immediately to the creek side, repeat go to Creek side as quickly as possible" served to throw petrol on the flaming fire of chaos that was starting to roar away. The warnings, first English, then Arabic, then English again got through to everyone. People running, shopkeepers trying to close down shutters soon gave up with their eyes and nasal passages seemingly on fire.

An Indian water seller walking near the corner of the intersection between the road that passes the front of the Souk and the entrance down to the Pedestrianized covered areas pushing his porters trolley called "Panni, Tanda Panni Ek Dirham" *(Water. Cold water one dirham)* saw his precious cargo of bottled Masafi water explode as a CS grenade launched 230 Meters away smashed through it and billowed out its foul smoke. Eleven seconds later the diminutive Indian water seller was exactly 100 meters away and heading through the labyrinth of alleyways that would lead him away deeper into Deira Side of Dubai and hopefully safety. Now there are 40 men running from the sectors between the road and the Gold Souk itself. The attack is in full swing. On the car park, mini diggers are being driven off the back of a low loader and they too headed for the main shop fronts. The men saw the lights go out as they headed for the Souk.

As Pickup finished their tire spiking runs the one coming in from the Highlander Hotel swerved a hard-right speeding out of Shindagha tunnel on the Gold Souk side opening the way for the old Mercedes Lorry that turned into the entrance and started accelerating its way down to the deepest part of the tunnel itself. As it did so, the driver could look across and see an identical lorry doing the same on the other carriageway, into the east bound section of the twin tunnel. Laden down with not only their 1,000 Gallons of cargo, the lorries were wedged, in every possible space left on them with old car tires that would burn for hours producing the thickest blackest smoke that only rubber could.

Reaching the lowest point, helpfully marked by "Emergency Telephone Number 3" They each jumped out of their Lorries and opened the emergency dumping valve and ran like hell the 700 meters back to the Deira side entrance. Once there he waited for his colleague to emerge 50 meters opposite. Ten seconds later both men were loading them flare pistols and pointing them towards the mouth of the tunnel which was already starting to smell strongly of petrol.
Clearly but calming the ex-Trooper spoke into his mouthpiece. "Tunnel GO 10 seconds , Tunnel GO ten seconds" meaning he and his counterpart were ready to fire the flares and once they hit the fume filled tube that Shindagha Tunnel had now become the effect was going to be incredible, a funneled explosion of the vapors that would turn everything inside into an inferno for several hours.

The transmission came back "Tunnel GO when ready. Out"

Sprinting across from the beach, clearing both now empty dual carriageways that are the entrance and exit to the Shindagha tunnels Stuart knew that at any second the roadways were about to become much warmer even than the hot Dubai night could ever be. As he ran he saw the lights of the Souk leap into darkness. "Good, perfect, jebel Ali worked" flashed through his mind.

In frightening speed, the Dubai lights went out and out, section after section. Traffic lights stopped working, petrol pumps refused to fill cars, queues would soon be forming and backing up, the chaos had started its march on the City. Added to this, when the electricity decides to give up the ghost, especially in the run up to

Iftar during Ramadan with the temperature running at 48 degrees C and humidity at almost 100 percent, then chaos rules supreme times ten and at 6.05 pm on the evening of the 22nd of July the King Chaos claimed its rightful place on the Throne.

The driving rules that forbid anyone from moving their car if its involved in an accident was already automatically encouraging grid lock sets in, minor road accidents immediately multiplied by lack of lights and signals, accelerated the gridlock to bite even harder with a vengeance that was now going for a total kill, a total clampdown on movement. By 6.15 PM the supertanker SS Dubai including every single suburb that surrounds it ground to an amazing and incredible "All ahead STOP"
....
....

Within seconds of the 41 smoke containers spewing out their acrid black plumes the smoke detectors kicked into action, no water sprinklers worked, there was no heat, nothing to inform them that they should operate. Instead the murmur that started in one room and led to the Syrian Ambassador and his secretary to leave their Junior suite, looking over the balcony he could see a mist of black haze from the floor below. "FIRE!"

Soon the murmurs were louder, inside 30 seconds the calling to each other from different guests shouting in different languages became a crescendo. Panic had checked into the World's only 7 Star Hotel and it was really enjoying its stay.
Along with the rest of the Emirate, the hotel lights went out at 18:05 and for the brief 15 seconds before the emergency generators kick in so smoothly without a glitch, the volume on the screams had been increased to full. Fire at the Burj.
....

Earlier in the afternoon, Brad, Oleg and his crew have been doing taxiing trials in the Ekranoplan. Now gently swaying in the early evening swell, a mile offshore, the aircraft was waiting for its call to life. As they sat in the wide flight deck there was lots of time and room to spread out the various maps.

"We need to start to drift off the planned course, or at least the route that the flight plan says. Here see?" Brad pointed at the low-level map and then to the higher-level airway's maps. "This is the airways that were supposed to be following. Out of Ras al Khamah, then up to "DARAX" (the waypoint out in the Gulf south of Bandar Abbas, and then Airways 419 and 453 which will take us to here, Zahedan on the border with Pakistan almost" Brad paused "But… what we really need to do is to drift to the right of the track, to get through the gap[p in the first mountain range. To do that we are going to have to look amateur, also I will need to give them lots of bullshit to use up their time. Once we get through the gap here we need to start our pretense at having a few problems, maybe call a possible diversion to Iranshahr further down this plain" again Brad pointed at the wide plain, Alexandre the Greats final resting place and to the Iranian base of Iranshahr marked on the map. We need them to think were a bit crap at our job mate, but that shouldn't be too difficult!" They both laughed.

They went over and over the most minuscule details throughout the afternoon. The sequence they planned to fly near the two mountains in Iran that they had named Titan and Venus, with Brad stressing distances from the monoliths that under any circumstances at all must be strictly maintained. Then on to what excuses Brad would give to the different Air Traffic Controllers, who would fly at what points of the flight and even down to when Oleg would don the night vision goggles to get his eyes accustomed to their strange green light.

Now, sitting in the wide cockpit they looked at the City from a mile offshore and at 18.06hrs Brad and Oleg watched the same City jump section by section into darkness "That Jebel Ali out Mate, Looks its game on, eh Matey?"

Before Oleg could answer the flash of yellow flame that shot out of both all four openings of the tunnel as it could be viewed from their vantage point was nothing short of spectacular, the four bright yellow and orange tubes of flame shooting like four giant golden stiletto flick knives into the darkened Dubai skyline almost horizontally before floating upwards in a twisting ball a hundred meters across.

"Whooohhhhhhh…… Holy Fuckin shite!!" came from Brad with "Bllyed!!!!!" Meaning something very similar in Russian from Oleg at the exact same time.

"Come on mate, now it really is show time" Barked. The flight engineers had seen it all from the same windows and had already jumped into the control panel and had already started the process for winding the powerful contra rotating turboprop into action.

On the prime week when most Europeans had gone away, most Locals had done the same. Ramadan is a month when everything has to slow down and this year in July with temperatures topping 55 Celsius in the shade, Ramadan had fallen in the hottest, most humid and uncomfortable part of the year.

In total, only four Police Officers could be found in the area. Crime free Dubai was notoriously safe, and the show of a Policeman was simply a token and definitely, almost deliberately, nothing more. They had been spotted, shadowed and targeted for the last 15 minutes without even noticing.

When the onslaught began, quite simply they didn't know what the hell was going on. They transmitted on their "hand helds" or portable radios, to the Police station at Al Twar just 4 kilometers distant and got absolutely no reply. The ECMs had made sure of that. They were transmitting normally but before it could be received, the signal had been trapped by the portable interceptors and basically ripped to shreds and thrown away. A CS gas container bounced past them spewing its horrible mass of chemical smoke and as they tried to call their HQ again. The first Police Officer didn't even feel the blow that felled him, the second officer, gun in hand discharged a shot that ricocheted off the dense block paving and disappeared through a plate glass shopfront on the other side of the street at the same instant as he thought he felt a blow to the back of his head and for a nana second tried to work out why the pavement was rushing up to meet his face. A week later recovering in hospital that impression was still all he could remember of the night's events.

All four were now stripped of weapons, radios, mobile phones; trussed with plastic wire ties at ankles, elbows, wrists and finally together painfully at the neck. The cheap red ball gags provided by Lenna from a newly opened sex shop in Kiev certainly didn't help the Policemen's embarrassment one bit.

Glancing down at his handy work Tommy couldn't help but turn to the Sarge and quip "I reckon he likes that Sarge"

Ignoring him the Sarge turned and waved at the first of the four mini diggers that had been disgorged from the two large Mercedes vans on the car Park and had now crossed towards the Souk and were bobbing down the wide pedestrianized area with the sign that enticed the shoppers to enter "Dubai City of Gold"

Running ahead of the mini Digger the Sarge saw it stop, quickly slew to the right and with its raised bucket smash the first of the Shopfront windows into thousands of pieces. Pulling back to lower its bucket the "Cleaners ran into the shop and within 4 minutes the vast majority of its contents, including its safe, were filling the bucket of the digger.

Other diggers and other cleaning teams were doing the same, systematically shop by shop, working from the back of the Souk back and back towards the front where they had entered.

The Ford low loaders had now arrived from the Hyatt and reversed in to position themselves in the widest part of the Souk walkways. On the back of each vehicle were strengthened aluminum wheely bins, each exactly 1.20 meters wide, 1.60 Meters deep and 2.25 meters long. Made by some of the finest sheet metal workers to be found in the Ukraine and made to fit perfectly four abreast and fasten together in the hold of the Ekranoplan. In all, 4 Rows of 8 Containers would fill the Hold of the Aircraft and full of 24 Carat Gold they would weigh 32 metric tons if they were all full, with no voids which would not be achievable at all. In an educated guess, saying that there would be a 20% plus shortfall of each container. The team had prepared an extra 8 containers, plus another extra 2 in case any were lost by damage or accident. In all 42 modified wheely bins needed to be filled and the target was to load at least 40 of them onboard.

Now all of the gas-masked drivers emerged from their trucks. Carrying several tear gas canisters, they entered their respective shops and heaved their tear gas grenades in.

Shocked store owners immediately broke for cover, fearing a fusillade of bullets would follow — but the choking gas forced employees, owners, and the few customers who had been in the

Souks shopping that night to their knees. All were rushed from their stores into the covered market area outside, where they were "escorted" out of the market, pointed in the general direction of the Creek. They didn't need any encouragement to run, and to run fast towards the safety of the creek inland away from the cruel effects of the CS.

Now the assault was in absolute and full force.

Dubai was shocked. Turned upside down and thrown into absolute turmoil. At every third set of traffic lights there had been at least a minor accident and in innocent party of every single one was refusing to move the injured vehicle a single inch in case he lost on the insurance claim. Slamming the gridlock home even harder were the Iftar racers who had achieved over 380 separate road crashes (their best previous record was a mere 290)

Already overwhelmed Dubai Police Department had already committed every fire fighting vehicle and ambulance to the Burj al Arab, it was clearly understood that this was the absolute priority. The flagship of the Emirate must not suffer.

They had already sent out the call for the help of the Army but that would be hours away yet. Every off-duty officer had been contacted, but with so many away on leave that help was drastically reduced. The fact that many of them on leave were Senior Officers only helped to flood more water into the sinking ship "SS Dubai emergency Services"

Fourteen Police cars and three ambulances had run out of petrol.

The CID had come out of hiding in their plain vehicles and these were providing the only real and helpful reserves that could be mustered but even so they were on the "back foot" It would be a very long night for them and a long time before any sensible control was asserted.

Major Khaled Abbas was Officer Commanding Al Twar Police Station who had dispatched every available Officer to the Burj al Arab almost an hour previously. Pandemonium was echoing through every office of the Police Station. He had already been able to send out only two Officers to a serious Tanker fire that had been reported in Shindagha Tunnel. He had ordered his men from the Gold Souk to attend to it as they were the closest but 30 minutes later he had been informed that they couldn't be contacted and so had to send out two of his last Officers, telling them to head "round the back" to avoid gridlock, to take the beach road past the Hyatt. The reports coming in were about a Tanker on fire in the eastbound tunnel, but there had been another report about the Tanker on fore in the Westbound Tunnel. Reasoning that someone couldn't tell east from west he told the Officers to find out which one had the problem and just keep people away from it somehow. Just let it burn, there was nothing else that could be done anyway.

When a young Syrian Police Officer ran in and told him of reports from an Indian who worked in the Souk that there was news about "Men stealing in the Gold Souk" He snapped "Then tell the shopkeepers to close their fucking shops! I've got more than enough to worry about now GET OUT! OUT! YALLA OUT!"

The young Syrian took his humiliations out on the next Indian who came in to report the events at the Gold Souk. A breathless Indian water seller who came in screaming some nonsense about the Souk being robbed. The Major was not pestered with any other complaints about the Souk for over 2 hours.

....

The gas curtain shrouded the Souk and thanks to Mother Nature herself was easing its way further and further inland like a massive invisible hand pushing all before it. After flushing the Souk, the security team unleashed fifty tear gas canisters around the perimeter, driving any would-be visitors back into the recesses and alleyways that provided entrance to the Souk. The gas also served to clear out anyone else who remained within the Souk. Fifty more canisters would be sent flying down alleyways for the next ten minutes until the team was ready to evacuate the area. All the time the loudspeaker on the van was reminding them of the terror, of the leaking gas.

With the perimeter secure, the only sound that could be heard was the engines of the mini diggers, squealing of tires as they slewed on the humid paving and then one after the other the crashing of plate glass windows. Bracelets, rings, necklaces, watches, anklets, gems by the tray full and even gold ingots that are popularly for sale as investments were all being thrown, pushed and dumped into the buckets of the mini diggers by the cleaning teams. At the end of thirteen minutes, the "cleaners" turned their attention to the store safes. Eighteen of twenty were open. And within the safes were diamonds, pearls, gold bars, figurines, and straight forward hard cash by the bundles. Whatever could be grabbed was thrown into buckets and quickly splashed like water into any digger bucket that was close by.

....

Unseen by anyone at all, the blacked out Ekranoplan had gently nuzzled itself towards the steep beach 350 meters away from the Souk. Edging it carefully over the last 20 Meters Brad eased the Power from idle to absolute zero and was ready to use reverse thrust if necessary, he dare not damage Oleg's baby at this stage. Almost imperceptibly the nose of the hulking aircraft softly it kissed the sand, less than 2 meters away from the dry area of the

unusually steep beach. With a mix of relief and pleasure that it had just gone perfectly as a "touch down" Brad thumbed the transmit button on his hand-held radio set to Stuarts frequency "Delivery Boy in place AOK. Will start the rampway over"
Stuart came back with a reassuring "Good, all's well here, let me know when the ramp is 5 minutes away from ready"

"Wilco" Brad knew better than to waste words or time on a radio.

"OK go go go" Brad called out to the engineers waiting inside the nosecone as he pulled the "open" lever in the cockpit and the nose started to swing open on its newly installed hydraulic arm. Quickly they raced out carrying the first timber batons and slapping them down sideways one after the other up the steep incline at the beach 13 minutes later the disposable timber rampway was complete. The two-meter-wide rampway was in place and 5 minutes later so were the 40 meters of temporary miniature gauge rail tracks that led deep into the belly of the cargo hold too. All was ready.

Leaving Oleg and the crew to make sure everything was absolutely safe with the aircraft in Oleg's hands he left the two engineers bolting together the last joins of the miniature rail track. He thumbed his Radio again

"Five minutes Delivery Boy will be open for business. Over"

Sounding out of breath came a quick "OK check ready in 5. Out" from Stuart.

Brad ran up the rampway to the Public Car park at the edge of the beach. He couldn't help but think to himself that in any other Country this would be a Lovers car Park, but not here, it lay deserted. To his right was the start of a Sea wall and climbing onto it he could get a good view of the Souk. The gas had thinned now, lights on the trucks and mini diggers were illuminating the façade of the Nada building which was dead centre of the block and looked towards the Souk from the sea wall. Further to his right he could see black acrid smoke billowing out of the mouths which made up the Deira side entrance to the Shindagha Tunnel. The burning lorries and tires were having a perfect effect; nothing would be coming through there for a long time yet. Glancing back at the chaos in the pedestrian area of the Souk Stuart said to himself quietly "Good". As the first low loader was having its last aluminum container topped up by the Caterpillar mini digger, it was almost ready to go. "Seventeen minutes, we're two minutes behind — let's make it up". Secretly he had allowed the extra three minutes, never having believed for a minute that they could clear the first 8 tons of gold and jewelry out of the Souk in fifteen minutes. Still, what they had just done was amazing. And more importantly, in those seventeen minutes there had been no challenge at any point along the perimeter. The police had not been prepared with gas masks. No one was prepared to penetrate the gas shield the group had put forward but if the cat was out of the bag and for safety's sake he had to at least assume that it was. He also knew full well that the gas wouldn't last forever, time and speed was crucial, they had to be out of here before there was any reaction to avoid a bloodbath.

Turning to the driver Stuart looked at the pressure in the double rear tires of the Low Loader.

"OK the aircraft is ready and in place, hurry up but for Christs sake be careful of the tires they're fit to bust. If they do just carry on ………don't stop."

Nodding the Driver didn't need to say anything at all. He knew that he wasn't going to stop for anyone or anything, no matter what. With five more men jumping quickly onto the back of the lorry he revved gently and set off towards the beach, weaving his way carefully on the roadways, making absolutely sure not to clip a curb or make any swaying motion to over pressure the straining tires. Stuart knew that it would take all the muscle possible to man handle the bins onto the rails and the five biggest and strongest of the team had been chosen carefully for this detachment.

Standing on the intersection that separates the Souk on its Northern shoulder from the Car Parks and the Spice market Stuart could look to the east and see the Hyatt Regency Hotel, only 2 Kilometers away. Its emergency generator working perfectly as it lit up the building as if nothing was going on. He flicked his radio to channel three and sent a transmission.

"Voyeur this is Badboy, How do you read? Over"

Not very professionally the answer came back from room 3004 of the Hyatt Regency Hotel

"Hiiiii Malenki? Are you OK???"

Stuart smiled, at least she's on the ball he thought to himself and then quickly asked "Any news? Over."

Again, quickly the reply "We heard something; they were all shouting about the Burj is on fire. One said it was going to fall down. Some others were saying it's a big, huge problem and for the Police and Fire people to come to the Burj fast. Lots of others saying that they will come and that they were on the way. All stuff like that, but then it went *more quieter* and then we heard some people asking if anyone could hear them. They are all sort of mixed up, you know, big confusion sort of?"

Stuart was glad to hear the news "OK good, anything since? Over"

"No that's it, we didn't hear anything for a long time now. So Lenna opened some Champanski from the fridge, it's really excellent!" Stuart could hear the laughing before the transmit button had been released but he wasn't worried, he knew these girls could operate pretty well even with a couple of glasses of Champers in them.

"OK good. Call me if you hear anything. Be in place in one hour from now and wait for me where we arranged. OK? Over"

"Ok Niet problemski mallenki…kisss kiss kiss "and then a few more giggles before Stuart flicked back the Chanel on his radio to Number one.
…………………………………………………………………………
………………..

The first low loader took the preordained route to the Ekranoplan and reached the car park where Brad was waiting just 4 minutes later. Backing the cumbersome vehicle carefully to the rampway until he heard "Stop!" the driver immediately jumped out and up onto the back of the Ford behind the cab. Another was already feeding cable out of the Car recovery winch and another still took the end offered to him and fastened it to the titanium ring on the base of the wheely bin. Gently but quickly the men pointed the bin down the metal ramps normally used for recovering a broken-down vehicle and watched as in concave metal wheels of the bin married the convex profile of the miniature rail track.

Setting the winch to "manual Brake only" The wheely bins using good old Mother Nature's Gravity hurried themselves into the hold of the waiting Ekranoplan. Within 12 minutes the first 8 tons was on board, in place and strapped down with western cargo straps each possible of taking a 10-ton breaking strain. It was now 19.22 Zero hour plus 1 Hr. 22 minutes.

....

Getting back to work in the Souk no one had much taken notice that Stuart, Tommy and Sarge had one small item of clothing different to any of the others in the team. A shoulder to opposite hip band, at the end of which was a self-sealing Velcro mouth to a pouch 8 inches by 8 inches and 2 inches deep. Tommy had christened it his "Lucky Bag" after a popular children's treat from his childhood. To get a lucky bag meant that everything was potluck, you were never sure what was in it until you opened it. And now, in Tommy's lucky bag was almost every single gem that he had spotted during the rape and pillage that he had noticed was bigger than Sarges thumb nail and that meant big, towards an inch in diameter at a guess. According to Tommy, the Sarge had hands like a bunch of bananas, although he wasn't too impressed when Tommy had mentioned it to him!

....

Looking directly up Brad saw a Boeing 777 he could see clearly the logo of Singapore Airlines on the Blue tail plane illuminated by its own floodlight as it is climbing gently out from the airport at the far side of the City. Looking quickly at its configuration Brad could see that it had just taken off and he knew that it was more or less a regular flight that was also more or less on time according to Dubai standards. "Good" he thought to himself, "That means that the shit hasn't really hit a fan yet" He knew the emergency generators would have kicked in instantaneously at the airport, it would be a couple of hours' before the chaos in Dubai itself would bring its effect into the departures of flights from the City. Quickly he passed the information to Stuart who acknowledges that it was "Nice to know, cheers, Out"

Leaving the four heavy lifters behind, the first low loader set off back towards the Souk, this time with relieved tires and only the Driver to carry it passed the second low loader under a similar strain as before, just 4 meters before they passed there was one, then two loud bangs. Both of its back tires on its left side had given up the ghost and destructed themselves within half a second of each other. The first blow out instantaneously triggering the second. The driver didn't miss a beat, didn't slow down at all and ploughed on with the low loader making an agonizing noise carrying itself on its two metal wheel rims. It would still make it, but it would also take extra time.

Even with the setback of the slower truck, by 21.38 hrs. the last of the 5 loads was painfully running on its metal wheel rims towards the car Park above the Ekranoplan mooring. Brad, again on the Sea wall heard Stuart's voice on his hand-held radio

"That's it, we are on our way delivery Boy, get ready. Got a few things to do here but will be with you soon. Over "

Brad flicked a double click meaning "Acknowledged" into the hand held's transmit button

Racing from the back to the front of the Souk the remaining men pulled back from the perimeter slinging opened Gas containers as they went. Reaching the rendezvous point at the intersection used earlier by Stuart to talk to the girls in the Hyatt two men now pointed their RPG launchers away from the Souk, towards the dual carriageway and fired off another 10 rounds of CS grenades. They were in the Mazda van and away before the gentle evening breeze could urge the gas more than 20 meters in their direction. This wave of gas would reach the Souk later and keep everyone out for just that bit longer.

As he jumped on board the back of the Mazda with Sarge and Tommy, Stuart looked back at the Souk. "Jesus, we haven't even moved 10 maybe 15 % of what's in there "

The Sarge nodded "Well, best leave em with a bit to be going on with eh Boss?"

Stuart nodded agreement but had to laugh when he heard Tommy throw in "Fuck em, we can always come back for the rest!"

Turning to Tommy and Sarge Stuart directed "Lucky Bags Boys" and held his hand out. Quickly Tommy and Sarge slipped the shoulder harnesses over their heads and handed the bags to their Boss as the van followed the tree lined slip road that curved its way round and into the Hyatt Car Park. They're near the trees that were watered automatically every night to save their destruction by the natural dessert, were the two Motorbikes and their Riders.

The pickup eased to a stop and the men were quickly off the back, the driver jumped out and he, Tommy and Sarge were quickly dispatched to the Ekranoplan, just another 100 meters further down the Coast along the sea wall to the Car park where it ends.. Turning to the motorbike riders Stuart looked as they removed their helmets. Lenna and Natallia couldn't help but look sexy even in jeans and a reflective red and yellow day glow Pizza Hut delivery jackets. Handing the two lucky bags to Natallia and one to Lenna he said:

"Look after these girls, put them somewhere safe and if, well if we get a bit *bogged down* on the next part, then, "…He paused. No need to elaborate "See you soon ladies" turned and left, disappearing between the trees to cross the road towards the sea wall and the waiting aircraft..

....

On the flight deck Brad and Oleg were going through everything literally by the book. Oleg reading out the checklist which was a good idea seeing as it was in Russian and Brad didn't read a single word of the Cyrillic's.

Glancing up he could see the four men left near the sea wall acting as a rear guard as Four men ran quickly past the end of the wall through the gap on the Car Park. Stuart, Tommy and Sarge with the Driver were all quickly inside and were being followed by the last four of the rear guard.

In the hold men were clambering around, still strapping down the last of the containers, others getting in positions some actually sitting on top of the different wheely bins. One of the Russian engineers was closing the nosecone and checking it was locked and watertight. The other was trying to make himself understood that all the guys should try to position themselves basically in the centre of the aircraft hold. He pointed at the red mark on the wall that denoted the "Empty Centre of Gravity "point, but with it also being written in Cyrillic's it didn't have much effect. As he did so Stuart looked back as he climbed the ladders to the flight deck and shouted out to the guys.

"He wants you in the centre Boys, it's about balance OK?"

"Sure Boss "came back and very quickly the team more or less spread itself across the centre (ish) area of the aircraft hold.

Satisfied now, the FE muttered "Nakanyetz!Khazyol!" "*at last! Stupid fucking goats*" as he turned towards the stairs to the cockpit. Tommy glanced and nodded towards the Engineer "Wots up with that miserable fucker? Somebody nicked his Vodka??"

Within seconds the turboprops had whipped into life. Brad busy on the flight deck got the all clear on temperatures and pressures, the engine could operate at full power from this point on. Levering back, lifting the lever into the "reverse thrust" slot he inched the leaver backwards and heard the engine tone accordingly rise. 50, 60 then 70 % reverse thrust had no effect, the aircraft didn't want to budge, 70 and 80 was no different except infinitely louder. And then all the way, full reverse thrust setting. Oleg checking the time, only 20 seconds could be allowed at this setting according to the book and at 35 seconds, Oleg had to call Power Down.

They were stuck.

The 30 Tons of Sparkling Cargo had turned the Ekranoplan gentle kissing of the steep beach into more like an ostrich burying its head with a 30-ton weight on the back of it.

Brad looked at Oleg, Oleg at Brad, engineers to each other and on and on.

No word was spoken and then a call from the Russian who had cursed the lads earlier.

"Move the fucking goats to the back. Move everything back"

Stuart called down into the hold "get cracking lads, shift everything as far back as you can as fast as you can. Move!"

Everyone worked lightning fast. Straps holding the bins in place we unhitched, The first bins started to move.
Stuarts radio crackled, channel 3.

"Melenki?? Malenki??"

Stuart watched the work, knowing it was being done as fast, if not just a little bit faster than was humanly possible "Yes here. What news? Over?"

"Police Malenki. Lots of them. There are blue lights flashing everywhere. They're going through the Spice Market towards the Gold Souk we can see 7 cars, no stop two more now".

"OK got it, let me know if any of them head here".

"One is now, I think to here, the hotel" Came Natallie's voice, more nervous now.

"What are you doing there? Why didn't you do the Pizza delivery" Cursed Stuart

"We. We thought we could finish the Champagne Malenki.... sorry"

Biting his tongue Stuart commanded now "Move, both of you, Make sure you wear the helmets and MOVE. NOW..GO!"

"Yes, Malenki we are going, Don't worry.. we go now"

All the men were straining every muscle; every other hand that could be squeezed onto the container was helping to lift it onto the top of the other containers at the back. The further back all the containers go the better. Slowly the aircraft started to tilt, almost imperceptibly at first, then a little more and a little more. From the vantage point in the cockpit Brad and Oleg could see the effect on the view towards the seawall. It was slowly inching its way lower in the cockpit windscreen, the front of their aircraft was getting higher as the weight moved backwards with the Centre of Gravity.

"Faster Stuart faster" Brad shouted back over his shoulder.

Heaving the last of the containers finally onto of the ones already pushed to the rear the sweating men working like maniacs. Cutting fingers on pieces of glass from the broken windows that had been mixed into the pillaged booty as they literally shoveled it by hand from the front bins into the rear bins. Every ounce counted now, but not for money, it counted now for their very freedom.

Calling up to the cockpit from the base of the ladders to the cockpit "Try again mate" Stuart shouted to Brad as he turned and ran through the now half empty cargo hold to the full end at the back. Men were climbing up and over the bins, some had found their way into the very tail of the aircraft too. Stuart climbed up to Tommy, the Sarge who had gone into the nose cone to check if there was anything of any weight in there now moved down the emptied area of the hold as the engines were screaming into full reverse thrust, just starting to reach 90 % power, inching towards another 100% flat out try. In his last 3 meters the Sarge took two bounds and almost made it in one leap to the cluster of men already crammed on top.

As the Sarge was pulled by Tommy and Stuart they felt the aircraft dip backwards, its nose rising into the air as its tail momentarily dipped underwater into the sea. They were out.

Tommy looking at the Sarge almost startled... "Well you *FAT* bastard Sarge"

Even the Sarge had to laugh and so did everyone else.

"Pumps on full" Oleg snapped at the Flight Engineer. Turning to Brad "The tail is not watertight, not ever supposed to be in water.

Floating out backwards on top the gentle swell the aircraft was slowly, very slowly turning a circle to ease itself parallel to the beach. Brad shouted back. It was also taking in water from the unsealed tail section.

Again, Brad shouted to the hold "Get the stuff back to the centre, FAST! shift it back."

Stuart whipped the men back into immediate action "Roll the top bins over don't bother trying to lift them down, just overfill the lower layer". It was faster, easier. As the men worked, again flat out at lightning speed they heard the engine tone change. Gambling on the fact that he could make a turn from this point, about 60 degrees and 25 meters from the beach, Brad kicked full right rudder and gunned the Kuznetsov NK-12MK 11000kW turboprop for 20 seconds. The two nose mounted jet engines, Kuznetsov NK-8-4K turbofans of 10.5 ton thrust could do nothing to help this situation. The effect was slow but real, he watched and held ho breath just a little as he looked at the left wingtip barely clear the steep sandy beach and then, as if it wasn't enough stress already he saw headlights shining higher up on the car park and made out a blue flashing strobe reflected in the air above their beams "Police Fuck it" 45 more degrees and the turn was enough now. Lifting the throttle from it neutral gate he moved it forward as far as he dared. The nose was still high; he knew the C of G was still too far to the rear. Oleg busily went through the startup procedure for the two jet engines located in the nose, darting through the complicated 1960s start up procedure doing everything in duplicate to start both engines simultaneously. All the time Brad was easing the aircraft round slowly the nose was turning, almost crawling its way to the direction of the open sea. A short 3 second blast at full power not only had the effect of making the Aircrafts turn faster, it also put a little distance between them and the beach.

"I reckon that's about right" Brad said to Oleg, estimating that the tail was now pointing to approximately where the temporary rampway and car Park were situated. Easing all three power leavers fully forwards as fast as he dared without causing stress on either of the three precious engines and at the same time producing the viscous sandstorm that whipped into the steep beach, up and onto the Car park which took with it the whole of every piece of heavy timber that made up the ramp, flicking them through the air they rotated like hell bent propellers up the beach and tore through the Parking towards the 3 Police cars that had reached the edge of the beach via the car park. In the hail of sand and pebbles being shot towards them the Police BMWs would never be the same again.

The carnage the rampway brought down forced the Police to scatter, backwards and away. Once it was over, the Ekranoplan was easily out of range of any pistols. Keeping a high-speed taxi, the aircraft started to bump in the heavier swell further out from shore. Brad strained his eyes to look at two spotlights in his 10 o'clock. Lights that stay still and don't move either left or right mean one thing. They are either heading straight towards you or heading directly away from you and these lights were heading his way. Feeding in right rudder, the lights slipped backwards into the 9.30 position. Again, they remained constant, it confirmed that they had also altered course to keep aiming slap bang at the Ekranoplan.

A minute later, closer now, Brad could see, they were high speed launches.

Orders were being strung out. "Oleg pumps still on full? Stuart, stuff moving. Oleg check the cargo, get it nailed down fast" Glancing to his left, comparing the previous view of the launches, they were closing.

In the hold the second Russian flight engineer was choreographing everything and everyone in fluent Russian. Tommy with sweat dripping off his nose leant forwards across the top of a bin they were trying to strap down back in its original position. As brad gunned the beast harder to keep a distance between it and the converging craft it hit a swell and bounced sharply just as Tommy said to the Engineer "You're really starting to piss me off now *Doris*. Make yer fuckin mind up will ya??"

With the sudden lurch of the aircraft both men's faces were pushed together. It was embarrassing. The Russian cursed "Gryazniy Podonok!" (*Dirty Bastard*!) as he quickly wiped Tommy's sweat from his face as Tommy heard the Sarge bark "Stop fucking about Tit and give us a hand here!"

Now their work was becoming harder, they were being bounced around violently by the higher swells that the Ekranoplan was hitting as it headed further out into the deeper water banging its way along in the attempt to escape the lights of the Police launches that were closing slowly but surely in on them.

....

It was also 20.00 hrs. local time on the flat plains of Uzbekistan and that meant that it was also Vodka time too. Matt sat at the same table as his three Chechen "hosts" and their interpreter, Vasily urged Matt to take a glass that had been poured and pushed in front of him by another burly and decidedly foul-smelling host.

"Its good manners Matt, please take it. Its best if you do" urged Vasily.

Knowing it wasn't a good idea at all, given the circumstances of what was about to happen if the news from Dubai was bad, Matt hesitated. There again, doing anything to directly insult the three Neanderthals at this point wasn't a good move either. Curling his fingers round the small thick glass Matt raised it and chinked it against the other three in turn around the table.

"Dovrstretchi potsdalom" (Till we meet under the table) came the blessed toast to which Matt added:

"To absent friends, may we meet again soon"

"Very good toast" Vasily quickly translated it to the morons as Matt glanced down at his deadly accurate Tag Heure watch and wondered just how things were going almost 2,000
miles to the south. Matt thought to himself quietly "Oh believe me sonny boy I *did* mean that one!"

....

In a normal swell, every so often there will be a rogue wave, it's a simple fact. Old wives tales say it is every seventh wave, sometimes they are right too but effectively the rogue waves are at random, however, the one thing for sure is that they will be there and when the Ekranoplan found one the thump of hitting it was severe. Lifting men and gold-filled bins off their rails, slamming them all back down on the reinforced deck with frightening force. This was not only making things infinitely harder for the men having to man handle almost 30 tons with nothing more than the strength of their own backs and the single electric winch of the cargo hold but it was also getting outright dangerous. Fingers, Toes or feet and hands would be lost if a wheely bin decided to amputate them. Stuart had come this far without a scratch on his team and didn't want a stupid accident to spoil that score now.

Dashing up the ladder to the cockpit Stuart grabbed onto the KGB seat. (Usually reserved in the Soviet aircraft in the centre of a standard X star seating arrangement on the flight deck for the KGB officer to overview the crew)

Automatically Stuart scanned the visual area that could be seen from the Cockpit windows. On the right he could see the City of Sharjah, lights burning bright in contrast to the sporadic lights of Dubai where only buildings with emergency generators were illuminated. On the left he saw some moored supertankers, three Dhows coming in on their final slow roll down the Gulf towards Dubai and he saw the two high speed interceptors, as he looked at them he asked Brad "How's it going?"

Brad nodded towards the 9 o'clock "Reckon they want to do us for speeding Mate?"

"Are they closing?" Stuart needed an answer.

"Yes, I reckon 5- or 6-minutes max. We can't take off with the aft C of G mate, it's impossible. "

Brad and Oleg were both pushing hard forward on the yolk. It seemed incredible that as they bounced and banged along the Pilots were actually trying to stuff the nose deeper into the swell that now felt like concrete instead of water.

Oleg's got his guy down in the tail trying to pump the water out as fast as possible. If we go any faster we will hop and if we do, with the aft C of G the nose is going to head for the sky, we won't be able to stop it. If it does that, then sure as apples it will nose in on the way back down."

Brad was in a catch 22 and Stuart knew he needed to have more time to balance the aircraft and get rid of the unwanted passenger, an estimated two metric tons of water according to Oleg's second Flight Engineer who had been down to treble check the pumps were at full bore and had made a fairly accurate assessment of the depth of water sloshing around in the outer bulk head skin of the aircraft.

"No worries mate, I`m pulling them round into our 6" *(dead astern on the tail)* "Then we should be able to put them off a bit".

Easing the right rudder in Brad slowly turned the Skipping Ekranoplan parallel to the coast. Equally slowly but surely the two pursuers slid gently and automatically directly behind the tail.

Down in the hold, the change of course had helped a little. The bounces were less severe now that the Aircraft was hydro foiling more along the line of the swell than against it. Carefully Brad inched in just a tad of left rudder now to keep their track true and at a safe distance from the shore with just that little bit of nose into the wind.

The team had prepared for an unfriendly welcome at the delivery point. Stored in the hold were a second batch of CS Gas Containers, plus some "Flash Bangs" These are similar to the CS but contain a special mix of a small amount of explosive, mixed with a high intensity portion of magnesium. These were very useful tools, designed specifically to disorientate a victim. If close enough they could leave someone deaf and blind for at least 60 seconds, if even closer, permanently deaf with exploded eardrums.

The whining sour faced, and downright fucking miserable Russian Flight Engineer also just happened to be one of the best at his job too. Of course, the perfect place for the weight of the Gold was for it to all be strapped down around the Centre of Gravity of the Ekranoplans Airframe and then for it to be equally spaced out from that point forward and aft. With all the weight now at the back of the aircraft and time being the demanding factor Flight Engineer Alexei Motchenka, top of his class at the Bearink Aviation Engineering Academy, Alexei quickly worked out that it was easier and faster to move 15 containers on the rails right to the very front of the aircraft than to move 30 of them to the Centre and even then need to keep readjusting their position for an absolute balance. He also knew that it was more dangerous too, because all he could do was to estimate that the right amount in weight had been moved the right distance forward. If he got it wrong to far forr`d , the Ekranoplan would nose down into the swell and try to wreck itself on the rock hard concrete wave; if he got it too far aft, then as Brad predicted at take-off, the nose would rise uncontrollably and the aircraft would try to stand on its tail before slamming down into the Sea.

He had made his decision and had already strapped the first 6 containers into place in the nosecone and was now watching number seven physically hauled into place by nothing more than brute strength and determination. In the cockpit, Brad and Oleg were starting to feel the lowering of the pressure needed on the Yolk.

Stuart ordered the Sarge to go up through the removed upper gunner's position and get a visual fix on the chase boats. Now that they were almost directly behind the Ekranoplan Brad was working blind, they could see him, but he couldn't see them.

Imperceptibly Brad eased back on the throttle of the massive turboprop and increased just slightly the twin jet engines in the nose. It was balancing act supreme; he needed to keep the aircraft skimming the waves but now just a little lower speed to draw the

Launches in while at the same time let them feel it was then catching up and not him slowing down. More power was needed via the jet engines for his plan to work. The moves were very subtle, only Oleg could notice them

Sarge came over the intercom into Brads headset "Range about 700 closing slowly. Separation wait………..9 to 10 seconds"

Brad clicked the ancient switch on the Russian chronometer in the left side of the instrument panel; it started counting the seconds by their hundredth parts.
Busy as he was Brad acknowledged Sarge with a brief "Check. Call at 500" as he turned to Oleg "Pressures off here (meaning the massive force needed on the Yolk) set the afterburners to standby, Start dumping through the afterburner inlet when I say, repeat when I say. Only ignite *only* on My Command. Clear?" Brad didn't want a misunderstanding in the language to screw this one up, everything was said crystal clear and affirmed as understood equally as clearly.

"Check start dumping on you Command, Ignite on Command only" Oleg confirmed.

"500 mark. Now." Was called in from the recently removed "upper turret' against a background of savage wind blast.

Glancing at the Clock Brad noted 16 seconds for 200 Meters closing rate of the chase boats. 8 seconds per 100 meters. The rate of fuel dumping set at a massive 2,000 kg per
minute meant that each second from the two oversized 100 mm fuel feeds would inject 67 Kilos of Fuel to be jet blasted into the air behind the Ekranoplan every second as the fuel pipes were set to inject the fuel directly into the exhaust outlets of the two

engines. It wouldn't however ignite, until the sprays of sparks were shot into the same jet exhaust from a separate device.

The Mark One computer was working in overdrive to mentally calculate. At a range of 300 Meters, expected in 16 seconds from the last mark will be…4 seconds of fuel dumping will put about 280 kilos into the air over a 50 plus meter stream, ignition at 20 seconds puts the ball straight in their faces.

"Be Ready. On my call, repeat only on my call start injection both sides"

"Check. On your call ready" Oleg confirmed.

"Ready?" Brad asked as he watched the stop clock creeping up to 20, 21, 22.

"Inject Now" snapped Brad, preempting the single second that would be lost between the command and the action of pressing the button plus the other second for the mechanism of the dumping system to kick in, making it all exactly on the 24th second.

Mentally counting now, 1, 2, 3, 4 Ignite. No premature order on this one, extra would always be better than less Brad assumed.

From the upper turret now converted into a rudimentary hatchway the Sarge could smell the paraffin filled air and saw the massive ball of flame ignite. For a moment he thought that the Ekranoplan itself had blown up as the orange fireball seemed to emit first from the lower sides of the aircraft before careering away through the air filled with the particles of fuel started their almost instantaneous transformation from the invisible and into the terrifying threat of flame and destruction.

Inside the cargo hold the flash of orange light illuminated everything; the amount of gold in there reflected it into an eerie amber yellow light. Everyone inside had the same impression as the Sarge and froze, just for a half second. In relief Tommy sagged forward against a container full of their wonderful cargo and muttered in relief that they hadn't just exploded.

Watching the Fireballs Orange glow flash into every side window along the fuselage Tommy had to comment "Do they breed these crazy fuckers in Australia?"

"Come on Lads shift it" Barked Stuart as he helped get behind the last of the Containers to move forward that The Engineer Alexei had demanded.

On the Flight Deck Brad asked on the intercom "They gone Sarge?"

From his vantage point Sarge could look back to a view either side of the tail plane. The last of the orange fireball was popping itself out 100 Meters up in the air, now almost half a kilometer behind in their wake, a good area of isolated wave still appeared to be on fire and both to the left and to the right he could see the sides of the Patrol craft each veering off in their own direction. Answering his question Sarge replied.

"Oh yes Cap. They've turned, they're out of it"

"And I don't fuckin blame them either" thought the Sarge to himself.

Scurrying up the ladder Alexei rattled out quick fire in Russian to Oleg.

"I've moved an equal amount to the front, *may*be equal, fuck knows I had to estimate, it should be OK, *should* be about right. How does it feel?" meaning the pressure needed on the yolk. Now everybody was working as much by instinct and feel rather than by computers and scale rules, they had no choice. Oleg slipped his night vision goggles on now, switched them on and after only 1 second they kicked into a green eerie light of their own, looking from inside them Oleg could see speckled around ahead of them, numerous tiny fishing boats scattered off towards the horizon. "Just in time" he thought to himself. Turning to Brad he confirmed. "I have control?" In return Brad acknowledged "You have control" and made a gesture with his hands lifting from the yolk clearly for Oleg to see. There was no system that could interpret the importance of what the pilots could feel in the pressures of the controls. No clock, no dial, no meter could help them at this point. Only experience and feel could tell them anything.

Now they all had to rely totally and absolutely on Alexei's experience and mental estimates.

After 3 seconds of silence, Oleg said quietly "Good……… I *think*"

Brad thought quietly to himself "And *they* call *me* mad!" before saying

"OK Lads, we *think* it *might* be OK agreed?"

"Yes, Da "came back

"How's the water doing? What's left?" Brad needed to know. Loose water in the bilges had a mind of its own and would move wherever Mother Nature encouraged it. "Through the translations between Oleg and Alexei and calling the second flight engineer, 40 seconds later the answer was "They say OK, definitely less than 200 Kilos left"

"OK Boys, time to go" easing left rudder in as smoothly as the power the bouncing of the Ekranoplan increased in frequency until such a point it seemed smooth. As closely into wind as he could position it, or estimate it Brad fed in the full power to all three monsters as he noted Fujairah passing in the distance to the right of the cockpit as the aircraft left the water, the smoothness of flight left the concrete waves 6 Meters below them.

23.03 Airborne. Mark this long and lat"

CHAPTER 17: NIGHT FLIGHT

July 22nd

As the aircraft lifted Sarge felt the wind blast increase dramatically and struggled to close the hatch, just having time for a quick final glance to the aft, their wake and was pleased to note that it was now completely empty of any other craft. Making his way down into the hold he saw the men, almost all of them slumped in the temporary canvas seating which formed two lines along the sides of the fuselage facing inwards. All were drinking water; some were pouring it over their heads, and all were obviously exhausted from the gargantuan efforts of moving such weights nonstop. All were so wet with sweat their clothed looked as if they had just been swimming with them on.

They all knew the importance of avoiding de hydration and heat stroke and they were all borderline on both. Devouring water until they didn't want another drop, they would wait just a few seconds and then force down even more. The first signs of heat stroke normally mean that it's already too late. Palpitations, feeling like jelly, lightheaded – the core body temperature was rising and needed to be reversed and that meant stopping still and cooling down. The rest wasn't only needed, it was now crucial in order to avoid anyone going down with severe heat stroke

Stuart was leaning forward, taking Mars Bars, Glucose sweets and passing them to the man on his right, who in turn passed them along. The men needed these too. The adrenaline that had been coursing through their bodies would now have its secondary effect, again lightheaded, sometimes nausea always a feeling of weakness after the adrenalin burn. Hence the glucose that were now so important.

Looking at the hold Sarge could see gold, bracelets, rings, chains, trinkets of every kind imaginable strewn around the deck. Some were even disappearing down through various gaps and small holes in the metal reinforced flooring into the cavities and voids below. Even the air seemed to have a faint golden hue of dust particles.

Stuart stood up and called out "Get filled with water lads, get the sweeties down too!" Looking at his watch "10 minutes and we get cracking" before opening the waterproof hatch in the overly strong bulkhead that separates the whole of the nose and forward engines of the Ekranoplan from the rest of the fuselage and stepping into the hold beneath the flight deck to work his way up to Brad.

Taking his KGB seat behind and in the centerline between both pilots Stuart noted that they had now changed roles. Oleg was flying, looking out and forwards. Brad was scrolling through the menus of the Garmin making sure that everything was treble checked and in order of sequence to work stage by stage through each frequency with each Controller at each pre-arranged spot along the route. Glancing past Oleg and through the starboard side cockpit window he saw the lights of Um al Quwain Port passing behind the right wingtip, the inlet which leads a further 6 Kilometers to the Rulers Palace situated imposingly at the end of it and then the mangrove swamps and sting of Northerly running islands that make up the marshlands North of Um al Quwain itself. Noting the last but one of these low flat islands Brad knew that just 4 kilometers distant behind them lay Umm al Quwain Airfield. A brand new 2.3-kilometer asphalt paved runway was there, clubhouse and hangars for various light aircraft and sport parachute jumping. He also knew that the airfield was closed for the night, there were no runway lighting systems, radar or effective radio. The airfield was basically a place for the rich boys to play with their expensive toys and sometimes killing themselves in the process too. Slightly further along he looked to see if he could make out the almost isolated lights of the Barracuda beach resort, which would give him an exact visual confirmation of the data being displayed by the GNS. For a moment his mind flicked back to the "open all hours" duty free booze shop that is situated at the entrance to the resort, the queues of cars filling their trunks with spirits, wine and beer at rock bottom prices, one fifth of what it costs in Dubai even though it means a drive through the Emirate of Sharjah, the only "dry" Emirate in the UAE before getting back to the cosmopolitan Dubai.

Stuart brought him back to reality "Everything OK? And, don't mind me asking but what the fucking hell was that flash bang?"

"Ahhh" Brad laughed" You've never seen me display with an F111 have you mate?"

Stuart looked a little puzzled, he knew that Brad had been a senior pilot in the RAAF and had flown a lot in the American aardvark or F111 Fighter Bomber but didn't quite see the link. Brad sensed his questioning look and was happy to explain.

"Well, when the Prime Minister used to let me use his aero planes for free *(meaning when Brad was in the air force)* we used to do displays. The party piece of the F 111 was to fly solo down the centerline in front of the crowd and inject fuel into the exhausts of the jet pipes, it was almost invisible from the crowd watching, like a mist of fuel particles, and then, after 3 or 4 seconds, depends how long the runway and crowd are spread, you hit the igniter and the lot sets fire. Looks like you've just blown up very spectacular but also its safe. So, Mate, what we just did was to basically give them their free air show after all! The boys in the boats got a grandstand view I can tell yer!"

His head hanging forwards and waving slowly from side to side in a "no" gesture Stuart was smiling and thinking *"Incredible, quite fucking mad, but incredible"*

Brad was already working away leaving Stuart with his thoughts. Now he was listening into the frequency of Ras al Kheima International Airport. Asking Oleg as he pointed between the 1 and 2 o'clock position on the horizon "Can you see any mountains running right to left about that area?"

Oleg had already seen them in the green world he was working in "Yes, about 1,000 meters, maybe 1,500?"

"Yep, that's about right Mate" Brad listening constantly to RAK approach knew that they had two aircraft inbound. One from Turkmenistan and one just setting up on long finals, an Antonov 78 freighter inbound from Uzbekistan. Leaning forward to look upwards in the 12 o'clock position overhead Brad spotted the navigation lights of the Antonov making their usual high approach 3,000 feet above. The Ekranoplan skimmed its way beneath it unseen by anyone so far.

Treble checking his tiny GNS screen and their position on it, Brad could see that they were now exactly eleven kilometers abeam RAK the most Northerly Emirate in the UAE and the last UAE City before they would pass into Iranian airspace now only 45 kilometers distant. Inadvertently when RAK International Airport approach radio had transmitted to the incoming Antonov they had also given Brad the regional Barometric pressure or QFE and the wind conditions too. Now, to make the next part real they needed to waste some fuel.

"Turn 300 degrees and climb to 5,000 on 1003 Millibars please Oleg" the command was polite, exact and smooth, but also with the natural authority that was required. Brad was Pilot in Command with the agreed brief that they had run through over and over as they had waited in position 2 kilometers off the beach earlier that day.

"For the Flight it is agreed that I am PIC. From the beach and up to the point of handover from me to you, prior to the takeoff, I shall be the Operating Pilot. The Pilot In Command (PIC). Before handover you will wear the Night Vision Goggles to become accustomed. After the handover you shall be the Handling Pilot, I shall be responsible for all navigation, radio, headings and so on. But I will remain PIC. You shall fly my headings and heights. After we have made our final turn, possible around here (pointing at a region of the map) You will remain as Handling Pilot until we change over, somewhere around here, pointing at the map again. The landing will be mine. Agreed?"

Engine settings increased, Oleg paused for the desired speed and then gently eased the nose upwards and started a 30-degree bank to the left rolling equally as gently out on the heading of 300 desired by Brad. Watching the altimeter pass 4,000 Brad flicked the flipped the frequency over to the Iranian controller and RAK approach radio was cut off. Now he was direct to Basra Control, Southern Iran. Listening for a brief while, he heard the tail end of a transmission clearing an aircraft to a point 220 miles to the North, obviously an internal flight. Made sure he wasn't stepping on anyone else's conversation and then sent.

"Basra Radar this is Romeo Alpha Zero Wun Ayte Wun Tree (*01813*) how do you read? Over"

(*3)

*3 *In radio telephony it is normal to "introduce yourself" by your full name, or full callsign, after that, when you have been acknowledges as that particular callsign the Controller will then abbreviate your name, shorten it to waste less time on superfluous chat that clogs transmission time, especially for any other pilot waiting to make his call. Therefore, Romeo Alpha Zero One Eight One Three would be confirmed as understood, then shortened to "Romeo One Three after the initial introduction.*

His heart was in his mouth. If the plan hadn't worked inside Tehran centre, then this was all going to turn messy and the flight would become infinitely more dangerous. The ten second pause seemed eternal. Again, the transmission:

"Basra Radar, basra radar, this is Romeo Alpha Zro Wun Ayte Wun Tree (*01813*) how do you read? Over".

Two seconds later "Romeo one three Bandar Abbas radar. Go ahead" *(pass your message)*.

Brad complied: "Bander Romeo Thirteen is a Charlie One Thirty out of Ras al Kheima bound for Zahedan. Presently 6 miles West abeam RAK heading 285 degrees. 4,000 feet on 1033 squawking 5565. Requesting Flight Information Service. Over".

Bander quickly came back: "Romeo One Three turn right heading 350 degrees for radar identification. Squawk 5650 Over".

Again, R13 came back: "Right to 350, holding 4,000 Squawk 5560 Romeo Thirteen".

The Bander Controller was no slouch: "Negative Romeo One Three squawk is 5650 with *(mode)* Charlie. Over".

Brad apologized and confirmed the correct "squawk" number as 5650 and that he would transmit it in mode Charlie height information as directed.

Two minutes later Brad received: "Romeo One Three we have you identified at 11 Miles North West of ras al Kheima. Hold present height and heading ".

(*4)

*4 A "Squawk" is a predesignated transmission from an onboard device called a transponder which emits a number (as designated by the controller) for the aircraft pilot to select and send. This then appears on the controller's screen to identify your particular radar mark or blip from any other. In mode "C or Charlie" it also gives your present height or altitude on the controller's screen as well.

His brain racing as he confirmed the turn with Oleg who was already rolling to the right, thoughts flashing through, quickly he confirmed to Stuart who was now plugged into the listening headset and told him: "They were slow (*to reply*) because they were reading the paperwork, they've accepted it, must have…"

Brad raised his hand in a "silence" gesture as Basra came back. "Romeo One Three you are cleared for initial climb to One Zero on 010 route direct Bandar. Report 20 miles to run".

Brad confirmed the directives again then leant forwards to work on the home-made looking box bolted to the side of the sleek polished LCD façade of the American made transponder. He dialed and entered numbers, then pressed "Go' The transponder started sending new flight levels out to Bander radar screens. R13 was climbing *electronically* and Bandar believed it. The rate of climb and difference in transmissions had all been preprogrammed months earlier by Brad, Oleg and a team of technicians in the Ukrainian Research Bureau, avionics section, to duplicate a typical rate of climb for a C130. Seven minutes later Brad confirmed to Bandar that he was now at 10,000 feet, Bandar checked and absolutely agreed with him too. In reality Romeo Thirteen was flying at 4,000 feet and tricking the radar at Bandar Abbas into believing it was at 10,000 feet.

"Who's a clever boy then". Brad chuckled to himself as he acknowledged Bandar's confirmation on his height.

A double click was enough from so far *lucky* Romeo Thirteen.

While Oleg tweaked the little turn to the North, Brad and Stuart pushed back one earpiece each on their Dave Clark headsets and spoke while they listened to any radio transmissions in the background.

Explaining to Stuart "Right. That's Bandar sorted out. They think we`re a C130 at 10,000 feet. We will go up to 7,000 but then they're going to tell us to go up to 16,000 later, that's for sure. So, we`ll just play the same trick again. Simple isn't it? Now let's hope that the UAE is still in the dark. We will have just come up on their radar 3 minutes back. The flight plan is in and they've accepted it so that parts OK. At worst they might think there's a screw up with the paperwork, at best they'll think were still *Kosha*. But, even if we `re unlucky, they can't send anything after us now, not into Iranian airspace." Brad was satisfied "For now we're OK Mate."

Brad continued "We've told Alexei that he needs to shift everything again, its balanced us for this part and believe me he did a cracking *guestimate* with his balancing act, but later on we might have to make some stronger maneuvers and I would rather have it all strapped down hard in a real Centre of Gravity. So, I`m sorry Mate but its work time again, the blokes must be well knackered eh?"

"Don't worry, How long do we have?"

"Sooner the better mate, sorry, but we don't know what will crop up or when. The worst at this stage is that the UAE get on the phone and start to talk to Tehran, then it will filter down through to us via whatever controller, they will probably ask us top land rather than sending us back, that would probably be their first choice. I can keep them talking but it won't be for long if that happens. Then if we refuse to land they will start to get nasty. Ultimately, the worst case, we will have one of their Tomcats looking for us and then we would be fucked, as in proper fucked! But don't worry, if I think it's going that way I can still try a few tricks".

"Mind you, Christ knows what they'll be". Laughed Brad.

"OK fair enough I won't ask!" said Stuart. "Alexei?" as he nodded towards the cargo hold:
" Pashlei shall we?''

Alexei smiled at the spoken Russian for "Let's go" and responded accordingly "Da, Pashlei".
Brad swigged down some water as he watched them leave the flight deck, glanced at Oleg who was flying absolutely accurately in the still night air and noticed by the movements with his head that he was scouring the night sky for any glimpse of an unwanted visitor in their vicinity, an Iranian Tomcat with its look down look shoot radar systems.

"No worries Mate" he told Oleg" If they decide to let one rip at us it will be from a hundred and fifty miles away and we won't even see it coming, *you'll* be dead before you feel it!"

Brad laughed, Oleg laughed with him at the black sense of humour and continued the joke "Oh, so *I* will be dead? *You* think I will be alone?"

....

Down in the hold the men had recovered, the air conditioning units (name of manufacturer of unit here) that had been shipped to the Design Bureau were working beautifully in the hold, ploughing out their promised 4,000 cubic feet of cooled air every minute which was more than needed. Even at night and even at 5,000 feet the Straights of Hormoz could still easily generate a hot and humid 40 Plus degrees.

One bin from the back had already been moved into its exact place in the centre. Alexei had worked out very quickly where each one should be and in what sequence. One from the back left, one from the front right and on through all 40 of the containers. With the flight smooth, straight and level now, the miniature railway tracks were working perfectly making the job infinitely easier than before. At the same time as bins were being positioned and strapped down firmly into place, some of the team were grabbing gold and jewels by the handfuls and trying as well as possible to even out the same volume in each of the bins.

The movements in balance were unfelt in the cockpit; the auto trim was removing them from the feel in the yolk instantaneously.

Brad monitored the screen on the GNS and mentally plotted a radio call in 7 minutes. Flicked the Russian stopwatch to zero and then flicked it again in minute and second mode to count up to six minutes in full, before turning to the fuel system and starting to top up the inner wing tanks from the specially fitted fuselage fuel bladders that had been part of the modifications in Crimea. If things turned sour, he didn't want to have to mess around with this job later in a stress situation; best get it out of the way now.

"Well, that's about right". Brad muttered to himself and then told Oleg: "I'll call Basra".

"Basra, Romeo Thirteen Over".

"Romeo Thirteen Pass your message. Over" came back. Brad smiled; he was using "thirteen" instead of One Three as his call sign. He knew it was unprofessional, but he *liked* it and now it seemed Basra felt OK with it too. That was a good sign.

"Romeo Thirteen reporting 20 Miles to run. Requesting an early turn for Minab". Brad knew that Bandar was getting busy with the radio traffic making them far more occupied due to the regular flights of immigrant workers that live in the Emirates and by Law need to regularly renewal their Visas and as such are forced to leave the country and then return immediately for a new Entry Stamp on their passport. Kish Island off the Coast of Iran is a favorite turn round point for the cheap and sometimes ridiculously unsafe Iranian Airlines flights but is the closest cheapest and easiest way for this mass of labour to move out and then back into the Country. They may not pay tax, but somehow with rules such as these, there was certainly a profit in the underpaid workers for the Governments of the different Emirates.

Thankfully eventually Bander Radar agreed that R13 could make an early turn and route direct to the preassigned point that had been set to cross the Coast and into Iran itself. From their point of view

Brad was an unwelcome workload that they could get rid of sooner rather than later.

Brad was pleased as he heard "Roger Romeo Thirteen QSY Minab on 123.45 have a safe trip".

Confirming he had the information correct and would do as requested Brad replied with a quick "Romeo Thirteen QSY Minab on 123.45 many Thanks. Out".

In an instant Basra was history as Brad flicked to the Minab frequency that was ready and waiting in the GNS communication System. Again, waiting briefly to make sure no one was transmitting Brad again introduced himself to the radar Control at the coastal Air Base at Minab on the Southern Coast of Iran and at the very neck of the Straits of Hormuz. This time the controller was a bit more terse, less hospitable and with much less grasp on the spoken English.

After a long pause Minab confirmed that he could overfly their field and asked him to climb to the pre allotted FL at 17,000 feet. Knowing full well that his false information was working on the Iranian Radar Brad "complied" and again, electrically the C130 on their screen started a slow climb to 17,000.

Time for part two of the act "Minab, we need to check out our pressurization, just a warning light needs sorting out, we do not see it as a problem but wish to check things before the climb. Request 11,000 until we sort it out over?"

Another pause, Minab didn't like it, "R13 should have been much higher before those idiots at Basra dumped him on us" thought the Controller.

"R13 there is high ground ahead of you range 7 Miles (nautical) at 2,300 Meters above sea level. Suggest you orbit until problem is fixed".

"Nahh" whispered Brad to himself and pushed again "Minab, we have good visual with the high ground and are well clear. Request continue track. Over"

Still Minab didn't like this but it was the Captains call, that's the rules. Again, a pause.

"Very well, continue present track. Be aware high ground to your right 1 o'clock range now 5 Miles, also to your left at 2,000 Meters range 4 miles in your 10 o'clock. Note you are not cleared, repeat not cleared for lower levels after my control space." Now Minab was getting pissed off.

"That is copied Minab, Romeo thirteen ".

But the Iranians were right, the high ground was there and R13 was now struggling up to 7,000 feet. They couldn't electronically lie their way over them, but they could physically fly between the gap that Brad had selected in his hour after hour of flight planning.

Calls were passed constantly to R13 and all were acknowledged by Brad accordingly.
From the cockpit even without the night vision goggles Brad could see the first Mountain ranges of Iran, the first run being almost directly ahead across the coastline, or seemingly to be at the water's edge. And all of them higher than the Ekranoplan could fly and all of them very close indeed.

Brad issued the directions" Turn right 5 degrees to 030, your gap should be dead ahead. Can you see it?"

Asking Bandar for the early turn had put R13 on a course set directly after Minab, through a gap in the mountains that leads into an unknown plain. On the screen they looked like they were at 11,000, in reality at 7,000 but the route was true, the position was the same for the false C130 and the real Ekranoplan. Straight through the gap.

Even before the turn had been completed Oleg could see the gap in the Mountains clearly in the night vision goggles "Yes, exact, I have it" confirmed Oleg.

Brad on the other hand, couldn't. He was working with the GNS, the paper maps and Mark One computer between his ears. He wasn't wearing his night vision goggles yet as it would be impossible to read the small Garmin screen with them as they multiplied the light, the screen would be more like a spotlight shining straight into his eyes. This was a teamwork that had to be on complete and absolute trust. Brad was far more experienced at Low level tactics and navigation and the use of advanced avionics than Oleg. Conversely, Oleg could handle his darling beloved airplane better than anyone else in the world. In this team they were both doing what they were best at.

"Good, Just fly the centre of the gap, it's a double range, the first run is the highest, the second we can clear easily then it drops down to salt plains and marshes after a few K" twelve seconds later they were entering the cleft between the shoulders on the Mountain range itself. Oleg felt good, even at this early stage he could see in the distance that the ground fell away and the route through was clear. While Brad couldn't see the same amount of detail, he was also confident that this opening wasn't a dead end and would lead them to the salt Flats and marshes of the long east West depression behind. Just North of the straits of Hormuz and running parallel with it, hidden from it by the massive granite curtain of Mountains. History rightly has it, that this is a murderous plain that has burnt people alive for Centuries. Including Alexander, the Great who entered it on His return from the wars in India and Pakistan, and never left.

....

Down in the Cargo Hold, with everything by now strapped down and centralized in the cargo hold it was time for food. The Team's logic was eat while you can; you never know how long the next meal might be. Three large cardboard boxes containing various Sandwiches, Boxes of cold KFC, cartons of fruit juices were passed around. For the first time the men could relax "just a little" and now start to feel that they could just be on the home run after all but not a single one mentioned it. It wasn't over till the fat lady sings and well they knew it. Some decided not to talk at all, others in low tones as was their habit. They were not noisy people; an occupational trait that they all seemed to share was to be softly spoken. Tommy looking put of one of the few side windows from the hold saw the almost sheer rock face moving past the right wingtip of the Aircraft just a kilometer distant. Rushing over to the port side window he looked and saw another, this one slightly closer. Quietly he turned and sat beside Sarge.

"OK tit?" Asked the Sarge as he chewed on a sandwich.

"Yes…OK Sarge" and pausing before informing the Sarge "Whatever you do…don't look out of the windows" which of course is immediately what Sarge did.

It didn't take long for the others to pick up on what was happening. The Cargo Hold became an even quieter place than before.

....

Soon the gap had been passed and as predicted the ground fell away, now just over a mile below them as they set up a course for the beacon at Iranshahr, some 220 Kilometers to the East, at the other end of the long low plain. To the right of them was the granite curtain that faced the Gulf Of Oman, over to their left, even higher mountains that form the southern rim that surrounds the massive Dashti Lut Basin of Eastern Iran separating it almost completely from the rest of the Country in a huge tear drop shape of mountain ranges that rise up to 14,000 feet at their highest point, but are less than 8,000 at the lowest points. To enter and leave this awesome tear at night in a 40-year-old aircraft capable of flying barely 8,000 feet was a prospect that would simply terrify most pilots. One wrong decision, one misinterpretation of information one unnecessary hesitation, any small and seemingly insignificant point that was overlooked; all could lead to everyone's death. Brad and Oleg had been planning this route over and over for months. Every tiny morsel of information they could get, they examined, and they shared. They had read maps until they could almost draw them from memory. They had memorized shapes of marshes and hardened acrid salt lakes, town names, village names, headings that roads took across their planned route, times between turning points and where to look for roads, railways, lights of towns and villages, absolutely any unusual features that would still be visible, especially in the night vision goggles.

Brad was well aware how good the Garmin navigation instruments were, but he was equally well aware that anything mechanical can break or stop working for a myriad of reasons, just when you needed them most. Brad was revising everything over and over again, just in case, for some unexpected situation, he would be forced to navigate this flight using the most basic of navigation aids.

One such memorized point was the highest peak at the Northern end of the plains that lead towards the Pakistani Border. It was unmistakable and easy to find. At the end of the 200 Kilometers of mountain walls on their left side would be a last, final and tallest peak towering above them at 11,446 feet above sea level. As it rose dramatically from the rest of the range, it also fell dramatically too, and it was here that Brad had found the entrance to the Tear Drop itself. The only opening in the South for one thousand kilometers. They had named this tallest Southern Mountain and key turn point; Titan. Just to the South east of Titan was an isolated smaller peak, this had been christened "Venus".

By now contact with Minab was well and truly lost, blocked by the mountains that R13 had passed between. Not to ring any unnecessary alarm bells yet, Brad was transmitting to Iranshahr Air base now 160 kilometers' ahead of them at the end of the cruel basin.

Informing them of the same, suspected problem and requesting to remain at a lower level than they were demanding brad knew that their patience would soon be exhausted. Iranshahr came back and now wasn't asking but was telling R13 that unless it could get the problem sorted out and get back on track then it was time to land. They even passed on all airfield information that R13 would require for a landing there. To refuse this instruction would provoke an automatic intercept from the Iranians but he needed to stall, just another 11 minutes was needed to get into sight of Titan itself.

Informing Iranshahr that he had copied the information and would comply with their request to land if the problem couldn't be sorted out within the next ten minutes of so, they eased the throttles forward a tad, knocking off 4 of the precious minutes that were slipping away. The Salt Lake at the centre of the flat plain had passed behind then, as had the tiny village of Berovahi which lies at its edge. Gently they were "accidentally drifting a little North of the course for Iranshahr all the time.

Iranshahr was losing patience "Romeo One Three, be aware you are drifting North of track. High ground, 4,000 Meters is to your right running parallel to you at range 12 Kilometers. Head 050 to track direct. Confirm our NDB is 332 Over".

Brad paused, 5 more minutes to his turning point yet, he needed to stall them, and he also needed to stay off track. Telling them nothing he transmitted back.

"Copied Iranshahr, We have the NDB. Should have this sorted out soon - our Engineer is onto it. Stand Bye".

Oleg turned to Alexei "Get down into the hold. Everyone strapped in and check everything is tied down".

Moves that Brad had deliberately made so far had given the three different controllers the impression that R13s Captain, to say the least, was not very good at his job. Courses had been just that little bit off track, heights had been missed by just that bit more than was normal. Even his radio speech calling himself "thirteen" instead of One Three meant a certain sloppiness in attitude. Reading back their instructions and getting the odd heading wrong so that they had to correct him, showed that they were switched on and he wasn't and then, as if to stamp the seal of inadequacy that this one was a borderline stupid Pilot, was the decision to fly through the cleft in the Mountains outside Minab. This alone confirmed the Iranian suspicions.

Unknown to the crew of R13, even before Brad had contacted Iranshahr, they had been called by Minab on a land line and informed them that they had an idiot *Britisher* Pilot on their hands and not to allow them to continue the flight unless they could sort their problem out and climb to the required flight level and track very soon. Either way, Minab would be putting in a serious report of a violation of Air Law. The idiot had endangered his aircraft and crew unnecessarily and was guilty under International Aviation and Maritime Law.

"They must think we're a right bunch of wankers Mate" He said to Oleg who was actually already thinking the same thing.

"But that is good". Oleg laughed "They will believe the next part!"

"Yeh, let's hope so eh?" Brad replied as he thought to himself "Hope *that fella at Shah thinks I'm a Pommy Bastard*" Judging by the Iranian controller's pronunciation of words during his transmissions, Brad knew that the Iranian controller probably wouldn't be able to differentiate between the accents of British or Australian.

Alexei had returned and confirmed to Oleg that everything was secured now. Nets and canvas covers had even been sealed over the top of every wheely bin which were now not only strapped and wrapped in place, but every wheel had been hammered and locked into place with aluminum U shaped chocks too.

Looking at the GNS, the Charts gave him a double check, he asked Oleg "Were about 2 minutes to run to the turn point. Ready Mate?"

Oleg nodded: "Ready".

Pressing the fuel dump button Brad gave a four second Burst and then pressed the After Burner "Igniter" He knew that they were still too far away from Iranshahr to be seen, but at 8,000 feet on a clear night the fireball *would* be seen by someone. To make sure he repeated the process again, then again. It wasted a hundred gallons of fuel but he knew that this part just had to be believable otherwise all sorts of problems could be called down on them, notably an Iranian Tomcat which, according to Stuart had reasoned that their operations would have been ramped down too with " Remember that Iran was a strict Muslim country and that Ramadan is Ramadan in Iran as well"

Immediately after the third fireball had been thrown into the Iranian night sky, Brad started to transmit. This was also Oleg's que to start his part of their private little airshow.

"Mayday, mayday, mayday Romeo Thirteen…Mayday, mayday……..." then Brad stopped.

At this Oleg had started his sequence. Dipping the left wing firmly and deliberately towards the base of Titan, losing a thousand feet in 5 seconds he then rolled back to the right to level the wings in the dive, to now see Titans sheer wall in full view rising impressively to its full 12,000 feet dead ahead, filing the windscreen. Due Starboard and now passing behind the wingtip were Titans little sister, an isolated smaller mountain codenamed Venus and putting Iranshahr airbase now to their South East. This meant that Venus would soon block any radar that could track them from Iranshahr.

Oleg's job was to dive, then enter a steep climbing hard right turn climb would "paint" the aircrafts radar return onto the face of Titan, then to disappear into the blanked return from radar, on the dark side of Venus. By the time they flew out of this shielded from sight area, behind Venus, they had to be lower than 500 feet from the ground. Over 500 then Iranshahr would see them again and the whole plan of deception would be wasted, then their alternatives would be to land and explain an aircraft full of gold, or to run and bring down the wroth of the Iranian Tomcats. There was no option, when they departed the cover provided by Venus, they *had* to be low level beneath any surface based radar scanning. Iranshahr had to think they had crashed somewhere high on the mountainside of Titan.

Leaning forwards to look out and around from the cockpit with its limited span of vision from only the forward and sideward facing windows Oleg constantly craned his neck, turning his head for better views and reference points for the attitude of the aircraft. Seemingly he was impervious to the G being brought to bear by the twists and turns he was putting the huge aircraft through. Seeing Venus starting to curve away on his right, Titans almost vertically sheer wall was now thrusting up ahead of him he started the entry of the maneuver. He needed to make it look like a flight into high terrain, but, if Oleg judged it wrong, it might just end up being just that.

The fate of everyone was now literally and totally in Oleg's hands. Still without his night vision goggles Brad was constantly calling the air speed to Oleg, knowing that he couldn't look down at the illuminate panel with his night vision goggle on. Oleg paused 2, then 3, seconds "After Burners Ready"

"Check"

Oleg started his pull as Titan filled the screen, as he pulled as he rolled the aircraft into a steep climbing right hand banked turn. On came the G forces 2,3,4, in fast order. Straining against the G as he pulled it on he called to Brad

As nose came up to a seemingly steep 35 degrees with a right bank of 70 degrees Oleg called out.

"Stand byyy……..NOW!"

Immediately Brads worked the two buttons marked "Feed" and after a three second pause, pressed "Ignite" splashing the burning jet fuel for three hundred meters across the Iranian night sky. Someone would be down there, even in this remote place, someone would see it.

Oleg eased back on the throttle, the last thing he wanted was to be too high, as he rolled the wings level. He needed to be "on the deck" when he came out from behind Venus. The aircraft had made its lazy sort of half chandelle, turned in perfect balance. The plume of yellow and orange fireball dumped behind it was strung out for a quarter of a mile.

At the zenith of the maneuver, Iranshahr lost contact with Romeo Thirteen as the blip that was R13 disappeared from their screen completely. In the cockpit Oleg looked to the right and saw Venus, the smaller mountain still stretching up higher by a good thousand feet than the Ekranoplan, blocking them from the constant search of the Iranian radar. "Transponder Off"

"Off now" Brad confirmed as he jabbed at the button of the Gramin transmitter, closing it down for good.

Oleg knew that the next part was crucial, not only to avoid radar but to actually *live* to avoid it.

As rehearsed, Brad was constantly calling the speed to Oleg. Hearing them, working only by vision in the green light of the night vision goggles and feel on the yolk. Pulling the throttle back to, quickly the speed bled off. At the same time releasing the pressure on the yolk, the nose lowering itself down to somewhere near to straight and level as Brad called "150" The exact speed that Oleg wanted.

Now keeping a constant and gentle back pressure on the controls, feeding in more and more rudder with opposite turn on the yolk to keep perfect balance. The Ekranoplan started its full side slip.

The technique, using fully crossed controls, basically presented the massive flat side area of the fuselage of the aircraft to the airflow, using it as a huge, shuddering air brake. Losing the maximum amount of height in the minimum amount of distance and by converting his 44 Ton all up weight 1960 vintage troop carrier, into a flying brick, Oleg achieved just that.

The Vertical Speed Indicator that shows the Rate of Climb or Decent was on it stops and pointing downhill. Brad now called speed and height and speed "two Thou 190" a second and a half later "17 hundred 210" At 1,000 Feet above ground level the preset radio altimeter sounded it warning. Within half a second Oleg had started to release the cross-control inputs as the airframe felt a relief from its shoulder charge against the airflow. As the dive continued the aircraft quickly accelerated itself back into flight speed as Brad called

"8 Hundred 290…" Oleg pulled slightly on the yolk to slow down the rate of acceleration "7 Hundred 320.." "That's better" Oleg quickly thought to himself as he lowered the nose deliberately to aim now for the exit point of the whole sequence of maneuvers. Seeing the ground clearly as it was racing towards his screen he started to pull holding a steady 3 G back pressure on the yolk for a full 4 seconds. Suddenly it was over. Titan was speeding past their left wingtip in a backwards direction at 450 KPH.

As they exited the dark side of Venus just above 200 feet above the ground they were invisible to Iranshahr radar but could now again pick up their transmissions. To the watchers on the radar screen at the airbase Romeo 13 and everyone one in her must be dead. They had already got two telephone calls from the Police about "fire in the sky" and more would come in later even including an accurate eyewitness report of a Boeing 747 being "shot down by a missile". In vain but according to the book, Iranshahr continued to transmit to R13.

Still no time to relax Oleg watched the side wall of Titan as it started its curve away to the North, Banking Oleg smoothly followed it, adjusting the bank as required to keep as close to it and as low to the ground as possible.

Romeo One Three, how do you read, Iranshahr transmitting to Romeo one three, how do you read over" after 30 seconds would come the same and again after another 30. before Putting Titan and his little sisters fully between R13 and the Airbase for a final time Brad heard them transmit blind. In the hope that someone on R13 could hear but not speak back.
"Romeo One Three it is believed you are down near high ground 72 kilometers to our North west; emergency services will be sent do you copy? Iranshahr over".

In Basra Radar, the telex stamped out. "UAE Centre requesting status on flight Romeo Alpha 01813…"

Two hundred miles to their South, Jason Billingham, a junior operations assistant at Ras al Kheima International Airport was now sitting in a cruel hot sweat box called a Police cell feeling just a little stupid. Tears were running down his cheeks.

In another tear Drop, the one that made the shape of the Dashti Lut in Central Iran, Oleg was streaking Northwards now, towards the small town at the tip of the oval depression, Bardeskan, 704 kilometers away.

Still no time to relax Oleg watched the side wall of Titan as it started its curve away to the North, Banking Oleg smoothly followed it, adjusting the bank as required to keep as close to it and as low to the ground as possible. Seeing a heading of due west roll onto the Direction Indicator Brad knew on the mass of Titan would soon be between them and Iranshahr, twenty seconds later their radio transmissions started to break up.

"Okidoki, the little whiz box here is telling us 340 degrees for the next way point mate."

Not wanting to look at the glare of the direction Indicator with his night goggles on, Oleg gently rolled the aircraft to the right "OK…Tell me when"

Three degrees before the desired heading Brad calmly told him, "Okidoki that should do ya" and the aircraft settled exactly on 340 itself.

The sight of the plain, in the moonlight, stretching out past them was incredible. Occasionally Oleg would raise the aircraft when he thought he saw anything that could mean power cable across their path. In the distance he could sometimes spot the lights of a car or a truck, Brad would be warning him of an isolated road or track that could be plotted on his land survey maps. Roads usually went hand in hand with power supply lines, even out here in the back of beyond.

After pumping fuel back into the wing tanks, reading the fuel content dials, doing his math's Brad felt happy with the fuel situation. Glancing at his watch he then started to work out how much "dark" was left, he knew from his hours of revision with his nose buried in the books, manuals and maps over the previous 6 months that dawn on this longitude in Iran on this day would be at exactly 05.00 hrs. local time. Working through
the remaining pages of his flight plan notes they were now only 8 minutes behind his estimated time at this given place. Tweaking the throttles, he informed Oleg they needed an extra 10 KPH to put them at the next turn point at the exact correct time. Oleg nodded an agreement and didn't turn his head from the windscreen at all. The only on-board radar that they had was Oleg's "Mark One" eyeballs constantly scanning and searching for any unknown obstacles, power lines or God forbid, an unmarked radio mast.

The ground was flashing beneath them at an incredible rate and to anyone who wasn't used to high-speed low-level flight would have seemed terrifying. At times gentle rises seem to float upwards sometimes slowly, sometimes in a flick that threatens to slap the belly of the aircraft into destruction. Brad was sure that Oleg probably hadn't even blinked behind his goggles for the last 2 hours. There was no doubt that this was a feat of endurance for Oleg. He had to fly through this night wearing the image intensifiers for a full 4 hrs. 15 minutes from start to finish and of that period, over 3 hrs. would be at brain sapping low level flight when just the slightest loss of concentration can be fatal.

Turning around to almost face backwards in his left-hand seat, Brad told Stuart

"OK Matey we should be sort of boring straight and level for the next hour or so. Best tell the lads to get some rest if they can. We've got a few ducks and drakes to play after the next turn point up there "pointing into the darkness ahead "So it's best if they rest now if they can. You too mate, try to get a bit of kip eh? We`ll look after this"

Sitting beside Tommy, Stuarts mind went back to Dubai, wondering what the situation was there; If Nat and Lenna were home free. Were the authorities in gear? For sure they had worked out the connection between R13 and the heist. Would the power be back on? Question after question ran through his mind. And then, looking at Tommy flicking though the pics section on his mobile phone, the penny dropped "Why not call Dubai and find out!"

Opening the safe breast pocket of his overalls, Stuart pulled out the small waterproof sealed bag containing his mobile, his wallet and his passport. Putting everything back
after re sealing the bag he made his way back to the flight deck to check with Brad about making a call.

"Sure why not " said Brad after Stuart asked "This aint a fuckin Airbus mate, help yourself, that is, if you can get a signal here" Pressing the green "Call" button Stuart waited while the phone searched for a signal "Welcome to *Iran sat*" came back and 30 seconds later he heard Natasha's voice "Da Malenki? Are you OK??"

"We're fine, all of us. How did it go there?"

"Ohh" came a laugh and another from Lenna in the background "It's been so crazy here! So crazy. All the Souk was fighting, Indians were stealing everything the Police were fighting everybody, you should have seen it. It was so wild"

Unseen to Stuart were Natasha and Lenna, sitting in a candlelight apartment and drinking even more Champagne, a ring on every single finger, necklaces and bracelets dripping off almost every appendage. Lenna had even tied her blonde hair back with a huge marriage necklace designed for a Shaker and was in the process of deciding whether or not nipple jewelry could be the next step seeing as she had run out of other places to wear stuff.

"Is the power back on?"

"Nooooooo! It's horrible here, no lights and no AC. We are stripped and keep splashing water on us to stay cool, its melting here!" Stuart couldn't resist that mental image but continued quickly.

"Did you hear any news?"

"No Malenki, the radio is on but they're not saying anything at all, just that there is a power cut which will be fixed soon, and to be careful driving and stuff like that. We have only just got our phones working" the giggling raised again as Lenna had decided that nipple jewelry would work after all.

"OK I will call you soon." Stuart added "And Natasha………."

"Da melenki?"

"Hide that stuff NOW!"

Three hundred miles away to their right on the and thirty-five thousand feet higher above the Afghan Border with Iran the call had been recorded onto the listening systems of the Boeing AWACS that had been watching them since they had approached

Bandar Abass. Air Sergeant William T Kazinski smiled to himself as he zipped the recording and forwarded it on to AWAC Command Middle East. He didn't understand the meaning of the conversation at all, but he did know it sounded odd. He could understand now why they had been detailed to "plug in" to Romeo 13 by Command Control and everything he had seen about this R13 flight so far was extremely suspicious. For sure they were up to something very special indeed.

The salt Lake situated in the top left-hand tip of the Tear Drop was looming towards them now. Again, Oleg translated Brads command to Alexei to go down and tell the team 10 minutes to run before the Ducks and Drakes started again. They had flown a curved route, putting them in the lea of the mountains that framed the Western Border of the Kaveri-e Lut that made up the Tear Drop itself separating it from the rest of Central Iran.

In their 11 o'clock Oleg could see the 9,000-foot mountains running parallel to their track. Brad confirmed the small town of Deyhuk on the higher ground at the base of the mountain range flashed past their left wingtip, 12 minutes further on the small gathering of lights marked the town of Boshruyeh as the ground fell away back to a level of 3,000 above sea level.

The vision was so good in the image enhancing goggles that Oleg could even follow the road that curved gently to the North towards its destination at Kashmar at the foot of the Kuh-E Gachi range that forms the rearguard of three separate strings of Mountains which make up the natural fortress of Iran's Northern Borders.

Flying between the road on his left and the salt flat lake on his right Oleg smiled; the Russian word for "Nightmare" was "Kashmar" his old Airforce nickname. "Good Omen" he thought quietly to himself.

There was always something to do. Brad had rebalanced and refilled the fuel again, pumping it from one temporary tank in the fuselage to the wing tanks and feeding the massive Kunutzov powerhouse high in the tail behind them. The two jet engines in the nose were there for the ride right now, but he made sure they were on standby ready for action. Navigation, position way points, everything was down the second accuracy now.

"ETA Initial Point 22 seconds "as he pressed the antique but wonderfully accurate stopwatch in the control panel. Three seconds later Oleg spotted the cluster of 8 yellow lights that were the village of Sa`d Ed Din, their IP. With the very lightest touch he moved the aircraft to the right just 10 meters. That would put the IP directly between Brads eyes, that is *when* Brad could see it with the naked eye.

"9 seconds. Check, IP ahead. Ready to turn on my mark, repeat on my mark ONLY turn left onto heading 308…………..Now!"

Instinctively Oleg allowed the nose to rise, giving the huge machine extra clearance of 75 feet, which would soon be eaten up by the lowering of the left wing as it pointed downwards towards Mother Earth, as he simultaneously rolled into the left and pulled, The Aircraft felt like it was on rails, 3 G came in fast as he held the bank at a full 60 degrees. In the Cargo hold the G force felt even worse, they had no warning of it at all so physically the effect feels greater. The Sarge was bracing against it with his legs this time!

Anticipating the heading of 308 Oleg started his roll back to straight and level at 303 degrees called out by Brad. As the wings hit "level" the DI hit 308 and the height was again spot of at 200 feet above the ground.

Looking to his right the lights of Bardeskan were making an arch shaped glow in the pre-dawn air as the next "V" shaped cleft in the iron rich rock faces presented itself in their 12 o'clock position ahead. This one definitely easier, actually fun to fly through as the base of the V was over a kilometer wide and as flat and level as the land that lead up to it too. Keeping to the left of the cutting Oleg easily and smoothly curved the bulky aircraft through the wide gap between the two peaks. As he did so Brad, head down in the maps and GNS screen informed him: "Left turn to 300, repeat 3-0-0 degrees".

A quick "Check 300" came back from Oleg. Eyes still glued to the green vision of the plain in front of him.

Brad continued "High ground 12 o'clock range …45 kilometers, height should be less than 5,000 agl" (*above ground level*) 45 Kilometers meant exactly 6 minutes at their speed of 450 KPH. They had time to double check their plan. According to all the information they had, this particular area was a labyrinth of mine workings. From his position right now, Oleg could see three separate, enormous mining projects. One was about to pass quickly straight under their nose. Ahead were two peaks rising to 5,700 feet on the left and 6400 feet on the right. The area between them had been marked vaguely on the map as "dissected terrain" with "elevation unknown" Brad had reasoned that this should be a ridge, joining the two peaks and should be lower than both peaks. But still, what neither of them liked, the height of the ridge was unknown. They could climb and clear the ridge even if it was as high as the peaks, which was doubtful, but if they did they would then expose themselves on radar screens at Marshad, the biggest Air Base in North East Iran 240 kilometers away to the east.

The plan was already agreed over a month before, but still Brad ran through it one final time.

"OK let's go through it again. I will call the range *(to the ridge.)* Once you get a good visual you will make your decision. If there is any doubt, repeat ANY doubt you will orbit left at 400 feet and take up a heading of 225 degrees and we take the alternate route. Agreed?"

"Check agreed" Oleg confirmed back to the Pilot in Command.

Brad knew full well that the alternate if chosen, would add almost an extra 300 Kilometers around this final high obstacle. In turn it would put another 40 minutes on the flight which also meant an extra 40 minutes to potentially to be discovered by the Iranian Air Force.

With one and a half minutes to run to the Ridge Oleg called visual. With 45 seconds to run he called "Its lower than the peaks, estimate 4,000 and………..Its mine working…. there is a gap"

Brad strained to see, he could see the rough shape of the ridge, vaguely, in the pre-dawn light that was seeping its way into the darkness of the Iranian sky now, he could make out the gap that Oleg was telling him about. The same filtered light that was slowly and surely workings it was into the previous darkness was also having a secondary effect and slowly it was starting to "haze" Oleg's vision in the image enhancing goggles.

"The gap is good, no need for afterburners, we can go through it".

As Oleg raised the aircraft, now too close to the ridge to show on radar it was safe top climb Oleg called again. "It's lower, the gap is at about 2500 base. Brad could now also see the gap, Oleg was right, seconds away from it now he could see it was wide enough by a good 600 meters from shoulder to shoulder, a huge part of the ridge that had been excavated for its rich copper filled ore. Oleg was aiming at a point almost perfectly between the two shoulders, being safe, not too close to the base and not too high to pop up on a radar screen. It seemed perfect but there was a little bell that just started to ring. Something in Brads head, something telling him, talking to him.

Instinctively he reached down for his night vision goggles, the seventh sense somehow asking him to satisfy the inner bell that had just started to tinkle rather than ring out. As he took the goggles in his hand the aircraft entered the exact centre point between the two shoulders and at that same nano instant the high voltage power cable that was strung from one side of the excavated ridge across the gap to the other side hit the upper part of the bulbous nose of the aircraft. Within a quarter of a second it had whipped up over the slanting windscreen, past the area where luckily the upper turret had been removed and cut through the empty Radar dome housing sending it careering backwards into space as the 1 inch thick whip shot backwards to the upwards curving tail plane behind the propeller of the Kunutzov and hanging on to the very base of the engine mounting to pull, like a giant garrote.

As it held the tail the aircraft nosed upwards as it braked in the air from 450 to 150 KPH in 2 and a half seconds. At the same time as an almighty bang was heard from the bulkhead behind and below Oleg's position on the right of the aircraft Brad was firing the

Afterburners, Oleg had thrust all levers fully forward to full to the stops power. As viciously as it had attacked the cable then broke. Cut by the tail pane itself. The cable gave in and left them, as if satisfied that it had cast its fatal blow.

The aircraft pointing nose up at 45 degrees screamed its warning of a stall and instantly started to shudder violently as it was pulled into a full wing drop stall to the right. In a flash photo glace to the right as the wing dropped Oleg saw downwards and slightly backwards. The image fixed in his head. On Brads side nothing could be seen, just black sky forwards and left.

Instantaneously Oleg made a decision and kicked right rudder fully and slammed the control yolk full left at the same time pulling back all the throttles the wing dropped down, straight past the vertical as the aircraft rolled 45 degrees inverted. The aircraft was entering a spin and Oleg was encouraging it.

The aircraft rolled over the nose started to drop, even at this point there was half a plus G factor kept onto the airframe. At three quarters around the first turn of its spin Oleg's inner clock flashed to Full left rudder full forward with the control column and full power all at exactly the same time. As the lag time used up the final quarter of the 360 pirouette the windscreen now filled with one stable picture. Iranian ground now 1,000 feet below and accelerating upwards fast. After a fifth of a second pause, enough for Brad top call out "170" Oleg passed for another portion of a second, he needed flying speed but not too much of it. Too little and they would enter a secondary spin, too much and they would hit the ground before they could pull out. A pause for another quarter of a second and then came Oleg's firm but measured and smooth pull.

3 seconds later they were flying at 300 feet on a heading of 300 degrees, just 10 degrees of track.

The Ekranoplan had just completed its first single turn aerobatic sports style spin. Both pilots sat and didn't speak.

Alexei was the first to move. Un- strapping from his seat behind Oleg he placed a hand on his shoulder "I will check the damage" Oleg nodded, and Alexei leaned forwards to say in his ear "Kashmar, *Kruto Sdelano Drugg*" (Thank you friend)

Running through the engine temperatures and pressures, Brad was satisfied that at least from what he could tell from the clocks and dials, all seemed to be OK. Next he quickly attended to the constant job of the navigation and called "Right Zero Four Five "

"045 check "came back as Oleg rolled right bank in, this time extremely smoothly not knowing what damage may have occurred.

In the hold it was an enormous mess. A single Bin had come loose in the deceleration and hurtled forward hitting the main bulkhead pillar that separates the huge nose cone from the cargo hold itself. It has passed within inches of the guys strapped into their seats on the right side of the fuselage, actually hitting three of them on their legs and ankle but thankfully banging them out of the way as it flew forwards. After hitting the main bulkhead, it had basically exploded its load everywhere inside the forward part of the hold after knocking a massive 2 feet dent and bend in the bulkhead and surrounding frames. Alexei with the help from the guys inside had managed to prize open the twisted bulkhead door, which had missed the major impact but had still been twisted out of line by it. Once open the door would never be able to close again.

In the cargo hold everyone was laughing, it couldn't be helped. The 22 Stone or 310 Pounds of Sarge`s bulk had been increased to 110 Stone (1,540 Pounds) under Oleg's 5 G pull and the old and worn Russian canvas just couldn't take it. The Rim of the seat had held but Sarge had fired through the canvas like a baby on a pot. His knees had hit his chin and he was stuck. Only now the hysterics had calmed down could anyone try to help him. Tommy being the most helpful was taking pictures on his mobile phone as the tears of laughter ran down his cheeks. What didn't help is that the Sarge had gone through with such violent force once the fabric gave way that he really was stuck inside the tubular metal ring of the seat. His cursing at Tommy promising to stick "That fuckin *camera* up his fuckin arse" just added to it all. Even Stuart had to laugh as he made his way past and up to the flight deck.

Brad and Oleg laughed too when they heard about Sarges predicament. They also knew just how lucky they were that the main spar of the 40-year-old Caspian Sea Monster hadn't followed the same fate as the canvas seat that the Sarge had just demolished.

Stuart made a sign to Alexei, a question "Kharashol?" with his thumb up. He then stopped by Tommy who was looking down flicking through the selection of pictures that he had collected on his mobile phone. His smile was broad, the cat that got the cream for sure.

"I think you'd rather have those than that lot wouldn't you Tommy?" Meaning the pictures of Sarge, sitting like a baby on a pot, rather than his share of the gold. Tommy laughed "Its close Boss! Very close!"

"Da, da, Kharashol" Alexei spoke to himself as he passed Stuart and started to investigate through every single nook and cranny of the fuselage towards the tail end to check for any other damages.

Stuart un-strapped and made his way up to the flight deck and arrived in time to hear Oleg explaining his version of the events in detail to Brad.

"I saw the cable but too late, as I saw it, it hit us. Then it held us and pulled us up, nothing I could do, then with the stall I could see down, the mine is bigger on this side, it was almost clean down 2,000 feet and the cable had pulled us up to about 4,000 from the ground. I think we had minimum 3,000 feet clear to make the spin a full turn, it was safer, so I made the spin. I could have recovered from the dive sooner, but I didn't want to be too high. I think we might have shown on radar after the cable pulled us up, what do you think?"

To Oleg this had been a perfectly logical decision. To anyone else, it was terrifying. Oleg had seen what Brad couldn't see and had made a snap decision on the visual information that he alone had. At the same time Brad hadn't interfered. That was total, absolute and professional trust and teamwork. Both pilots had done what their years of training had taught them to do in an unexpected serious and dangerous situation. There had been no panic, no confusion and no disagreement. It had worked and Oleg for one was not surprised. To him it was far more sensible to encourage the aircraft around a single full turn spin, than to fight it after it had already gone past the point of no return at the entry. This could have led to more height loss and more time to regain control and could have put them easily on a heading straight back into the mountains to the right. By "flying" the aircraft round a single turn spin, height loss was still massive, but it was controlled, as was the heading on the way out of the spin which took them into clear air, albeit at 300 feet.

Not really knowing what to say to Oleg's explanation, Brad was just happy it was behind them now and so far, the aircraft seemed to have survived relatively undamaged.

"OK then, well…. As for showing on radar you might be right, but if we would have shown for more than a single, maybe a double return. It shouldn't have been any more than that. Either way not long enough for them to get a real fix or to set any alarm bells…. I hope"

Brad paused for thought, nothing much that could be done if it had now.

"So, back to work shall we? And Oleg, no more fucking around eh Mate?" both Pilots laughed, and Brad got back immediately into navigator mode. "We intercept *the* 36th parallel in 3 minutes," accentuating the *36th* as if it were important was just Brads way of talking when he was concentrating, he didn't even realize he did it "And then take a right turn onto due east. That's the last leg before the Turkmenistan Border. Good news is that there is no more high ground to clear. Bad news is that it's a busy area. If anyone will spot us, then it's on this part of the run that's the most likely place we will be tinkled (spotted). Marshad is one busy place, lots of roads, small towns and villages and a huge airbase just 15 or 16 miles North of our track. After we're abeam Marshad we track right along the 36th parallel until we pass the end of this range of mountains "Showing Stuart as he pointed at the map "And then, hang a left and head straight up to the Turkmenistan Border here". Pointing again. After that its straight as an arrow for about an hour direct to the Lake."

Again, advising Oleg "There is going to be lots of power cables here mate, they will be the usual, strung along roads not too high but there will also be the bigger ones stringing out in pylons all over the place. Try and hold 300 feet as much as possible"

"Check, 300 feet and looking" Oleg confirmed as the radio altimeter was re set by Brad to go off at 270 feet.

Twenty seconds later Oleg took up Brads new heading of 090 degrees, due east to the Turkmenistan boarder exactly 354 Kilometers and 47 minutes and 12 seconds away.

In the hold the men were clearing up the mess. Putting it into buckets, bags, anything that could double up or work as a container of some sort but not having enough, all they could do was to throw most of it to the sides of the fuselage. It seemed surreal, almost comical, that pure gold and precious stones were being treated this way. As they walked they stepped into it, it stuck between the pattern's ion the soles of their boots, it got everywhere.
Tommy stood in it, turning to Sarge who was also collecting with a small bucket.
Like a complaining housewife Tommy said "Look at it…. Will you look at it, what a mess! And I've spent all afternoon cleaning this floor as well!"

Sarge patted Tommy on the head "Never mind dear, *Sargey* will help you".

Keeping in character Tommy came back with "And I should think so too. You out gallivanting all day and me working like a slave, that's what I am, a slave"
………………………………………………………

In Marshad air Base operations Centre the telex had arrived from Tehran Centre.

"Believed intrusion of airspace by illegal flight entering South East Iran at 00.14 Zulu via Bandar Abbas - Minab Airspace. *STOP* Believed that incursion flight is crashed into high ground 48 NM NE of Iranshahr *STOP* Increase radar observations to level 2 until further notice as precautionary action *STOP*".

By the time the telex had been removed from the sheet and carried by hand to the Officer in Command on the quiet early morning shift R13 was passing just 16 miles south of him at an impressive 465 KPH at 300 feet.

Looking down Brad could see small fields, patches of home-grown crops, roads with traffic seemed to be coming to life, railway lines and clusters of houses with darker areas of vegetation around them. The broad valley was a hive of activity compared to the desolation of the Tear Drop.
"Any later" he thought to himself "And they would have definitely copped us here".

Looking at the telex the Officer sat and read it slowly as he yawned and thought of his bed and being able to sleep straight through another food free day of Ramadan. Looking for a pen that eventually worked he signed the telex as "Received" and wrote the time on it. Then wrote slowly and clearly.

"Passed to radar Block to increase surveillance to level two. Time noted 03:55".

Then looking for his office stamp, which he also couldn't find, he pressed a button to ask a corporal to come in from an outer office to ask where the hell he had hidden the stamp.

By the time the bureaucracy had been satisfied R 13 had been given another 9 minutes and covered 69.75 Kilometers of their race to the line that separates Iran from Turkmenistan. At the same instant that the Officer clicked the sealed plastic box which could be pressed down to stamp onto the printed telex Brad called Oleg to "Go left to due North, Border 45 Kilometers. ETA 6 minutes." They had rounded the last mountain of Iran's fortress wall.

As Oleg turned and took up the new heading he glanced for a second to the right. The sky above the horizon now seemed bright through his goggles; soon the dawn would be with them.
Brad felt a physical relief as he watched the yellow dotted line that pinpoints the Border across the GNS screen, waiting just a few more seconds he was genuinely pleased to call out to Oleg and Stuart "And…this is……wait for it……. the Border! Welcome to Turkmenistan gentlemen!"

From this point on they all knew that Tomcats wouldn't be sent and whatever happened, even if they were forced to land. Lecho's tentacles were long enough and strong enough to help them out if needs be.

Within 5 minutes Brad identified the tiny town of Miana, Turkmenistan passing a few kilometers to the left. Even in the half-light he could see the difference in colour, the greenery in comparison to the previous landscapes that were more like the moon. Almost immediately the land turned flat, absolutely flat and green with mile after mile of swampland and marshes.

Easing back on the throttles to set 420 KPH Brad set about moving fuel around, there was still oodles left even after all the dumping and afterburning. The ease back on power was more to nurse the single Kunutzov powerplant than anything else. Even though it had worked without missing a beat even though it had been abused more than once, there was no sense if pushing their luck and so accordingly, he eased up on it just enough to set the ETA, Estimated Time of Arrival to the delivery point on the edge of the remote Lake at exactly one hour to go.

Turning again to Stuart "OK mate, best go down and tell the lads. One hour to run." Then to Oleg: "OK mate, I have control".

"You have control". replied Oleg and after satisfying himself that Brads hands were in control of the aircraft, he leant back for the first time in over four hours, pulling the goggles from his head. Turning to look at Brad, squinting, the sun that was now rising would hurt his eyes for several minutes. The red impression lines across his nose and cheeks highlighted the tight fit of the headwear that had almost cut into him over the last 4 hours. Even from here, Brad could see Oleg's eyes were red and bloodshot, he looked exhausted.

....

In the hold everyone was getting ready. Actually, they were all prepared but more like double and treble checking everything over and over again. Through the right-hand porthole shape windows, they could see the dawn over a flat and green Turkmenistan, from the right, the rising black shapes of the Iranian Mountains that were now starting to reflect the colours of the dawn.

For them all, the next hour passed quickly as the sun rose and the Ekranoplan terrified the wild birds into flight as it streaked smoothly across the flatlands on Turkmenistan towards the lake.

CHAPTER 18: THE DELIVERY

July 23 rd. 0545, Uzbekistan

The bulk of the Ekranoplan had now been skimming the Northern plains of Iran for just over an hour. Now and then Brad would ease it up to gain a little height whenever they passed over or even near the clusters of cream coloured clay walled villages. Even out there they had power cables strung along at what seemed to be complete random.

Looking down at his creased charts even though the state-of-the-art Garmin Global Navigation System was infinitely more accurate, Igor confirmed to Brad.

"ETA coasting the lake at 12 past the hour, should be a small town or a large village about 2 Kilometers to our starboard when we get to the lake"

Brad was pleased to see Oleg's nose in the map, he knew only too well that sometimes satellites decide not to play and if the Garmin losses one or 2 of them momentarily then the electronic brain starts to tell little lies. The mark one computer, the human brain was always there and on this flight there was no room for fuck ups, not one.

Sure enough, good to Igor's word, the lakeside village dutifully passed away on their right wingtip, about a mile distant. Now they were on the home leg, now they needed to be spot on with the landing that would take them to the beach and Lecho.

Working out the effect of the almost nonexistent dawn zephyr Igor set the course for Brad to follow "Take up Oh… Zero Wun Tree (013) degrees and hold 200" Brad instinctively glancing to the right to make sure there was no other traffic there even though they were miles from beyond it was a habit knocked into his brain to look before turning, eased the Ekranoplan gently to the right in a 15 degree bank and the course was set at. Igor jabbed the "start" button on the antique but extremely accurate stopwatch set in the control panel and started his military style way point approach to the landing run. The Garmin was there only to confirm Igor's skill at navigating as far as he was concerned.

Brad leaned over to Stuart sitting in the jump seat; or rather the seat that was reserved in all Soviet aircraft for the KGB member of the crew set back on the centerline between the two pilots seats simply to keep an eye on them and make sure the one of their red star aircraft didn't make any sudden unplanned turns to the Western side of the globe.

"Ask the lads to get ready mate, we will be landing soon, 25 minutes to the wage packet!"

Hearing Igor mumble *"Tventy Seieven* Minutes" Brad smiled.

Compared to Western Aircraft the flight deck of the Ekranoplan is a ballroom. Five seating positions in an X layout. Stuart turned to his left and changed seats to what now seemed an antique navigator / radio operators' desk.

The radio was already on, checked and tuned, Stuart knew full well that he needed to be close in before the radio would work on a line of site basis. Slipping on the cloth helmet with rubber headphones sewn into it, the typical ex-soviet military headgear, complete with thick rubber bands an inch deep running over the top of it to protect from banging the head itself on the numerous bulkheads inside the aircraft Stuart fastened the equally ancient throat mic around his neck. These had been banned years before in the west

because it collected transmissions directly from the voice box in the throat, they were really very effective and had none of the problems related to the touchy western mouth microphones and as a Soviet cherry on top of the cake, also caused cancer of the throat. This flicked through his mind as he eyed the set frequency on the old-fashioned dial up window on the radio and he then pressed the transmit button
"Beachboy, Beachboy this is Delivery Boy, how do you read?"

Instantaneously there was a reply in an easy, laid back Californian drawl.

"I gottcha fives delivery, BB over"

Stuart was relieved, it had been pre planned that changing the names to delivery instead of Delivery Boy and BB instead of Beachboy confirmed that his contact on the ground was status "We have not been compromised"

"That's good news, our status is also good, we have the delivery in full." Stuart knew only too well that the Ground Team he had set up as a precaution would definitely need to know the state of play and the success of the mission so far "Sitrep please BB" Stuart wanted a Situation report, what was on the ground, what awaited them?

The drawl calmly and coolly ran through the report.

"We've a total of 48 people as close as we can tell. 24 are workers we see them as Chechy Mafia, they're armed, side arms mostly, only 6 Kalashnikovs seen so far but could be more locked away that we didn't find. That apart we haven't seen anything heavier at all. We see another 20 to 22 as technical (meaning the beanny counters and jewelers that would be needed to wade their way through the 24 tons of shopping that Stuart was delivering.) So far no arms spotted with those guys. The set up here is a lil village, its set back from the LZ by 50 Meters. There are 5 large central tents, circular ex sov stuff, they've been filled with all the equipment that's needed, we saw weighing machines and scales plus some technical stuff, all looks real… There are another 30 smaller tents for accommodation plus 3 more big ones for eats, crap and showers. Back again by 10 Meters or so are the vehicles, 8 five-ton trucks, half a dozen 4 wheels and two Mercedes limos, one of them is armored. The boss mafia arrived in it 2 days ago. Looks like the works all set up. Yesterday there were Police here, three cars, we watched them, and they left after a few hours, looked like a small delivery or collection or both, probably a payoff from what we could tell, they sure looked happy when they left. Either way they're gone now, but they usually show up every few days and then leave."

This was no shock to Stuart, in fact if there were no Police he would have been worried. Good to his word, Lecho had bought the Police Force and they were more than likely his delivery boys now.

"Any military at all BB?" Stuart asked even though he knew that BB would certainly have told him in his sitrep (situation report)

"None confirm none" the Drawl replied, and Stuart also knew that if anything Military had been within 10 miles of the camp over the last 10 days, BB would certainly have tagged it.

"Confirm your positions are OK?" Stuart clipped the question

"Affirm BB is set up 20 Meters in and 40 Meters east and west as planned, RPG and 30cal are in place full teams are OK" Stuart smiled "full teams" meant 8 men in all, but 8 professionals who could certainly make a mess of the quaint little village on the shoreline, and everyone in it.

The Drawl continued "There are three tanker wagons, 2 with water one with fuel, we've been in and checked them, they're real, petrol tasted crap but it's better than the water!"

"Any visuals for me" Stuart asked as his mobile phone bleeped to inform him he had incoming messages; photographs taken by BB.

"You got it!" said BB with a very slight sarcasm to his drawl now.

"Stuart looked down at his phone and pressed the transmit button to inform BB "Stand by one".

A quick double click was heard on BBs transmit button meaning OK acknowledged.

Flicking through the pics Stuart saw the tents, the people, the weighing machines, so close up he could read the manufacturers name, a Canteen, Shower Block, Inside the larger tenting the tables and makeshift chairs neatly set out in lines. Even one of a Chechneyan guy holding a Kalashnikov in one hand and picking his nose with the other.

"Good lads ". Stuart muttered to himself "Very good".

"OK BB your assessment please?"

Quicker now the drawl came straight back "I reckon it's a *go* boss. Looks genuine. I think the Chechias have set up to do the deal Boss. Can't see anything to ring the bell here".

Brag reminded Stuart "The water, what's the depth?"

Passing the question on to Beachboy One Brad waited for the news.

"Looks like at least 10 feet from what they can tell" said Stuart.

Oleg caught enough of the conversation, looking at Brad with his now very visible blood shot eyes he questioned: "ten feet…err. Three Meters?"

Brad looked at him and nodded.

"Too close Brad," he flicked his head as if meaning towards the rear of the aircraft: "With this much weight".

Again, Brad nodded as his mind raced through the options which didn't really exist.

"We`ll keep it *on the step* (*1) for as long as possible, if we scrape the bottom let's make sure we do it towards the beach, as close as we can"

Now Oleg nodded his agreement "Kharashol".

Stuart paused, glanced down into the cargo hold and looked at his men. It was his call and he had to call it now. Turning back to the radio set he pressed the transmit button. Stuart knowing that this man had spent several years monitoring similar set ups in the central American jungles knew exactly what to look for. If there was any telltale sign of a double cross or an ambush, then for sure BB and teams would have seen it. Absolutely guaranteed.

(*5) *On the step* **roughly means keeping the aircraft in a <u>very</u> high-speed taxi mode, skimming the surface until the power is reduced and the hull sinks into the water.**

"Confirm repeat confirm that we're on our way in BB. Our ETA is 25 repeat 25 Minutes to run. See ya soon Delivery boy out".

"Affirm inbound ETA two four minutes BB out" and again the double click came back. Nothing more was needed to be said, it was "Game ON".

Climbing down into the main cargo hold behind the high cavern or rather the flight deck that was Brads office, Stuart could see that there was no need to tell anyone to get prepared, only to confirm to them that it was now 25 minutes to run.

Weapons constantly checked no potential jamming, grenades easily accessible. The lads were more than ready for anything.

Stuart ran through the briefing with them again.

"OK Lads, everything so far has gone straight from their end, just had a sitrep from BB that all looks good" meaning the Chechnyan's "And I know we can never be too sure but the general opinion is that this should go down as planned, it's in their best interests not to cause any problems so watch them, be ready but for Christs sake no one losses it without good reason. Is that clear? Just remember if we wipe these buggars out we need to find another buyer and there's not too many places we can sell this lot is there?"

The men laughed. They took it for granted that if the situation turned sour, it would be the other side that lost and most certainly not them.

"However, Green section take up a position to the left of the landing, Red to the right, you know the crack lads. Jimmy, Pete, pop your heads through the hatches but do not show your weapons. Blue section, that's the bulk of you, all follow me out and **be** casual. Carry your weapons, of course don't shoulder them but don't point them either. OK lads, good luck…and please, do try to be good boys for a change".

Smiles, mumblings of "Yes Boss" and gentle nods came back in return. Stuart knew full well that his lads were more than capable of dishing out any shit that might be required
but it was after all in everybody's best interests that the "sale of the goods" went smoothly. They had just pulled off a magnificent job without a single scratch and Stuart thought to himself what a "bloody shame" it would be not to get everything wrapped up 100% now.

As Stuart climbed back up the metal ladder and into the sprawling flight deck he looked forward. The Coast was a thin orange band on the horizon. Oleg was peering intently through the Cockpit windscreen looking forward at the horizon, his thumb gently pressed the transmit button on the flight column, pressing only the button as not to interfere with Brads inputs on the controls.

"Shopkeeper this is Delivery Boy how do you read over?" …he paused 5 seconds and again, slightly louder this time "Shopkeeper this is Delivery Boy how do you read over?" another pause and finger hovering above the transmit button Igor mumbled "Fucking Chechnyan's".

Brad glanced across "Probably line of site if they're using a cheap handheld (radio) Mate, keep trying eh?"

Oleg transmitted again, this time he could hear someone trying to answer but it was no more than crackle. Oleg hand was raised as he leaned forward peering through the screen, looking, scanning the horizon where they should be then he saw it, the first of the three streams of smoke from oil cans burning tires 50 Meters apart. Then the second and almost immediately the third started to crawl their way into the blue morning sky.

Jabbing a finger "That's it, almost 12 o'clock!"

"Almost?" asked Brad.
Oleg wasn't amused at Brads joke and pointed again "It's those donkeys, they're in the wrong position! The fuckers moved from plan"

Easing his left boot onto the rudder Brad placed the "donkies" exactly where they should be, slap in the aircrafts 12 o'clock, dead ahead. Glancing down he flicked the range on the Garmin screen down 2 levels and was immediately informed the 17.6 kilometers to run.

"Rightee Dokie" in full professional mode now, laid back, calm but precise to the absolute degree. "Confirm our landing is to be towards the beach as close as possible to reduce taxiing time, agreed?" Brad was starting the pre landing procedure with his fellow pilot.

"Agreed" nodded Oleg as he started flicking through the flight manual to the pre landing checklist.

"OK touchdown point 2K from the shore and we hold it on the step (ready for an immediate take off) until 500 Meters" he turned "After that Stu we are committed, if you spot anything and want me to blat past them half a K is the last chance, OK Mate?"

Brad continued "Unless you decide that the landing is definitely on, then the touchdown will be half a K from the beach, you're call mate, but better for this old croc to make a single landing with what it is carrying rather than bouncing along for a mile."

"OK no probs, Its game on, were delivering the stuff, make it a straight in" Stuart confirmed as he made a mental note to watch the range closely on the GNS screen.

"Fair enough" Brad acknowledged and then called" Checklist please" to Oleg who was ready and waiting to fire through the string of questions for Brad to check each lever, button, dial, valve, temperature and pressure as part of the pre landing drill.

At last, radio range kicked into place "Delivery Boy this is Shopkeeper how do you read? Over" came the transmission in good Russian.

"We have you 4 to 5 (radio strength), Smoke identified" Oleg replied. Normally he would have given them far more information or even general chit chat, but in this situation the less they know the better.

"Good, we are here, and everything is ready for you" the voice confirmed, leaving Oleg thinking, wondering, just what *"have everything ready for you"* could actually mean. Quickly he translated everything to Brad and Stuart and without either saying a word he knew that they were thinking the same thought.

.

"1K Brad" Oleg read out from the GNS as Brad was carefully monitor the slowest possible flying speed at the lowest possible height.

Oleg continued, calling the distance in Meters now "900,……. 800,……..700".

Brad didn't change his view which flicked every second between the Air Speed Indicator, the shore and the peripheral vision telling him that he was 1 meter above the almost calm surface of the lake called to Stuart "Anything mate?"

Stuart peering forward almost without blinking, he could see vehicle parked, figures standing intermittently between them. He looked at how the spacing of the vehicles were, could make out lorries 6 of them, and three 4 wheels. His mind racing trying to take in everything he could to see if there was any, even the slightest hint of an ambush.

"600".

"If it's a set up it's a bad un!" thought Stuart as Igor called "550!"

Together as Oleg called the final measure "500" Stuart came across loud and clear with the directive "Land" As if it was only Brads muscles that were holding the Ekranoplan in the air itself, a half second later the boom of the hull hitting the surface of the Lake for the first time rang through the aircraft like a thunderclap. They were "On the Step".

"Hold it on…hold it on.." Oleg called out, Brad nodded as he concentrated on the balancing act between back pressure of the yolk and power on the throttle.

"Hold it…. hold it.." Oleg called again as his eyed were glued to the beach. He knew he needed to predict the exact distance to the beach that it would take the aircraft to slow down. This felt more like a game of chicken to Stuart who watched in silence as the shore raced towards them.

At the point where Stuart and Brad were thinking, it's too late, we won't stop in time, Oleg raised his hand and barked "Now!"

Instantly Brad pulled the throttle as he applied even more back pressure on the yolk to hold the nose up and the Ekranoplan bit into the water. The beach now only 30 Meters away seemed too close, much too close and then the noise of the lakebed scrapping along the hull coincided exactly with a sharp deceleration.

Four seconds later, the huge aircraft had literally ground itself to a halt just 6 Meters from the shore.

There was silence on the flight deck, it took a second to realize. The flight was over, they had actually done it.

The beach had been prepared with a large, broad wooden walkway, or driveway.

Then suddenly, there was no time to waste. Inside the aircraft Oleg pulled the hatch lever to the "open "position in the cockpit as the Ekranoplan stood fast on the salty bed of the lake. One man was wading out towards the aircraft, Brad had to smile at the Chechy in nothing more than an old pair of underpants making his way to the front of the aircraft while pulling a cable from a winch higher up on the beach.

Oleg lowered the wheels of the aircraft, the hydraulics pushed them out and down from beneath the hull and slowly, against the screaming of the power system under pressure it had never been designed for, the aircraft stood up, on its wheels. Soon they could feel the tug as the cable started to bite in…seconds later the nose of the Ekranoplan crept towards the beach and the rampway.

....

On the shore, wearing his designer casual clothes complete with Armani shades the well over 6 feet of Lecho, besides him was Matt, also wearing sunglasses and looking as usual incredibly calm. They walked down the rampway built out of planks laid side to side making it almost 20 feet across as Stuart watched them through the cockpit.

Brad pointed "Hey Stu, its Matt, he's with the guy…..So, that's the rich Chechy he's with? "

"Hess the one and he's the same one who would have tried to slaughter Matt if we hadn't have pulled this off Matey" Stuart turned and quickly slid down the ladder into the hold.

Turning to shout down into the cargo hold Stuart called out "OK boys, A for Away and G for go! Remember the crack". (Meaning the rules, the drill.)

With a bang the Front-loading door swung open as the sunlight streamed in. In the cockpit Jimmy had stood on the KGB seat and was already peering out of the hatchway, Police
Sunglasses looked so cute on him as he smiled at the Chechnyan's looking towards him. In his right hand, safety off, was a fully loaded Kalashnikov. He looked down over the nose as he saw Stuart walking the few Meters up the rampway to face Lecho.

The men faced each other, Stuart glanced at Matt and looked, the look was enough, it said "Are you OK?" Matt smiled gently and nodded; no words were spoken.

Lecho's greedy gland was stretched to its limit for a fix now he had to know.

"Well Major? What do you have for me? I heard from my people that it was a busy night in Dubai" for sure Lecho had put enough 2 plus 2s together over the previous months to know that the only place so much Gold could be collected was the Gold Souk of Dubai, City of Gold, and for sure he would have had lookouts watching the progress.

"I think 24 plus tons Mr. Lecho and unfortunately we had to leave some behind".

"Oh, I know Major, I know you did" smiled Lecho. "But it was not *all* wasted. After you worked last yesterday night there was huge confusion which went on a big long time. There was how you say, you know, people stealing everything in the streets. Now are some very rich Indian laborer's walking round Dubai this morning". Lecho couldn't help but laugh and it was a genuine laugh.

As the men spoke red and Green teams were already out of the aircraft and not running, more sauntering had separated themselves from the main party to either side. The rest were behind Stuart as planned. No one was threatening but everyone was ready. Up on the crest behind Lecho his men were watching, standing and smoking. Stuart noted that they looked prone, disorganized and definitely not set for a fight. This was good.

Stuart turned and gestured with the palm of his hand pointing towards the open nose cone of the aircraft. "Well Mr. Lecho, here is our part of the bargain as promised"

Stuart and Brad followed Lecho into the aircraft and watched as his head darted down inside one portable Dustbin after another, a bit like a snake looking into bird nest for an innocent chick. Brad and Oleg watched also from the rear of the flight deck.

Looking at Stuart Matt whispered *"What wonderful thing greed can be"*

Tommy at their side couldn't help but point a finger towards Lecho's back and let out "Hey, I think that bloke has just cum!"

Lecho turned, his face was an absolute picture, beaming with genuine pleasure "Its real, all real!"
Straight out Tommy came back immediately "Well it aint fuckin scrap metal is it Matey!" turning quickly before he could catch any verbal abuse from Stuart he quickly exited out onto the rampway.

"Don't you worry about these boys shooting you Tommy" said Sarge.

"I don't" said Tommy, "Fuck em".

"No boyo, I mean don't worry about them shootin cause the fuckin Boss will get ya first" the Sarge grinned, at last one up on Tommy!

Tommy looked at Sarge puzzled at the pleasure on his face "Well Sarge, at least he wouldn't fuckin miss would he!" referring to the missed shot the Sarge had took at the escaping insurgent two years earlier and walked off up the ramp.

Muttering "Will I ever fuckin live that down" the Sarge looked at the Group of Chechens doing nothing "Come on me lucky lads, if ya can't talk in English let's hope you can fuckin work in Russian" he looked at them, mentally counted them "Ah that's handy, it's a ton apiece you have here!"

Back in the hold the atmosphere was a little more tense. Holding a heavy wedding necklace made out of 24 carat gold Lecho toyed with it, like a set of rosary beads "Your men will not need any arms here Mr. Stuart. Everything is very secure; you have our protection and in fact the Police and even Government protection too. I have set up a camp to show you, everything is ready including people from our City to value everything and weigh it accurately. Also, I have initial bearer bonds in half million-dollar denominations as agreed up to the value of 200 Million US Dollars. The balance is subject to certain, err, private negotiations that have been held with Mr. Light here."

Stuart didn't react, if he thought that he didn't know about Matts side deal, then that was good, he didn't realize that they were a solid team in that case and in turn it meant that their cover hadn't been blown, Lecho didn't perceive them as trained soldiers. Yet.

Lecho paused, as if still struggling to make up his mind just who this upper-class Englishman really was and then continued "As for everything else we know you Westerners prefer a certain degree of comfort, so I have arranged all to be as comfortable as possible. You will see"

The need to be comfortable, as it was interpreted by Lecho also confirmed it too, Lecho was still thinking that he was dealing with Western mafia, and that was good. If the men did turn it into a fight the shock would be even stronger and effective.

Graciously but without any inflection of threatening him, Stuart informed Lecho

"Thank you Mr. Lecho, please don't worry about our arms we will look after them. After all, I heard the hunting in these parts can be very good"

Lecho smiled, he had just been told incredibly politely to go and fuck himself.

Stuart turned to Matt as they walked away from Lecho "You in full contact with the Beachboys?"
Matt smiled "You bet, they're fine and they're listening to everything, even this!"
"That's great" Stuart was satisfied, an "Angel" was looking over them in the shape of American Special Forces wings and he could now start to relax, just a little.

Matt looked at Stuart "Now it's time to look at the last bit".

Knowing exactly what Matt meant Stuart nodded "Yes of course Mate, let's get it done".

Looking Stuart square in the face now matt was firm on the issue "No stu, this one is mine. ONLY mine. That's the way it is, full stop".

The unloading continued all the way through the day and into sunset. From the minute the first packages arrived into the sorting tent the jewelers were busy, first separating all stones from Gold, including them set in gold, the workload seemed massive. By sunset the dustbin for diamonds needed to be changed, it was full. Fifteen more of 24 carat gold had already been filled and weighed and all of this didn't seem to be putting a dent in the delivery itself. This was going to take a lot of time.

Outside a fire was burning bright made up of false heads and necks used in the Dubai Jewelry stores that had found their way into the dustbins in the haste to fill them.

Stuart and Matt now sat at the table in the private tent reserved for Lecho's dinning.

Lecho was still hovering somewhere close to nirvana; he could smell taste and feel the wealth and loved it more and more every minute. He constantly remembered Matt's words *"There will be enough to **buy** you a Country"*.

Matt looked at him "Now you know it's all online Lecho, it's going to meet the target plus a bit more, easy. There's far more stones than we expected and so, SO Mr. Lecho" Matt looked him deep in the eyes "Its *time*".

Usman paused…"The last we heard is that he would arrive sometime between the 18th and the 25th. That was the last message. He has my contact numbers here and I have people in Tikrit ready to meet him. I think your plan worked but…we shall see. He hasn't turned up yet and Usman isn't contacting anyone, even his mobile is kept switched off, he doesn't want anyone to know that he is here and "Again smiling but now almost laughing "You will see why".

Matt smiled back politely, giving the impression that he trusted Lecho absolutely and whatever the "surprise" was, he trusted that Lecho would explain to him when the time was right.

"I'm sure you will tell me how you managed to get him here in secret when the time is right Lecho".

Proudly, the first President of Chechnya (in waiting) assured Matt that he would explain everything when it was necessary. What Mr. President didn't know is that Matt had been kept informed of every single move that Usman had made since he arrived at the dacha four days ago, care of the Beachboys.

Stuart stepped in "Well, I'm sure we can wait a little while longer and give Sonny boy a chance to turn up. They're never on time anyway so let's leave it say another two days?" Raising his glass of fairly decent Vodka he toasted "Besides, we still have an awful lot of yellow stuff to weigh in!"

....

As they spent their first night, July 23rd, in the camp Dubai had recovered from its shock.

Almost in a state of emergency, although no tourist would ever have been able to tell. Dubai Police were quickly unfolding the evidence they had at hand.

Major Abdullah al Sayeed had been summoned to the Majlis in Zabeel Palace, only a mile from Sheikh Zayed Road. He was nervous as he waited to be called; it had taken even him, almost 15 minutes to pass through the security checks and be shown to his seat outside the heavy teak doors with the solid gold handles that was the last barricade before the Majlis. He was nervous and his wait seemed to go on, and on.

Almost an hour later, the doors silently and smoothly opened to allow three leading dignitaries to leave the Large room. Another fifteen minutes passed before Abdullah was called.

The room was massive, almost 30 meters long and 20 wide. Heavy chandeliers hung from the ceiling which was 40 feet above his head. The chairs were situated down the left and the right of the massive room, over a hundred in all and they joined another line of sumptuous chairs that ran from side to side along the bottom wall of the room. On this line, 12 dignitaries were seated, all of whom Abdullah recognized. He was in the presence of some of the world richest and most influential people on the Planet earth.

As customer had it, Abdullah walked to the central chair ahead of him, bend submissively forward and kissed the hand of the man in the centre seat, and then those of his three brothers to either side.

A voice instructed him politely to take a seat, near the main line of chairs but to the right of the room. Water, tea or coffee was offered, he politely accepted water. The same voice then asked him for the news, exactly what had gone on?

Abdullah was prepared; he had done nothing else for the last 24hrs than to be absolutely ready for this. He knew he would be repeating what they were already aware of, but anyway, the best place to start was at the beginning.

"Your Highness. We have had basically three separate, but connected incidents.

Firstly, the Power Station at Jebel Ali had been sabotaged with three separate bombs. They were very small but had been placed crucial points. The damage that they had caused was accurate and crippled the Station, they had no chance of restarting Power any quicker, one of the devices was also placed deliberately to cut any back up supply that we could have got into our grid from Abu Dhabi."

He paused and cleared his throat.

"The second was a string of devices that had been concealed in the roof spaces above guest bathrooms in the Burj al Arab Suites. These were smoke canisters not explosive devices. They set the automatic fire defenses off and lead to the evacuation. We have interviewed all the staff but especially the Maintenance Department and the receptionists. The manager of the maintenance department is under arrest, but as yet he has told us nothing. Two receptionists have strongly indicated that a group of Americans were something to do with this incident, they had all stayed at the Burj a month ago and each room that they had occupied, although there were other rooms too, had a smoke device in them. We have contacted the FBI with their names and passport photocopies that were taken when they booked in at the Burj and should have news later tonight – morning Eastern Standard Time. Just in case they are Americans, if the report comes back that their identities are false, then we have already started a full check on every American that has entered the UAE for the past 3 months. Compared to other nationalities they are relatively few, only around 11,000 in the period.

Thirdly, the Gold Souk was attacked by we think, around 60 to 70 men. The amount of gold stolen is still being assessed, but it will possibly be as much as 40 tons. The store owners are saying their losses were massive, but they're probably exaggerating it a lot. The thieves then made their escape by seaplane, the one that arrived 6 weeks ago at Hamriya. It left the UAE airspace last night and flew into Iran where we have received reports of its crash but after today's searching they've still found nothing. I suspect it didn't crash, if it had, the helicopters looking for it should have found something by now."

"We have arrested an English man, Jason Billingham in Ras al Kheima. He has admitted filling a false flight plan for their escape. He is telling us everything that he can, and we know that there is a Russian Hooker involved, she got him to put the flight plan in, he said he was blackmailed but I don't believe him, there's no proof. All he told us was the girls first name, he said he didn't know anything else about her, if she's real, then there can be an East European link, if she isn't, then we are considering he might be part of the gang itself so we are giving him what he deserves, a very hard ride.

He has told us that he had been introduced to the girl by an Australian called Brad Johnstone, he owns the Company called starlight Aviation that imported the seaplane here last year. He has disappeared of course and almost certainly was involved with flying the stolen gold away. We have searched his offices and home; they were virtually empty. But, the aircraft was imported from Russia, it is registered there, and the crew were also from the Ukraine, we have their details and are checking them, but the Ukrainians are not very helpful. However, it does show that Russians are involved. Probably their mafia.

One strange point, in the Souk, the main attack seemed to be focused on the Al Shattaff group, all of their stores were hit, 11 in all. I feel there must be some reason for this, it's too much of a coincidence. I've spoken to Mr. Al Shattaff, but he is very upset and can't explain why he has been chosen as a victim. He is asking for an audience at the Majlis for help. I also tried to contact his Partner, me Usman al Ghazzal but he is traveling at the moment and no one can contact him.

Questions and answers continued for well over an hour.

Towards the end of the discussion, a young Arab as all the others present in his pure white national Dress entered the room and quietly passed a sheet of paper to Major Abdullah, he read it carefully.

"You Highness, the eight Americans had been identified, or rather not identified, their passports confirmed as forgeries. According to the computer they were still at large in the UAE."

The voice in the centre spoke quietly.

"Thank you Major Abdullah, you have done well, but the question is – Are they really Americans at all? - Now you will focus on restoring normality. It is necessary to continue the hunt for these people; we do want to know who has been involved as quickly as possible. However, when you establish who, you must report back to us immediately but do not take any action, no arrests until we say so."

There were lots for the Majlis to discuss, affairs far beyond Abdullah's limits of comprehension. He was thanked by all, and he left. Dubai was to return to normal as quickly and quietly as possible. The spin doctors started work; the diplomats moved into gear. Dubai was to do its part in finding a sensible solution to this messy affair, but other were going to have to play their part too. The quiet and softly spoken voice at the end of the Majlis would make absolutely sure of that.

The next day tension was visibly relaxed in the camp. Lecho quite rightly and very sensibly had made absolutely sure that his men did nothing to antagonize any of their guests. He made no attempts at disarming them; in fact, he made a point of disarming a few of his own guys who were brain dead enough to let a few rounds off without thinking. Others he had carrying weapons as a show of "security" for the lads and others, the best, he had carrying their weapons concealed (or so he thought).

Work had been going on through the previous night none stop. Stuart and Matt could now see the jewelers beavering away, extracting every single diamond and gem from every single trinket, necklace and chain, then segregating them for colour, clarity, size and weight. There were even boxes marked Rolex, Tag Heure, Cartier, Dunhill, Breitling for what seemed to be a thousand watches. Stuart looked in the Rolex box marked "Rolex Male" and pulled out a solid gold Rolex oyster with a ring of diamonds around the face. It was heavy, worth probably a hundred thousand dollars and looked incredibly cheap.

"Who????" said Stuart "Who on Earth would *ever* wear something like this!" and dropped it uncaeremoniously back into the pile beneath.

Matt looked around the sorting tent. "If the gold alone is over the 20-ton mark, these stones and extras are going to make the gold seem cheap. I don't think Lecho is going to be able to afford this entire do you?"

Deep in thought Matt told Stuart "We really need to think about how we can move out the stuff he can't pay for ".

Stuart smiled "Matt, its already sorted out, we got that fixed in Dubai just before the Job. Tommy and Sarge s old boys' network will send a UN plane to Tashkent. By International Law their cargo can't be checked. They will deliver UN Boxes as medical supplies and we send the same boxes back in the same aircraft. Stick only to the stones, smaller and easier to shift"

"Where to?" Matt wanted to know.

"First" paused Stuart "Kabul, it'll be safe there, then…"

"*Safe* in Kabul" Matt was almost sarcastic".

"Safe with 8 of the lads sitting on it yes. I've arranged for the men to fly back on the same flight. They've all got their UN security clearances and I have set up a contract for them with a friend of mine whose out there running a mine clearance and private security outfit." Stuart replied.

"OK and once it's *safe in Kabul*? Then? We sell it to the Afghanis?"

"And then" Stuart was almost laughing "Tommy came up with a brilliant idea about that".

"Ahh "said Matt "Now why do I get the feeling that this is gonna be a *real* good one?" resigned to the fact he was about to hear something crazy Matt still had to know out of plain curiosity now "And Tommy thinks what exactly?"

"You're going to love this" laughed Stuart……..."We sell it back to the Gold Souk in Dubai!"

Shaking his head, "Fucking Tommy the Tit head strikes again! Are you serious? Or have you been using that nuts cup and caught something?"

"Well, maybe" Stuart beamed, think about it "They are going to need to buy some new stock aren't they? None of them carry any insurance, no one does in Dubai. We can sell it back at half price and they'll be happy, it halves their losses. They put their retail prices up another 15%, which will gross another 45 % on cost, they've hardly lost anything. On the other hand, if they don't buy it back, they lose 100% full stop".

Matt stopped walking, stunned, the math's worked out. Cocking his head sideways he turned to Stuart "Goddamn" looking across the camp he could see Tommy talking to Sarge as they drank a mug of tea and chatted together.

"Tommy the freekin tit" Matt said quietly and turned to Stuart to ask, "You reckon his mom got laid by Einstein?"

The men laughed as they walked, then saw Lecho leaving his tent. He had his mobile phone in his hand and raised it then pointed to it as he saw Stuart and Matt. He had news.

Following Lecho into his spacious tented accommodation the took a seat at the small table.

"The deal is complete gentlemen. Khalid arrived in Tashkent, the capitol of Uzbekistan 10 minutes ago. He is being taken to Radisson or Hotel Tashkent to stay the night, then driven out here tomorrow morning; they will be at the Dacha around noontime."

Lecho got straight to a point that was far more important to him than simple murder and turned to Matt "The gold seems it will be less in weight, maybe 22 or 22.5 tons. I will be losing"

"Why look so pissed Lecho? Isn't an extra two and a half tons? What's that, 30 Million US? Not enough? Besides, I told you 10%

extra on more OR less whichever way it went." Matt was pushing his luck; this was Lecho's home ground and Matt was right on the verge of calling him a greedy bastard outright. Seeing what could develop Stuart stepped in quickly

"Mr. Lecho, let's not worry about this now, think how much the diamonds and other stuff is worth, we can always…. balance the payment so everyone is happy"

It seemed to satisfy the greedy glands craving. Stuart felt relieved, Lecho felt satisfied and personally Matt didn't give a shit, all he wanted was Ghazal blood.

"Very well" Lecho conceded "our deal is almost completed. When do you want to go there? I will take you"

"Now" was Matt's simple answer.

CHAPTER 19: THE AMBASSADOR

24rd. July 1100 Virginia

Director Abrahams looked over the desk at the woman in the smart business suit "Glad you could make it Maria, how are you?"

"I ..I`m fine, just fine, fine..and.. and.." she knew she was nodding too much flashed through her mind her nerves triggered her into asking "And errrr and …How are you?"

Abrahams noted her nerves. His steel blue eyes didn't blink. "Oh, I`m fine Maria, just fine".

Maria had been called to give a briefing about Usman al Ghazzal and forewarned to be prepared with a presentation and facts, figures, numbers, times, dates and so on. She had suspected a trap but had to do it anyway.

Her eyes flicked momentarily towards the intercom as Abrahams pressed the buzzer to the linked to the outer office "Please ask our guest to come in Mary" and Abrahams immediately left his desk and walked towards the office doorway. As it opened and a tall Arabic gentleman in a 2,000 $ suit calmly walked into the room. Extending his hand "Your Excellency, thank you for coming, please ...May I introduce Mrs. Maria Donnelley, she is one of our key people in our constant paper chase of money movements worldwide and will try to help us today".

"Pleased to meet you Mrs. Donnelley" came in impeccable Oxford English towards Maria's direction as the man gently shook her hand and smiled at her as Abrahams explained "Marie, please meet

His Excellency Omar Qasim al Ayood, Ambassador Extraordinaire of the United Arab Emirates to the United States of America.".

Firstly, "Oh shit" went through Marias brain, then quickly "What the hell, who fucking cares!" followed it.

The threesome took their comfortable seats around the Circular meeting table to the side of Abraham's plush office. And it was Abrahams who started the dialogue.

After offering refreshment politely turned down by His Excellency, Abrahams began

"Firstly, your Excellency may we be allowed to express our sincere apologies for any embarrassment that recent events may have caused to you Country. Very importantly I must add that this was not an officially sanctioned operation by the United States Government. These are also the sentiments of the Secretary of Defense and the President himself, who by the way would like to meet up with you within the next few days on an unofficial basis if that's possible?"

"Yes of course I am at the Presidents disposal Mr. Abrahams. But for now, perhaps we can agree to some open and…off the record explanations within these four walls?"
By now, the phrase "OH fuck" had bounced through Maria's mind twenty times, The Secretary of Defense, The President!
"Oh,,,fffffffuck!"

Abrahams continued "Your Excellency we can assure you of our absolute openness and cooperation on this matter. You are correct in your requests yesterday to investigate an American involvement in these events and we have discovered several links that we intend to pursue for you on behalf of your Government. First of all, the aircraft that left your airspace last night was tracked and we can confirm that it didn't crash in Sothern Iran as was previously reported. Also, the Iranians as yet have found no wreckage at all. Our AWACS did track it and confirm it was last registered in the system heading towards the Afghan Border passing just South of Marshad in Iran at 0430 hours local time. Unfortunately, we had a tactical situation that arose at that point and the AWACS was diverted to what could have been a more serious issue, I trust you understand that I cannot elaborate on this?"

The Ambassador nodded, so far unimpressed and so far unconvinced either.

"As for American involvement, as I said previously, most certainly there is no official involvement here at all. This is unconditional, absolute fact. The United States is your trusted and valued ally and we would not and have not considered jeopardizing that position with your Country. We want you to rest assured that we will leave no stone unturned. We shall investigate it and again give you our assurance that should there be any American citizens involved then they will be brought to justice for this crime against a Sovereign State."

"That is very kind of you Mr. Abrahams, we feel comforted that you are being so open and honest with us" the Ambassador epitomized grace itself. Polished, smooth and thoughtful.

"Good". Abrahams continued: "Now perhaps Maria will explain some of our finding relating to a particular UAE national who I'm afraid is involved with the financing and money laundering which is Maria's area of expertise".

Allowing Maria to conclude her presentation on Usman al Ghazall without any interruption Abrahams then stepping in.

"Your Excellency. We believe that Mr. Al Ghazall is involved with the larceny of the Gold Souk, his involvement with certain outlets there shows, and I think you will find that these stores or outlets have formed the central point of the robberies there. Perhaps if you could request this information to help us with our investigations? Our information at this stage strongly suggests that we need to consider that Al Qaeda is in some form of disagreement with Mr. Ghazall and this apparently appears to be some kind of falling out between the organization and their main money cleaner. Perhaps he has not completely honored some form of business deal with them? Who knows? Whichever, doesn't really matter, all we are concerned about is that you feel secure with our intentions not to let this become public. We do of course absolutely realize the damage that this could do to your Country if it were perceived that some form of; how can I put it better? Inter terrorist falling out, had taken place on UAE soil".

"However, what we do know is that there has been some involvement by ex-patriots in the United Arab Emirates, and as I said earlier, if they are American citizens then we shall definitely hunt them down under our anti-terrorist rules but sensible, it could be assumed that any Westerners involved would more likely be from Great Britain than America wouldn't you say? However, judging by their chosen escape route, again I think it's a pretty good bet that what we should be looking for is some form of Russian or ex-Soviet State mafia involvement here, wouldn't you agree Your Excellency?"

"Sensibly, we will be looking for leads on those angles. Russian mafia, probably suppliers to Al Qaeda? If there is a western involvement then it doesn't make sense that they should be Americans, doesn't ring true to me Sir".

Calmly the Ambassador smiled "Oh yes. You could well be right Mr. Abrahams. Thank you for your reassurances; I shall look forward to hearing from you soon".

As they walked to the door Abrahams passed on his most important message, the difference being this one was the truth. "The.... Secretary of State has inferred that it may after all be in our Countries best interests to allow the sale of the new F22 Raptor to the Emirates after all, I hope this is good news for you Sir? And I have a feeling that this will be on the President's agenda when you meet".

His Excellency turned and shake Abrahams hand "That is also very reassuring news Mr.. Abrahams, thank you" Offering his hand to Maria "And thank you for your.... *enlightening*.... information Mrs. Donnelley. I hope that perhaps you can join your husband on his next visit to my Country. Please take my card, do not hesitate to contact me if there is anything further to discuss?"

Maria was rooted to the spot and now thinking *"Godamit he knew Matt was there!"* and it was Abrahams turn to think "Oh shit!"

Abrahams returned into the office; Maria followed; they both knew her game was up. This time Abrahams took to his desk and sucked through his teeth as he flicked open the file.

Looking down at it he made Maria wait an agonizing five seconds before he started to speak "hmmm OK, here we go. Maria, first off. My heart goes out to you, it was terrible, and you have to believe me we sympathize deeply. "

Maria nodded.

Abrahams slowly shook his head "But…. You really have set fire to the rule book."

Marie interrupted him:

"Hey, who cares? It's over, I did everything I could, and I just don't. Do not..care anymore, I broke the rules, I broke the Law, I broke the Official Secrets Code. I did it to avenge my Son, who cares? What ca you, the President or Jesus H Christ do to me??? Hurt me more than I've already been hurt? You really think you can do that? Hurt me more I mean?" Maria was now glowering at Abrahams – she had no fear of him at all – in fact no fear of anyone – nothing in this world could face her absolute determination for revenge and Abrahams knew it full well.

"Stop Maria". Abrahams had to be firm he knew damn well that she didn't care, in fact, he didn't even blame her, deep down for sure he agreed with Maria but somehow he had to maintain control of this situation.

"*You and* others broke a whole mess of rules. John, Nadia, Julia are as guilty as you now. But what you've missed is some very important things here. Let me explain, just how lucky you are."

"The last thing that Ambassador wants for his Country is bad publicity. What was lost in the whole freelance escapade means nothing to him in comparison to a drop in the housing market of Dubai, a one percent drop would cost them a thousand times more over the next twenty years. Believe me; he is going to sweep this under the thickest carpet he can find. In return, he will do an amazing deal for his country on a new aircraft provision that's going through. Sure, the US will bend, but that's Politics, its normal and to be honest, what we lose on the sale price the accountants will make back on the spare parts forever and a day that they will have to buy from us to keep the things in the air. Uncle Sam won't have lost a cent."

Knowing Maria simply wasn't interested in the logics involved, Abrahams quickly moved on and pushed a satellite photograph across the table. Pointing at a lake in the center of the photograph he quickly bought Marias attention back to him.

"This is where Matt is Maria, its where he is right now as we speak"

Continuing and pointing again....*That* is an Ekranoplan – that's their aircraft sitting in no more than ten feet of saltwater in Southern Uzbekistan. That's where your husband is, he's been there for over a week now which is why you haven't heard from him".

He paused; he couldn't resist showing Maria just how sharp his team had been "Not even on
that secret borrowed mobile that you have, let's see." Turning a sheet or two in front of him "7715354 no calls since a week last Tuesday correct?"

Maria wasn't shocked, and neither was she bothered what Abrahams knew. All, she cared about now was matt and what was going to happen in some God forsaken plain in Uzbekistan.

Abrahams continued: "From what we can tell, and I think you'll be pleased to know, your husband is fine. He and his friends have managed to completely empty the world's best hotel, throw the Emirate of Dubai into the previous century with no electricity for almost two days, empty God knows how many tons of gold and gems from the World's largest Gold Market and then fly plumb straight through Iran with it to this place". His finger jabbing at the map.

Our officer from the Embassy in Tashkent spotted this guy arriving 12 hours ago, another photograph was slid across the desk. The pretty Khalid al Ghazal complete with baseball cap, Gucci jeans and hold all leaving Tashkent International Airport. He seemed to be smiling or was he? Maria looked closer and saw the hair lip, the disfigurement that Tomas had inflicted upon him.

"And….and? What else. Tell me.." Maria was urgent, she had to know.

"Last we heard he was heading West towards the area that Matt is in. Two guys, probably Chechen mafia left from his hotel with him three hours ago".

Abrahams looked at Maria, this time he wasn't angry, wasn't scolding, somehow he looked pleased, sympathetic towards her.

"Looks like your trick worked Maria, I take it the bait was Tomas's fictitious brother?"

Maria nodded.

"And Matts old platoon, strange, none of them can be contacted, I wonder if they might be somewhere near Matt?"

"What the hell". thought Maria and nodded again.

"Good, then the score is going to be settled properly. As it should be too". Abrahams said in a serious tone. "Now, you go home Maria, and *this time*, you let me know the minute you hear anything. No more secrets. OK?"

Immediately after Maria left he pressed the intercom to his secretary. "Get Tashkent station online please" and he glanced at the picture of Khaled al Ghazal still on the desk and thought to himself *"For sure you are one dead man walking sonny!"*

CHAPTER 20: BALANCING THE BOOKS

2300 24th July Uzbekistan

An hour later, Matt stood beside Lecho's Mercedes. He looked up to see one of the clearest nights in his life. The star disappearing into infinity, passing satellites and shooting stars, all could be seen easily with the naked eye on this gin clear moonlit night. It was a hunter's moon, sharp and bright, verging on a strange kind of daylight.

His thoughts were with the Ghazzal's, and now, for this Hunter the prey was temptingly close. Matt reminded himself not to lose the eye, not to be too quick with any moves. This had to be controlled, calm, cold - professional. He was setting his own mind straight; he knew all too well that emotions would only have a negative effect on his performance. He needed his mind to be as clear as the dark eternity that he was looking up at.

Stuart Tommy and Sarge arrived along with Lecho and helped place the equipment Matt had prepared into the back of Lecho's Mercedes. Their faces were serious, none of them spoke.

Four of The beach boys lead by Number One had already dispersed, the previous night. Their positions had been replaced by four of the men from the camp who had left the completely unseen the previous night. The Chechnyan *guards* never saw leave them leave, but to be fair, their priority was guarding the Gold rather than worrying about any of the guests.

Both Matt and Stuart had preempted Lecho getting news of Khalid's arrival and had reasoned that the clock was ticking, if needs be they would have to be satisfied to take Usman out alone, and besides, even if the plan had failed and the lovely Khalid hadn't taken the bait, Usman had to be dealt with anyway. Beach boys 1 and 4 and 5 had easily tailed Lecho on a previous trip to the dacha days before Stuart had arrived, that had been easy.

Matt turned and shook Stuart hand.

"You sure we can't join in Matt?" Stuart asked, already knowing the answer. Matt looked solemn.

"I don't think this one is really *your cup of tea* old chap. It won't be what either of us are used to you know."

Stuart knew all too well what Matt meant.

"And besides" Matt smiled, we need somebody to guard our investments here don't we?

"Yes, you're right there "said Stuart glancing round noticing one guy scratching his crotch while the other smoked his cigarette "Don't worry, everything will be safe here. See you when you get back"

The three watched as Lecho drove away with Matt and as they saw the car disappear over the ridge, just 50 meters distant Tommy commented.

"Fuckin glad my name isn't Ghazzal" and then looking across at the Chechnyan with his hand still raking his crotch he whistled to catch his attention as he pointed between the man's legs "Nasty dose of crabs is it? You need some blue unction on them mate, I'll get some from the Serge's bag for you, he's got the same problem"

The Chechnyan glowered but didn't reply, he simply said to his friend "Pro chto etot cozelbazarit?" (*What that bastard saying?*) Tommy smiled as he walked away with Sarge, "He's probably saying What's that little bastard on about, what you reckon Sarge?"

"I reckon he's right; you are a bastard and I *haven't got* fuckin crabs"

Forty minutes later Lecho swung the car to the right from the "main" drag, a two-lane road that was rarely used Lecho continued for another three miles on a hard-packed sandy roadway. He had explained during the drive that the hunting lodge where Lecho was staying had originally been a gift to the Uzbeki Director of the Soviet KGB for the region after having assassinated a Russian general that had proved too popular for Joseph Stalin's paranoid schizophrenia to cope with. It was an identical copy to another hunting lodge that Stalin had commanded to be built in his native Georgia.

"It's very big, large bedrooms and a big dining hall". Lecho described the building intimately, explaining the stairways, the kitchens, the layout in a great detail. And that Lecho was occupying the main bedroom in the west wing, his four minders, provided by Lecho, and worked alternating shifts, day and night. He had already contacted them and instructed them to pull out tonight once he gave them the say so."

"Khalid is with two more of my men, they will deliver him here at noon tomorrow, once that is done, I have finished my deal and you owe me the extra 10%."

"In winter, this is so cold here you wouldn't believe, no one ever comes here in winter, the Dacha is just another 3 kilometers, behind that small hill" and Lecho pointed as he turned out the lights and slowed the car down to just over walking pace as they approached a slight ridge before the large Uncle Joe's personally designed Hunting Lodge. Thirty meters from the crest of the gentle ridge they stopped the car and walked and used a depression in the ground to hide themselves from becoming a silhouette in the clear night sky. It was one a.m. and Matt looked down to view the lodge, now just a mile distant. Lecho explained, the lights in the upper three windows to the right were Usman's bedroom. Directly below were two more windows illuminated, that was the large kitchen are, that's where his men would be.

Matt stopped and viewed the building for another three or four minutes. "OK Lecho, ask your men to leave now"

Lecho took out his mobile phone and called a number from the memory, it was answered immediately and Lecho spoke quickly, in a harsh sounding tone then closed the phone. Less than twenty seconds later, a brighter light, shown by a door opening into the dark night could clearly be seen. Someone was leaving.

Within a minute, the lights went out in the downstairs and the door went blank. Car lights were seen to come on and then drive away from the Lodge. Matt watched for a while, just in case the car stopped for any reason. He also knew that the Beach Boys would be watching it too but omitted to inform Lecho of that fact.
"OK, I need to get my stuff out of your car" said Matt and Lecho nodded then made his way back to the Mercedes with Matt. Pointing the key at the boot it opened smoothly to its full expanse. The light was bright, but it couldn't be seen beyond the ridge. Matt reached in and Lecho looked down at what he took from the trunk of the limousine.

"Ahhh I see you intend to be some time with this business?"

Matt didn't smile and didn't answer either.

"When your guys get here, flag them down, I will need their car, you take them to the camp OK?"

Lecho nodded and almost at that instant the old soviet jeep came over the rim of the ridge. Slowing immediately as the driver spotted his Bosses car. The four burly minders got out of the jeep on Lecho's demand to "Give him the jeep and you lot come with me"

The looks they cut towards Matt were unfriendly, slightly arrogant but more so intimidating. It was their usual manner. They fell on very stony ground indeed, Matt was in no mood to be threatened and looked back coldly at the four, each in turn as the thought "*You first*" looking at the hulk in the furthest back position of the group, "*then you and you next*" One wrong move on their part would have brought a viscous surprise their way.

Luckily none was made, under Lecho's commands the men piled into the back and the passenger side seat of the Mercedes.

Lecho paused and spoke to Matt through the car window "This piece of shit and *its* son are all yours now. Tomorrow at noon our deal is done. Agreed?"

Matt nodded "Agreed" and the men shook hands.

Matt looked at the man as he spoke. "It is up to you what happens but for you to know….. If it is my choice, or……. If you do not manage to do this work" he flicked his eyes towards the Lodge "Then I *will* kill them both tomorrow".

Lecho swung the car round and drove off as Matt loaded the Jeep in silence.

Slipping the handheld radio from his combat waistcoat, Matt flicked the "on" switch. Checked the frequency then pressed the transmit button, two sets of double clicks.

"BeeBee One here come in?" came back immediately.

"Sitrep please BB one".

The drawl was back "Wellll,… the babysitters just left. Confirm four of them and best we know, that's all there were. Our guy is sorta home alone, should be just him and any entertainment he might have in there".

"OK copied, where can we RV? (rendezvous)".

"Do you have the Lodge visual?" BB one asked.

"Affirm visual" Matt told him.

"That's cool……." So was the drawl! "Well…..There's this big old barn thing, to the east corner, I will be there OK?"

"Affirm and I will drive, if the target saw the jeep leave then he will just think it's coming back, be there in three minutes" and Matt set off.

True to his word, just under three minutes later Matt slowed the jeep and very slowly took the way around to the back of the old barn. He knew BB one would definitely be watching and wanted him to see that he was alone, hadn't been compromised in any way. As the jeep stopped and Matt got out BB one spoke to him from the shadows. Looking at the old jeep and saying quietly.

"Well. ...I guess it beats walking.."

"Where are the others?" Matt wanted to know.

"We`ve got a three-point stake out going here, all the angles are covered, if he runs one of em will fetch him down but try not to kill him. That leaves me free to give you back up. The guy (Usman) is in the far set of bedrooms, sort of a private wing kind a thing" as he pointed, to the far side of the building, its lights shielded from the barn.

"Best way in?" Matt asked, and realized he was being too sharp, too eager. Reminding himself to slow down, there was a long way to go yet, and a long time until noon the next day.

BB one explained "Straight into the kitchen then work our way left through the house to the stairway"

Then BB passed the rest of his information "We were watching those guys all day; they didn't give a shit by the look of it, just disappeared. We have hardly seen the bad guy.... spends most of the day in the rooms upstairs. We can just go in there through the kitchen.... too good to be true almost".

Matt considered it, too good to be true. If Lecho had decided to double cross than now wouldn't be the time, he would have hit them at the beach, all in one tin can, cradled together, not now, it didn't make sense.

Not looking up Matt replied "It's supposed to be. We've paid good money for it".

"Fine by me" said the drawl as he picked up on Matt's blunt response "Fine by me".

After making all their preparations, Matt had run through the general plan with the drawl all questions that needed to be asked by him had been answered by Matt and they made their way to the house from its blind side, the West, the end furthest away from Usman's master rooms. Quickly they made their way along the house, stopping to listen and look into any downstairs window that they could, double and treble checking the house was empty of every one of Lecho's guards. Although they didn't suspect a trap, they still checked it thoroughly.

Inside the kitchen, they could still smell the stake cigarette smoke and the stale, cheap stench of the homemade Vodka. The kitchen was large, very large, built to feed an entourage of visiting VIPs in the Soviet era no doubt. Matt looked across the kitchen, the large wood burner stove, the massive old wooden dining table and 12 chairs. Herbs and spices hanging from the walls, and the obligatory bread oven for the Lavash unleavened Uzbek delicacy.

As he did so, the Drawl was already making his way from the kitchen and along the corridor that joined the spacious reception area and the stairs to the first and only upper floor. Checking to make sure Matt was behind him, the two men slowly, extremely slowly made their way up the old wooden staircase. Placing a foot so slowly on each step before any weight was taken by it. The ascent of the stairs took over 10 minutes to pass the 20 treads of the stairs to mount them in complete silence. Before they had reached the top, the noises could be heard from the bedroom occupied by Usman. The noises were screams and they were getting louder. Matt saw the Drawls eyes flash, in return he eyed towards the door. They slowly pressed on, close as possible to the wall where the wooden floor would creak less.

At the door, Usman's shouts and the females screams and begging in languages neither Matt nor his friend could understand were reaching a fever pitch. *"Stay cool, stay slow. Keep switched on"* Matt made himself think.

Matt was against the door now and looked through the large old-fashioned keyhole. The door was locked, the old iron key had been turned in the lock. Looking in Matt felt his temper flush.
"Stop…. don't!…. I must…. must slow down…..don't rush!"

It took another three minutes to press the door gently, so gently and slowly no one inside would ever have noticed, to check for a bolt having been slid across at either the top or the bottom of the door. There was none.

The hand signal was read by the drawl who very slowly moved back from the door and crouched side on to it. Matt stood beside him his pistol already drawn and safety off; ready…..took one last pause and then nodded as he started to move. The drawls foot hit the door precisely at the lock point and as the doorframe and wooden trimmings flew spinning through the air inside the room and before the door smashed full swing into the back of the interior wall, Matt was already two full paces and in full flight towards Usman al Ghazzal who, as he knelt on the bed beside his poor female companion looked at Matt with very wide eyes of shock as the heavy pistol hit him squarely on his left ear, splitting it like a ribbon and stunning Usman into the silent world of a conscious dream.

Curling into a ball the naked Usman felt himself being dragged onto the floor, childishly he raised his hands to half protect himself and half to beg for his attacker to stop. It didn't work, the pistol didn't stop as it cracked ribs, fingers, nose, temple and cheekbone.

The Drawl called calmly on the radio.

"Bad guy bagged, come to me, come to me. Bring medic kit".

"Check" came back.

Usman didn't cry, he was too shocked for emotions just yet. Stuart looked down at him, stood over him. The Drawl looked at Matt's eyes. He saw evil.

Matt glanced at the bed, the drawl didn't know really what to do, his hands over the female, frightened to touch as if she would burn him, he looked at Matt again. And then turned as the three other Beach Boys sprang into the room and stopped.

The girl wouldn't die from her ordeal, but she wouldn't enjoy her 10th birthday that she had been looking forward to in only a week's time.

In the kitchen the dawn was breaking through the double skinned glass of the East facing window. Matt looked at the sunrise. It was beautiful, the green and thin streaks of pale blue with the amber of the dawn sun, so much in contrast to what was inside the kitchen. Usman was naked, the bleeding had stopped, and the pain had begun, just as Matt wanted it to.

Bound with wire at the wrists, arms, neck, thigh and foot to the heavy wooden chair he watched as Matt sat and spoke to him.

"If you speak one single word, if you beg me, if you even move your mouth, if you say a single word until I tell you to, I will hurt you more and more and more." Matt leaned forward, Usman looked into his eyes, Usman wanted to wet himself, he knew, for the first time ever in his comfortable life that he was now in the presence of a truly dangerous man. A killer.

A tear ran down Usman's cheek, he wanted to plead; he wanted to bribe or to beg or reason.

"Good……….. I don't like you Usman, I would enjoy killing you" Matt paused and looked at the window and said quietly, more to himself than to Usman, as he realized something "Yes…..I would enjoy it…. really *enjoy*.."

He turned and cocked his head, looking at Usman.

"Your life is going to change today Usman,…a change you will never be able to live with my friend" and Matt smiled and slowly shook his head.

Taking a heavy soviet style hammer from the bag of equipment Stuart had packed into the trunk of the Mercedes the previous night Matt didn't show a flicker of emotion at all as he broke Unmans` right leg six inches above the ankle. It didn't need all of the eight hits to do the job and shatter the bone, but Matt didn't mind one bit. As Matt pulled the leg to see that it made an extra bend in a gentle V shape Usman finally wet himself.

Leaving Usman to regain sensibility from the spin that the pain had sent his mind into Matt turned and searched for coffee in the cabinets and Jars near the cooker. He wanted Usman in pain, not in the welcome comfort of dreamland where the pain would pass. Conscious is what he wanted Usman to be, very conscious and awake. Matt wanted him to savor the pain fully.

Taking his seat again opposite Usman Matt explained.

"If you think I am here for the American Government Usman you are wrong, Or if you think I am here for money? Wrong again" Matt smiled. and continued…" I am here for something much more serious," and tapping Usman gently on the shoulder he added softly "You will see soon, I promise".

Trembling uncontrollably Usman peed himself again.

The morning passed, the Beach Boys did several jobs, getting everything ready as Matt had asked. Usman, now writhing in a pain that wouldn't go away was now told to speak, and to speak in great detail and great length of everything he knew, and he gladly told absolutely everything he could as Matt recorded every word.

At eleven thirty exactly, the Drawl opened the door.

"Car," was all he said as he closed the door and left.

Matt turned to Usman, now you will be silent, absolutely silent or I will kill you instantly, do you understand?"

Usman nodded: he wasn't going to say a word.

Matt watched from the window down the long path towards the dusty area outside which pretended to be a road. No sign of the beach Boys, not a trace could be seen, but for sure they were all in place and all very close. Eleven minutes later the land Cruiser slowed down in a plume of dust and stopped.

Matt could see the driver, beyond him a baseball cap and in the back an obvious Lecho man. The rear door opened, so did the passenger side door at the front as the baseball cap made its way to the back of the land cruiser, the rear door slammed shut, the Lecho man staying inside and the vehicle shot away leaving the baseball cap standing alone.

"You fucking bastards, my bag….." Khalid shouted.

"Fuck..fuck fuck." He cursed as he turned to look at the house. Beyond him matt saw the drawl and one colleague slowly walking towards Khalid's back, rifles aimed from their shoulders. Khalid sensed it, turned and saw. Then to his right another and then to his left.

"Fuck…Americans" Khalid realized he was trapped. Turning his back to Matt's window Khalid looked at six feet six inches of Californian meat and he smiled.

"And what will you do? You think sending me into one of your secret prisons will help you? You think I am afraid of you? Fuck you!" but he didn't make a move, didn't try to attack the man pointing the Kalashnikov at his face, instead Khalid spat at him. As he did so Matt was closing in behind him, now only five feet away.

Khalid again sensed a presence and turned. Matt was now almost face to face with him. Khalid froze; he had seen this man before.

He then felt his hands pulled behind his back, the wire ties snapped tight and made him gasp. Strong hands held him.

Matt said softly. "You recognize me don't you boy? Look at me…think….." Matt said softly.

Khalid was someplace between a state of shock, or rather serious confusion and disbelief. He answered.

"I know y…….. your eyes……. They….." Khalid suddenly realized where he had seen those eyes before.

Matt saw the realization "Yes Khalid, you remember them don't you boy?" and headbutted the killer of his son, fair, square and deafeningly hard shattering his nose, the blow was so accurately vicious, pushing splinters deep into his nasal passages.

Minutes later Khalid sat and faced his father, chair to chair as Matt spoke

"Look at us all her, look at where this little life has brought us. You see Usman, I've done the same as you, did you know that?" Usman looked puzzled but didn't speak.

"Oh yes, I've encouraged people to kill, many times, hundreds of times in fact," Matt paused, almost talking to himself now as he nodded "yep…I've done that.."

He looked at Khalid "And I've killed too, even more than you…..Yep…. done that too.."

Matt was now in a different world; one he hadn't visited before. He was beyond law, order or reason, swimming in a sea of hate and evil. It was wrong, he knew it was wrong, but he wanted it, needed it and didn't care.

"The difference is, I do it better than both of you" Turning Matt took the gas bottle and moved it nearer so that the six foot of rubber hose could reach Khalid's chair, at the end of the hose was a flat cast iron burner ring and matt placed it carefully underneath Khalid's chair that had already been modified, hit with the same hammer that had broken Usman's leg, to remove all except two slats in the seat portion of the chair itself.

Matt spoke as he worked. "You see, you're a terrorist - so am I. Only difference is I guess I am supposed to be more sort of …legal… than you. Oh, you know, I got a real uniform to wear, monthly paycheck, medical insurance, maybe even a few medals and hey, a pretty crap pension at the end of it too. You guys don't get that do you?"
Khalid was starting to get the picture, could he really be in the hands of a maniac? Someone who had really gone out of control. Surely not, surely they need him alive so he can talk.

"So, as one fellow terrorist to another, how about you let me show you this time, the way I do things? That's fair eh? Yes…. Very fair…. Now I terrorize you".

Matt twisted the valve on the top of the gas bottle, just a quarter turn and then bent and lit the burner and then turned it down even lower.

"That should be about right I think?" he said to Khalid as he eyed the gentle ring of flame before turning towards Usman and pushing one of Lenna's ball gags into his mouth.

"Your bluffing, you know you can't do this, you and your fucking president are all shit, full of shit bastards.." Khalid wasn't frightened; he was convinced it was a bluff.

"You need me alive and you know it. You won't turn down the chance to get information out of me, I know it…your bullshit man..bullshit".

Matt sat at the table.

"Let me explain pretty boy…I don't work for my President anymore; I work for me. You are going to die today but guess what? Not until *you* ask *me* to kill you….and believe me boy, you *will* ask".

Khalid felt warmth beneath him gentle warmth. For the first time Khalid started to be frightened.

Standing and half turning to point at his father "And he is going to watch you die and while he watches he won't be able to say a single word to help you. Won't answer you, won't be able to tell you he loves you, or that he's sorry, won't be able to help you– just like I couldn't for my Son."

Matts green eyes looked into Khalid's as he said quietly.

"Trust me boy…." Matt nodded his head slowly up and down as he spoke "You *are* going to die, trust me – trust me" and Matt smiled.

Khalid tried to squirm a little, the warmth was changing into hot.

The screams, when they started, lasted for the rest of the day. All the way to the sunset over the vast lonely plain of Uzbekistan.

Outside they could hear the screaming, hear the pleas for mercy. At one point they even heard the offer of blood money, any amount no limit. But then the screams became whimpers, then they became screams again. The day seemed to last a week. Even the smell the flesh burning permeated through to the outside of the lodge as Khalid`s innards cooked.

A beach boy spoke, he had to say it. Shaking his head, he spoke quietly to his comrade "Man, he's lost it. Lost it really bad… real fuckin bad man".

The Drawl nodded gently and answered him "Aint he got the right?"

At sunset there was a silence at last.

Matt placed Khalid's severed head between Usman's legs and carefully tied it in place. Usman's eyes were glazed, rolling; he was almost in convulsion, gasping, panting as if in an attack of asthma, for breath.

Matt gently stroked Usman's head and looked at him. He spoke very softly to him.

"Yes, it is a nightmare….and it never goes away…...never. One that we'll both live with every day for the rest of our lives but you see Usman. …..See?" Matt looked down at Khalid's head, so did Usman and he vomited yet again.

Usman's eyes were rolling, shedding tears, sobbing uncontrollably.

"You stay here now with your lovely boy. Look at him every time you open your eyes. You will see him forever…. You know that it's **you** who did this to him, no one else…. Only you"

Matt turned after he had smashed every single remaining bone in Usman legs and hips with thirty or more blows of the Russian Hammer before he slowly left the room, quietly closing the door behind him.

CHAPTER 21: IMAGINE

Within a month and in many different parts of the World the imaginations of various individuals had either run riot of their own accord or had been told to develop various spins of certain events.

The CIA were convinced beyond any doubt *(publicly)* that Usman al Ghazzal had stolen hard earned Al Qaeda money and thence paid the penalty by losing his extensive treasure trove and his only son in an act of retribution – at least that's what they told everybody was their official conclusion. Maria, John and Nadia kept their exemplary records and would remain that way.

In Jebel Ali, an overworked generator that simply couldn't cope with the growing demand of the Emirate had given up the ghost. Its breakdown had led to an extraordinarily long power cut. DEWA, Dubai Electricity and Water Authority announced the plan to build a new Power Station away from the prestigious tower block developments that were crawling their way down the coast towards the outdated power station. They would be investing over 800 Million $ in the project. It apologized for the inconvenience caused.

Reported looting had been attempted in the Gold Souk during the Power Cut on the 22nd of July, some 144 individuals, mainly Indian passport holders, had been deported following arrests.

A separate account in the Khaleej Times reported that a petrol tanker had caught fire following an accident in Shindagha tunnel, leading to it being closed and inspected for repairs for the next one month.

The Fish Market was fined for disposing of waste in the public sewer system, leading to major cleaning being required.

There was no report of faulty fire alarms being set off in the Burj al Arab.

Dubai had reasoned. There would be nothing to gain by admitting the robbery, there could only be a loss in both confidence and more importantly, investment in the Emirate. The government had lost nothing, apart from having to replace an already aging power station, something that was needed anyway. The owners of the shops in the Souk, mainly Indians, could bear their own losses; after all, they had made a healthy tax-free profit for many years, so why complain?

More importantly, The United Arab Emirates was pleased to announce the purchase of new F22 Raptors from the United States. They alone had been granted the option for the new aircraft and their Gulf State allies had not.

Usman al Ghazall was found on the 1st of August in a back street of Tashkent, having suffered a nervous breakdown. Following emergency operations to his legs, he had been returned to Dubai. Following his divorce which was issued by special decree within a month, Usman had allegedly decided to gift his business enterprises to the Government following a decision to retire due to ill health. It was rumored that long stays in a mental asylum in Switzerland were to be normal for him.

The Dubai Government announced that the first four deportation requests made by the USA over the previous year were to be honored, in a gesture of Global security and cooperation.

As far as Dubai was concerned, it was business as usual, it never missed a beat. Nothing had happened out of the ordinary and the simple fact still existed. Dubai is safe, free of crime and a marvelous place to invest. Property here is booming and sunshine was still guaranteed 365.

Four known ex IRA operative were deported to the UK following a request from the British Home Secretary.

Rumors from the American embassy in Moscow suggested that a Mr. Lecho Dudeyev a successful Chechnyan entrepreneur had been approached by the Kremlin as a first gesture of finding a negotiated settlement regarding the Chechnyan crisis. It was hoped that a partial independence for the state would be achievable in the near future. Hostilities stopped and Russian troops were programmed for a limited withdrawal from the region within three months if the peace was maintained.

At St. Marks church in the parish of Martley Worcestershire the bands had been put up, announcing the forthcoming marriage of His Lordship Stuart Henry Bonham to a
Miss Natallia Fedorova Gradskaya (nee. Atamaniuk. Divorced)

It was never publicly announced, but Jason Billingham was released after serving nine months and fifteen days of his six month sentence. He was deported to the UK the next day after being allowed one hour to pack.

Dubai Tourist Board announced record visitors to the Emirate.

Welcome to Dubai, the Greatest Show on Earth.

THE END

Made in the USA
Lexington, KY
12 December 2019